DARK CRIMES

A gripping detective thriller full of suspense

MICHAEL
HAMBLING

Published 2016 by Joffe Books, London.

www.joffebooks.com

This book is a work of fiction. Names, characters, businesses, organizations, places and events are either the product of the author's imagination or are used fictitiously. Any resemblance to actual persons, living or dead, events or locales is entirely coincidental. The spelling is British English.

ISBN- 978-1-911021-43-8

The mirror doesn't lie. Every day it gives you back the swollen, puffy, discoloured eyes, the bruised cheeks, the split lip. Those tears you see reflected there show what the brain will not admit, that there is no excuse for behaviour that you know is wrong. The tears may have lost their meaning now, but the inner self cannot be fooled. It sees the hollowness there, the emptiness where love should be. You don't deserve this misery.

CHAPTER 1: Murder on Spring Hill

Monday Night, Week 1

The outer door of the hotel lobby swung shut behind her. She turned, descended the six steps from the ornate porch and glanced down the High Street. There were few signs of life. There was no traffic on the road, and no pedestrians making their way home in the late-night drizzle. Curtained windows were illuminated in several of the nearby flats and houses. She raised her umbrella and clattered down the remaining four steps to the pavement. Odd how cheerful she felt, how light-hearted her mood had become in recent weeks, despite the chill, damp November weather. She rather liked nights like this. The air was cool and refreshing and the ten minute walk home would be the perfect antidote to yet another busy evening shift at the hotel bar. Then a cup of tea, a chocolate biscuit, a short but warming bath and into the luxury of bed. The young woman walked briskly along the silent, rain-slicked pavement.

She stopped as she reached the more open area beyond the hotel. She paused and briefly tilted her umbrella aside as she looked up at the darkness. Rain fell on her curly brown hair. She hadn't realised just how wet the night really was. She was about to turn onto the Spring Hill footpath, its steep incline falling away in front of her. Was the path darker than normal? The misty drizzle seemed to suck the light from the night air, leaving each of the street lights outlined in a fuzzy orange halo. Her pause was only fleeting. After all, she'd felt so much safer, so much more at ease, since she'd moved here, away from the shock and violence into which her life had unexpectedly descended. She stepped forward down the path, her heels ringing on the hard surface.

* * *

Midnight. The rain still fell onto the glistening streets. The dark November night was wintry now, with the addition of a salty mistiness that drifted in from the sea. Water still trickled between the paving slabs, down into the gutters and the drains. But now, on Spring Hill, its progress was impeded by the curled-up form on the left side of the steep walkway. Surface water dribbled past the body, down the sloping path towards the junction with Kings Road at the bottom. Few people used Spring Hill on winter nights. There were other walkways that were less steep. The only folk out were a few late revellers winding their way home after a night in one of the nearby High Street pubs. They all had enough rational judgement left to take an alternative route. The body had continued to lie undiscovered and undisturbed until just after midnight when, finally, a small dog sniffed around the dark shape. The dog whined to its owner, who had remained at the top of the walkway.

'C'mere, boy!'

The disobedient terrier whined more loudly. Then it barked, pawing at the ground. It sniffed the body again and started to growl.

The man walked down the steep part of the path to his dog and saw the sodden form lying in the deep shadow of the wall. He paused, then knelt down beside the body and gently felt the neck for signs of a pulse. He withdrew his hand and noticed small spots of blood on his fingers. They were just visible in the dim light from the single street lamp that illuminated the walkway. He slowly stood up and backed away from the body until the wall prevented him from moving further, his eyes fixed on the lifeless form.

* * *

A silver saloon drew up against the kerb behind one of the squad cars, taking the prime spot directly across the end of the path. The uniformed constable at the bottom stepped forward as a slim, middle-aged woman started to climb out. She wore a pale-pink cocktail-dress, a sequinned jacket and evening sandals.

'You can't park there,' shouted the duty officer, hurrying across the pavement.

Sophie Allen looked up for a moment, and her right foot splashed loudly into a puddle.

'Shit!' she said. 'Bloody, bloody hell. I'm now going to have a cold, wet foot for the rest of the night. Help me out, you prat.'

A stocky figure trotted forward from the shadows.

'DCI Allen?' he asked. He offered her a hand, but she was already walking to the boot of her car. She looked back at him, then glanced up at the night sky with distaste.

'I've got wellies and socks in here, and a coat on the back seat. Get it out for me, will you, please?'

He found the coat, and held it open for her to put on. She then sat down on the rear seat, took off her strappy sandals and tugged thick, blue woollen socks onto her feet, followed by a pair of pink wellington boots.

She locked the car and turned to the man, giving him a tired smile.

'Well, good evening. Not for my right foot, though. It's having a particularly bad evening. Trodden on by my husband's boss, who can't dance for love or money, and now soaked in a freezing puddle. You must be Barry Marsh, the local DS.'

'Yes, ma'am. I should have been down here to meet you, but the local police doctor arrived just a few minutes ago. Sorry.'

'Don't worry. I ought to have been more careful. Up here, is it?'

The rain had abated slightly, but the weather was still cold and damp. She scowled at the night sky, buttoned up her long coat and tucked her blonde hair inside her upturned collar. As she walked away from the car she put up a large umbrella. She'd been at her husband's staff Christmas party when the call had come through from headquarters. Martin was by now probably sipping a hot drink in their lounge at home. She put the image out of her mind and followed Marsh up the footpath.

'What do we know? And for goodness' sake come in under the umbrella. You're getting soaked.'

Marsh ran his fingers through his neat hair. He moved in a little closer under the umbrella but kept well to the outer edge of its dry zone.

'Thanks, ma'am. A young woman's body, up there, about three-quarters of the way to the High Street. The local police doctor's just arrived and is having a look.'

'Remind me. Why do we think she's been murdered, and that it wasn't just a nasty fall?'

'There was an emergency call. When the paramedics arrived she was already dead and there was a lot of blood loss. They found what appears to be a knife wound to her chest. They backed off at that point until we arrived. Her clothes are soaked in blood, and there's some on the wall at what would be her chest height, we think. As I said, the doctor is examining the body just now and the forensics team are due any moment.'

'Who found the body?'

'A man called George Appleby, out walking his dog. He's sitting in one of the squad cars.'

'A bit late to be out, isn't it?'

'I thought the same thing. Apparently he's not sleeping well at the moment so is in the habit of taking his dog out late at night, even in weather like this.'

They reached the cluster of people at the upper end of the path. An awning had been fixed between the two high walls to keep the worst of the rain off, and two spotlights had been set up. Allen recognised Mark Benson, a local GP, wearing nylon overalls. His gaunt features were stark in the bright glow from the floodlight.

'Good evening, doctor. What are your thoughts?'

'Nice to see you, Chief Inspector. What looks like a knife wound to the upper thorax, probably deep, from the amount of blood on her clothes. Right into the heart, I'd guess. If so, she'd have died instantly. The body is still warm, so she's been dead less than two hours. Time of death was around eleven thirty.' He turned to face them. 'I can't believe it. Not murder — not here. Swanage just doesn't have murders. It's not that kind of place.'

Sophie glanced at her watch. It was one o'clock.

'Murder has nothing to do with place, Mark. Nowhere is immune. Have you finished here?'

'Yes. There's nothing else I can do. Forensic team arriving soon?'

Marsh nodded. 'Due any minute now.'

The doctor still looked grim. 'I'll wait for them, then get myself back home. Not a good night to be out. I'll get my initial report written up tomorrow morning and sent up to the station. The post-mortem will be at Dorchester, I expect?'

'Yes, I've asked for Benny Goodall.' She touched his arm. 'And thanks. I do understand the way you feel. It's always disturbing. If it helps, I still feel that each time I investigate a murder, and in a strange way I'm glad I do. I think I'd start to question myself if I started to view murder as a routine part of life.' She turned to Marsh. 'Let's have a look. You can tell me what you think.'

The body lay on its side. The victim's glossy brown hair was wet and spread across the path. She was in her early twenties, slim, obviously tall, and attractive. And very dead.

The two detectives stood several yards away. Marsh observed the scene carefully before he spoke. Allen guessed he was a little in awe of her. 'The spot's been well chosen. Further up, the path is overlooked by those flats. Further down, it can be seen from the two houses that front onto the lane. But just here it's more secluded. She's lying with her head uphill. To me that suggests an upward attack, as if she was walking down the path. Whoever stabbed her was coming up. If it had been the other way round, she'd be lying with her head downwards.'

'Maybe she struggled and got turned around that way.'

'Possibly. But look at the thickness of her coat. That knife went right through it, and whatever she's wearing underneath. There was a lot of force in that blow, enough to push her over backwards. I'd guess that he wasn't close and struggling with her. He had the knife ready, maybe at his side or behind his back, and swung it hard.'

'So he was ready to do this? He was prepared? You don't think that it was a mugging gone wrong?'

'It just doesn't fit the typical mugging scenario. I think it was premeditated.'

'Which means that either he knew her and targeted her here, or we have some sort of psycho on the loose,' said Allen.

'I'd go for the former, ma'am. The psycho idea just doesn't bear thinking about.'

'Rather convenient that this street light isn't working, don't you think, Barry?'

Spring Hill had two tall lamp posts, evenly spaced along the length of the path, with an additional motion-activated lamp attached to the wall of one of the flats near the upper end. The middle light was not working.

'The path's quite well-lit at the top, on the steep section, because of the light coming down from the High

Street,' she continued. 'This movement-activated one by the gate to the last of the flats means that she was silhouetted as she came further down. Normally she might have seen someone standing there as she got close, but not tonight with that lamp off. She may never have seen her attacker. Contact the council, or whoever, tomorrow first thing. Find out why it's off.' She turned. 'There's the forensic squad just arriving from HQ. We'll have a quick word then leave them to it and speak to the man who found her.'

They walked back down the steep path to the small cluster of vehicles at the bottom.

'By the way, was it you who put the roadblock out on the main road to Corfe?'

Marsh nodded.

'Well done. Quick action like that can make so much difference to a case. They haven't found anything suspicious so far but it was the right thing to do. I had a quick chat when they stopped me.'

They reached the squad car parked at the bottom of the path. Sophie climbed into the front passenger seat, with Marsh getting into the back to sit beside Appleby. Sophie noticed the small terrier curled up at Appleby's feet.

'Good evening, Mr Appleby. I'm DCI Allen and I'm in charge of the investigation. This is DS Marsh who is assisting me, and who will be taking notes. I'm sorry that we've kept you so long on such a foul night, but I expect you understand how important it is that we speak to you while everything is fresh in your mind. Now, can you tell us the events that led to you discovering the body, and what you did subsequently?'

Appleby was a heavily built man in his early fifties. His clothes were slightly untidy, and his shoes scuffed. She wondered if he lived alone, and kept the dog for company.

'I was walking Toby along the High Street. It was quiet so I'd let him off his lead. He's a good dog.' The dog raised his head, and Marsh patted it. 'We often go down

Spring Hill if it's dry, but I'd decided not to tonight so I walked past.' Appleby went on to recount his discovery of the body.

'Did you see anybody about, either on the High Street or on the footpath?'

'Not on Spring Hill, but I think there were a couple of men ahead of me walking up the High Street.'

'Did you notice them before they'd reached the path or beyond it?'

Appleby thought for a moment. 'It was while I was standing at the top of the path waiting for the dog. I can't say that I'd seen them before that.' He hesitated. 'But they might have been in front of me all the time. I'm not very good at spotting things in the dark.'

'Don't worry. Tell me, what made you decide to check the body for a pulse?'

'I was in the army. Came out over ten years ago but I still remember some of the basic drill. The funny thing is, I never saw a dead body. I was in Kuwait for the first Iraq war, but not on the front line. Just saw a few injured squaddies. Anyway, there was no pulse, and then I felt really spooked. There was a lot of blood. It took me a minute or so to calm down. I phoned 999 on my mobile and was told to wait at the scene. I felt more scared than I ever was in the army. I kept thinking that he was still around with a big knife, watching me. I was bloody glad when your guys arrived. It felt like forever, but it must only have been a couple of minutes.'

'Did you touch any other part of the body?'

'No. I thought something was up when I saw the blood on my hand. I backed away quick.'

'And your dog?' added Allen.

'Put him on a short lead. He was pretty quiet.'

'She doesn't seem to have had a handbag with her,' Sophie said. She added no explanation.

'I spotted that. But I didn't try looking for one. I left everything as it was.'

Sophie nodded. 'Why were you out so late, Mr Appleby?'

'To take the dog out.'

'Yes, I know that. But isn't it rather late? Most people take their dogs out mid-evening.'

'A bit of air helps me sleep better.' He paused. 'My wife left me a few months ago. It's hard getting used to being alone.'

'I'm sorry to hear that, Mr Appleby. It was good of you to wait, and I'm sorry to have kept you so long. I'll get one of the cars to take you home if you wish, once you've left your details with DS Marsh here. If you do remember anything else, please contact us immediately. Someone will be in contact with you tomorrow to take a formal statement. Thanks for your help.'

She climbed out of the car and walked back up Spring Hill to have a word with the forensic team.

'We don't know who she is,' Sophie told them. 'Can you have a look in her coat pockets? There doesn't seem to be a bag anywhere, which is a bit odd.'

The senior forensic officer felt in the coat's pockets. They contained nothing but a few coins and receipts. The photographer finished her work and they turned the body over. There was no bag underneath.

'No keys anywhere?' Sophie asked.

'No. And no other cash, as far as I can tell. There's no inside pocket on her coat, so unless we find something once we start examining her in the lab . . .'

Sophie thought about the lack of money, keys and other personal items. It looked like a mugging that had gone horribly wrong, but the mugger had still made off with the victim's bag. Yet it didn't feel right. Would a hesitant robber have used that much force in a single blow? From the doctor's description of the wound, and the spread of blood, it looked as if the stabbing had been violent and deliberate, as Marsh had conjectured.

'There doesn't seem to be an umbrella. Is that right?' she asked. 'Yet her coat doesn't have a hood.'

The forensic chief merely shrugged. Marsh came up to join them.

'Appleby only lives a couple of hundred yards away, just off Kings Road. He said he'd prefer to walk.'

'I don't think he was involved, but we'll need to check him out anyway.' She paused. 'Barry, this could be a difficult one, and we'll be working together a lot. I don't have a DI assigned to me at the moment because of staffing cuts, so you'll be my second in command. We need to bounce ideas off each other. When we're out on the case, like now, you can call me Sophie if you feel comfortable with it. I only need to be ma'am when it's necessary. Is that okay?'

Marsh looked awkward. 'If you don't mind, ma'am, I'll just call you ma'am. That's if it's alright with you?'

'Of course.' She smiled.

'It's just that you're a bit of a legend in the division. It wouldn't feel right to me . . . But I'm really glad to have the chance to work with you at last.'

Sophie wondered if he was blushing. It was too dark to tell. She felt a mixture of pride in the fact that her work was recognised and anxiety at the responsibility that came with it. She saw the genuine enthusiasm and respect in her new assistant's face. It deserved a response.

'Well, Barry. Thanks for that. I'll still call you Barry, if you don't mind. It's a lot more personal than sergeant. Okay, this is what we're going to do. We'll wait until the forensics have finished with the body and taken it to pathology. Meanwhile, I'll phone through to HQ and report our findings so far. I want you to walk around the top of the lane and have a look along the High Street. See if there's anyone hanging about. Note any houses that have lights on, within hearing distance. We'll have a quick word to see if they can add any information.' She indicated the houses that had side windows looking onto the lane.

'These houses here alongside the path, we'll need to get them up whether there are lights on or not. I'll make a start on that.' She paused. 'Is that a hotel near the top of the lane? On the High Street? There's still a light on.'

'Yes. It's the Ballard View Hotel. Quite plush.'

'See if the night porter saw or heard anything. After that we'll call it a night. Try and get some sleep, and be ready for an early start in the morning. It would be a good idea for us to visit the cottages in that lane at the bottom of the path first thing tomorrow, before the residents have a chance to leave for work. Say about seven thirty? Are you okay for that?'

'At Eldon Terrace? Fine.'

'We'll have our first incident meeting at nine tomorrow morning. You're based at the local nick. Could you get them to start setting up an incident room there ready for us? And, by the way, you've made a good start.'

They spent an hour calling on the nearby flats and houses with little result. None of the occupants had realised that anything was amiss until they heard the sound of sirens, and the ensuing activity in the lane. Even the occupants of the flats that had windows and doors looking onto the Spring Hill path reported hearing nothing prior to the police and ambulance activity. Most of the flats were unoccupied holiday properties, and the owners were only there during the warmer months. Marsh called in at the hotel, but the night porter had seen and heard nothing from his office behind the reception desk.

The forensic team found little of use in the area around the body. Shortly after two, the body was removed and the forensic team packed up for the night, planning to return the next morning for a more detailed search of the path. Spring Hill was sealed off with a squad car parked at each end. The few onlookers drifted away, followed by the two detectives and the rest of the uniformed officers.

Sophie Allen glanced at her watch as she climbed into her car. Maybe she might manage four hours of sleep before the mayhem really started.

CHAPTER 2: Mother and Daughter

Tuesday, Week 1

Swanage police station stood on a side street off Kings Road. It was a hive of activity the next morning. Used to dealing with the more common rural and seaside resort crimes of petty theft, minor disorder and alcohol-fuelled assault, the local force had been shocked by the murder. The news had spread quickly in the small hours of the morning, and they had come in early to lend a hand. When Sophie arrived at the attractive Victorian building shortly after eight, she found an incident room already in place. She sought out the station's senior officer, Inspector Tom Rose, to thank him. He was a local man who had returned to Swanage after three decades spent in different stations around the county.

'The least we could do. It's our town and we want this murder solved. By the way, a message came in for you confirming that the post-mortem is set for eleven in Dorchester.'

'Thanks, Tom. We're starting the review here at nine. Would you like to be there? You might have some useful input.'

Early that morning she and Marsh had visited all of the remaining cottages in Eldon Terrace. This narrow street ran at right angles to the lower end of the Spring Hill path. They'd called at the nearest houses on the south-facing side the night before, because their rear, upper windows would have had a view up the path. Some of the residents had been out then, watching the forensic team at work. No witnesses had been found but it was early days yet. Members of the forensic team had arrived shortly after daybreak, and were carrying out a meticulous search of the path, so she had let them get on with their work undisturbed. A number of officers were already searching the gardens of nearby properties, looking for the murder weapon.

By nine the meeting was under way. The atmosphere was calm and workmanlike. Sophie introduced herself and presented the core of her detective team to the assembled group. This consisted of herself and DS Barry Marsh, helped by DCs Jimmy Melsom and Lydia Pillay. Melsom was a young detective based at the station. Lydia Pillay was from the local divisional headquarters and had worked for Sophie on her previous two cases. She was in her late twenties and was bright and alert, a product of the fast-track scheme that recruited suitable graduates. She had driven to Swanage from the county headquarters at Winfrith.

Pillay had just finished pinning the photos of the crime scene to the display board. Sophie began by summarising the events of the previous night, then reviewed the initial lines of inquiry to be followed up that day. There was little to go on at the moment, and still no clue as to who the victim was. Sophie had decided to work with Melsom initially, starting with the post-mortem later in the morning. Marsh and Pillay were to remain in Swanage, overseeing the investigation into the victim's identity. Most of the other local police officers were involved in tracing the identity of the victim or in the house-to-house enquiries in the vicinity of the crime scene. Two officers were chosen to sift through the national database and look for previous knife-based murders. Sophie was not optimistic that this would provide any leads. She tended to agree with Marsh that this crime wasn't a random attack, but she couldn't discount the possibility.

'No assumptions, anybody. At this stage we keep open minds. We consider all possibilities and follow everything up thoroughly. And it will stay that way until I decide otherwise. Is that understood? Okay, let's get to work.'

Sophie and Melsom left the incident room soon after ten to drive to Dorchester for the post-mortem. Melsom showed none of DS Marsh's deference, despite being younger and less experienced. Sophie wondered if he was just a little too brash. She had been impressed with Marsh's careful reasoning, and had few concerns about leaving him in charge. Time would tell whether Melsom would warrant the same level of confidence. He offered to drive, but Sophie refused.

'If we take one of the pool cars then you can drive, but we're going in mine this morning so I'll drive.'

'Okay,' he said.

'I'll take that to mean "Yes, ma'am", shall I?'

'Yes, ma'am. Sorry, ma'am.'

'Apology accepted. Remember who I am and who you are, Jimmy. That way we'll get on just fine.'

Sophie waited until they were out of town before speaking again.

'Barry tells me you have the makings of a good detective, Jimmy. He thinks a lot of you.'

'I'm glad to hear it, ma'am. I'm willing to work hard and learn.'

'Good. I want you to act as an extra pair of eyes and ears today. When we're interviewing anyone, I talk first while you watch and listen. You take the notes. Don't interrupt unless you think I've missed something obvious. When I've finished my questions, I'll always ask if you have any. Don't ask anything just for the sake of it, only if it's something that you think is important. If you want to mention something to me on the quiet, just raise your finger slightly. At this stage, you're mainly here to observe, think and learn. We can discuss and reflect later.'

'Understood, ma'am.'

Sophie's car was unpretentious, a reliable and well-proven saloon, but it did have real power under the bonnet. It handled well along the narrow lanes of the West Country.

* * *

They arrived in plenty of time for the post-mortem.

'I'm probably only going to be here for the initial external examination, Jimmy. It can get a bit too ghoulish for me once they start on the insides. Have you attended a PM before?'

'No, ma'am,' said Melsom.

'In that case it would be better if you came away at the same time as me. We'll get the rest of the information soon enough anyway.'

As it turned out, most of the useful information came in the first stages. Sophie knew the pathologist well. Benny Goodall had worked with her on previous cases and he was a family friend. The two officers had a quick coffee with him before moving on to the lab.

The pathologist's assistant started by removing the clothing which was then searched and bagged ready for further examination. Nothing was found that would help identify the young woman. The victim had been wearing a dark jumper over a white blouse and a plain black knee-length skirt. Sophie wondered if these clothes were a uniform of some sort. She also had on black boots and pink, stripy socks. Her underwear looked relatively new and clean.

'Can I have a quick look at the boots, please? Leave them in the bag.'

The assistant passed them to Sophie, who turned them over to look at the heels.

'Look, Jimmy. The heels have a fairly hard surface, which means that they would have clicked as she walked. The attacker would have heard her coming.'

Benny Goodall made comments as he worked and his assistant took photos.

'As I think you suspected, death was most probably due to the single knife wound to the chest. It's deep but I can't be sure just yet whether it has damaged the heart. If it did, death would have been nearly instantaneous. I'll be looking at the internal organs later.'

'Can you make any guesses about the weapon used?' asked Sophie.

'Probably a large-bladed knife, maybe a kitchen knife.' He finished his examination of her torso, and transferred his attention to her head.

'Now here we have a contusion on the back of her head, probably due to it striking the ground. There has been some bleeding. But do you notice the slight marks on her face?'

He stood aside to let Sophie see.

'These are not fresh. There are signs of bruising on her right cheek and on the right side of her nose. She also has a slight bruise on her forehead. These are almost fully healed. I'd guess they are a couple of months old at least.'

'Any ideas as to the cause?'

'Not at this stage.' He indicated a point on her throat. 'There's also very slight discolouration at this point on her neck. It would be wrong to jump to conclusions, but it could also be the residue of a bruise that's nearly healed. If so, it's older than the facial ones. There's only a slight trace left.'

He worked in silence for a while.

'There are bruises on the outsides of both arms.' He wiped some dirt off her hands and wrists.

'Look here. There are some faint scars on her wrists. Only just visible, so again probably from months ago.'

'So she could well have been suffering violence for some time?'

Goodall nodded. 'It looks that way, but I'll need to do more detailed work to be sure.'

Sophie looked at the young woman's face. It was slightly freckled, framed by her dark curly hair.

This girl had been about to enter the prime of her life. How had she ended up on this cold laboratory bench? How had she managed to collect these bruises and scars? It wasn't just that she had experienced a sudden and tragic death. It appeared that she had been subjected to violence for some time.

'Can you tell if she is right- or left-handed, Benny?'

The pathologist measured around each arm and felt the muscles.

'Right-handed, I'd say. Her muscles are just that little bit more developed.'

She turned to Melsom. 'These kinds of details should help us to visualise what happened. The path would have been slippery last night, and there's a handrail in the middle of the path. She's more likely to have walked down on the left side so that her stronger arm was gripping the support. That ties in with the position her body was found in.'

Goodall completed his initial examination, finding a few more faded bruises on the shins.

'I'm going to get her X-rayed before I go any further. If my guess is correct about these bruises, there may be bone damage.'

Sophie turned to go. 'Thanks, Benny. We're going to head off. Can you call me when you've finished? You've got my mobile number, haven't you? You've done a fantastic job for us, thanks. I'd like to get a copy of all the photos. Is that possible? Can they be emailed to me?'

'Of course. I'll get my secretary onto it. And good luck with the investigations. Phone me if you need any more information.'

She turned back to have a final look at the victim, but said nothing further as they left. What was there to say? She had no words to describe her feelings about this young life that had ended in such a violent way.

* * *

They were back in Swanage within the hour. Sophie looked in on the incident room. Barry Marsh was on the phone. He saw her come in and gave her a wave and a thumbs-up sign.

'Possible identity,' he called excitedly across the room. Sophie joined him at the desk.

'That was the manager from the Ballard View Hotel on the High Street. One of their bar staff can't be contacted. When I asked for a description, it matched exactly. About five foot six with long, dark, curly hair. Name's Donna Goodenough. She lives half a mile away in Gilbert Road.'

'From the murder scene?' she asked, re-buttoning her jacket.

'From here as well. It's the far side of the railway station. A house that's been converted into flats. She has the first floor.'

'It's taken them a bit of time to report it, hasn't it? They must have known about the murder. Isn't that the hotel you called at last night? I'd imagine the whole town knew by this morning. Why didn't they report it earlier?'

'She'd been working the late shift this week. Started at three in the afternoon and worked through until eleven. When the manager heard about the murder, she started ringing round the staff but left Donna until last, since she liked to sleep in when she was working late in the evening. They weren't able to contact her either on her landline or her mobile. I saw the night porter last night, and he told me he hadn't seen or heard anything, but his office is tucked away round the corner from the entrance. And there's something else. That broken street light in Spring Hill was working earlier in the evening yesterday. One of the local house-owners reckoned that it must have gone out sometime between eight and ten.'

'Well, that's interesting. We'll follow it up later. Okay, let's move. I want us all there, and a squad car.' She called across to the two officers carrying out the database search. 'By the way, there are signs of old bruises on the victim's body. Face, wrists, legs. I want one of you to switch your search to look for stabbings with a domestic violence background. If nothing comes up, just follow up the beating theme. This may be the first time he's used a knife. We might be lucky and find something. But first contact the council about the broken street light. I don't want it fixed without one of us there with forensics. Make that absolutely clear to them.'

* * *

Sophie's car drew to a halt outside the house, and she led the way to the front door. The building was a substantial, red-brick structure with a small front garden. The historic railway station was directly opposite, with a restored steam engine hissing gently beside one of the platforms. The door wasn't locked, so they hurried up the stairs to the first-floor flat and rang the bell. When there was no reply, Sophie told Melsom to go down to the lower flat and see if its occupants had a key. Pillay was sent to the upper flat with one of the uniformed constables. Marsh hammered on the door, but there was no answer. Melsom was back quickly.

'We're in luck.' He handed the key over. Pillay came back down the stairs. 'No one in,' she said.

Sophie opened the door.

'Donna Goodenough?' she called. 'Are you here? It's the police.'

She went into the hallway, indicating that Marsh and Pillay should follow. 'You stay here,' she told Melsom and the uniformed men.

The flat was compact but had been well looked after, with clean surfaces and polished furniture. There were two bedrooms, one double and one single, a bathroom, a small galley-style kitchen and a lounge-diner. The main rooms showed signs of having been ransacked, with some drawers and cupboards partly emptied. Pillay spotted a photograph lying on the floor behind a chair. It showed an attractive, dark-haired young woman sitting on a sunny beach smiling at the camera. It was their victim without any doubt. Sophie had been looking at that very face little over an hour before, on a mortuary bench. Several other young people were in the background, sitting under a parasol and appearing to talk to each other. Their features were difficult to make out from their position in the shade.

'We need a very quick look for anything that we can use to trace friends, family and acquaintances. Mobile phone, address book, diary, that kind of thing. Lydia, you take the bedrooms. Barry, the kitchen. I'll do in here. Don't disturb anything. If you do, forensics will have a fit.'

She called through to Melsom. 'Jimmy, get gloves and suits for us from the car, then seal off the house. Call back to the station and tell them to get forensics organised. Tell the people downstairs to remain in their flat.'

They found nothing of any use. Whoever had ransacked the flat had left all items of value, but had removed anything that could have helped them.

'Find out what you can about her,' she said to Marsh and Pillay. 'Speak to the people in the lower flat. Next-of-kin details as soon you can. Find out if anyone saw or heard anything unusual here yesterday. Jimmy and I will pay a visit to the hotel.'

* * *

Sophie parked her car on the High Street outside the hotel, close to the top end of Spring Hill. She walked across to the start of the path. From here the steep gradient was more obvious, the pathway falling away quickly from where they stood. David Nash, the leader of the forensic team, saw her and came up the slope.

'We've just about finished, and I'm afraid that we haven't found anything of great importance. There was little significant blood spray pattern on the wall or the ground because of the thickness of her coat, mainly leakage out onto the surface. We did some blood treatment of the surfaces and took some ultraviolet shots. You'll have them later. There are some curious smudge marks there but nothing obvious. And nothing else to be found up here.' He paused. 'But down there a few yards beyond where her body was, is a rough track in what would be deep shadow at night. We found a couple of cigarette butts just at the junction. And they don't look as though they've been there long. Might be useful.'

'That's good, Dave. It might be too much to expect some DNA?'

'We can but hope, but we had a lot of rain overnight. I'll let you know as soon as I can.'

'No sign of the knife?'

'Not as far as I know. We've been concentrating just on the immediate area up here, but I think we'd have heard if it had been found.'

'Umbrella?'

'Again, no.'

Sophie nodded and turned back up the slope towards the hotel. She and Melsom hurried to the main entrance and entered a warm, panelled reception area. She introduced herself at the desk and the hotel manager, a soberly dressed, dark-haired woman in her forties, quickly appeared and ushered them into her office. She looked pale, but was businesslike as she spoke to the two officers.

'I'm Jenny Burrows, the manager. I can't tell you how shocked we all are by this. Is it true?'

'Officially, I can't confirm or deny until we have a firm identification, but unofficially we are almost certain. And that information is for you only, Mrs Burrows. If any of the staff ask, just say that you can't comment at present. I'd like you to tell me about Donna if you can. Start with her employment here.'

'She started with us only three months ago. We lost a lot of our temporary summer staff when the universities and colleges went back, and we were under-staffed in the bar for the autumn. It can still be quite busy here right through to Christmas. We advertised, and Donna was the best of the people who responded. I have to say that she's been terrific. Always willing to lend a hand and do extra if needed. I was only talking to her a couple of days ago about moving her into reception work to get more experience. I think she had the makings of a really good manager once she'd got the training.'

'What was her background?'

'Apparently she dropped out of a university degree halfway through. I don't know the reason. She wouldn't talk about it when I asked at her interview, just saying that it was in the past and she wanted to forget it. I only know that it was some type of business degree. She was obviously very intelligent.' She paused. 'Look, I need some tea. I just feel numbed by all this. Would you like some?'

Sophie nodded. 'Please.'

The manager called through to reception to make the request. Sophie continued her questioning.

'Where was she from?'

'She had some local connections. Her grandmother lived in Swanage and Donna's flat was left to her by her gran when she died. That's why she decided to come here. It's also possible that her mother lives fairly locally. I think that she might live in a cottage in one of the villages. I don't know which one. Donna didn't talk about her mother anywhere near as much as her gran.'

'Who would know which village?'

'She was often on duty with one of our other girls, Maria Jones. She might know.'

She pulled her jacket closer in. Her hands were trembling.

'This is just awful. I can't believe it's happening.' Tears welled up in her eyes.

'Is there anyone else, Mrs Burrows? Who else might know?' Sophie asked.

'I've heard that she's been seeing one of our junior chefs, Vilis Berzins. He's from Latvia.'

'I'd like to see them both please, once we've finished.'

Jenny Burrows looked ashen. 'Maria's in, but Vilis didn't turn up for the lunchtime session. Chef phoned through with the news just before you arrived.'

'Can you get his address, please, and give it to DC Melsom here? Meanwhile I'll see Maria. Is there another office I can use?'

'He doesn't have a separate address, Chief Inspector. He stays in our staff accommodation, and he doesn't seem to be there. No one's seen him since breakfast.'

Sophie thought quickly.

'I need that office, if you could find one quickly. Then, please, find Maria and send her along. Can you then get me a list of everyone on the kitchen staff? Find the person who was closest to this Vilis Berzins and send him along too. When did he finish work yesterday?'

'He was on the evening shift, so he would have been here until about ten thirty.'

'Sorry if my manner appears a bit sharp,' Sophie replied. 'You've been very helpful so far. Could you do one more thing, and secure the door of Berzins' room, please?'

She looked at Melsom. 'Jimmy, could you go along with Mrs Burrows? Get a couple of uniformed guys up here. I want all the staff to remain on site until we've spoken to them, and I don't want anyone to go into his room. If necessary, stay there until someone else arrives. Then get a description of Berzins from the chef and confirm his shift time yesterday, and when he left. Phone the description across to the station, and ask them to keep a lookout for him. Get them to put it out to the other stations and the port authorities in Poole. Okay?'

She was shown into a small room just along the corridor. She phoned Marsh, asking him to come up to the hotel as soon as he'd finished interviewing Donna's neighbours.

* * *

Maria was shaking with sobs when she arrived to see Sophie, who poured her a cup of tea to help calm her down. She was younger than Donna, about eighteen. She was short and a little stout, with straight black hair held back in a ponytail. She wasn't heavily made-up, but her tears had made her mascara run.

'Maria, we need your help. Mrs Burrows tells me that Donna's mother lives locally, but doesn't know where. Do you?'

'I think she lives in Corfe. I don't know exactly where, but I got the idea it was on the west side of the village. It's an old cottage, I think.'

'Have you ever met her mother?'

Maria shook her head.

Does she have the same name as Donna? Goodenough?'

Maria nodded. 'I think so.'

'What about Vilis, Maria? How long has Donna been seeing him?'

'About two months, I think. But it can't be him. He's so sweet. Honestly, he wouldn't hurt a fly. She really liked him. She was only saying a couple of days ago that they could have a future together.'

'I'll bear that in mind, Maria. Tell me something else, if you can. When she started here, did she have some bruises on her face and arms?'

'I don't know about her arms, she always had them covered. But she said that she'd fallen off a bike and got bashed on her face. It wasn't obvious. She used special make-up to cover the marks, otherwise she wouldn't have got the job here. Mrs Burrows is very particular about the way we look. I only saw them because we were going out one evening and I called at her flat. I was early, and she hadn't finished her make-up.'

She blew her nose.

'Did she ever mention it again?'

'No. I kind of got the feeling that she was a bit annoyed at me for mentioning the marks. So I never asked again. She was nice and everything, but she was a bit different to the rest of us on the bar staff.'

'In what way?'

'Well, she was cleverer. She knew a lot. And she kind of took control, a bit like you or Mrs Burrows. I never asked about the face-marks again.'

'And was this before or after she started seeing Vilis?'

'Oh, well before that. I've told you, he wouldn't hurt a fly. Lots of these guys from Eastern Europe really try it on with us, but he didn't. He's nice. I tried to get off with him once, but he wasn't interested. He's always kept himself to himself. Sends a lot of his money home to his family. But he fell for Donna big time. She's got class, and he saw that. And she's really pretty.'

Maria had brightened up as she was telling her story, but as she finished she started crying again. Maybe she realised that she'd switched to the present tense, thought Sophie.

'I think that's all for now, Maria. You've been very helpful. We'll need a statement from you. One of my officers will take that later. Meanwhile if anything else occurs to you that could help us in any way, then find me or someone else from my squad. Here's my card. It has my personal contact numbers if you need them.'

Maria left, still sobbing. Sophie called the station and asked for a trace on the mother's address in Corfe. It came back as Cornerstone Cottage in West Street.

When she'd finished her call, she opened the door to a young man dressed in kitchen whites who looked nervous. His face was bony and pale-featured, with eyes of a washed-out blue.

'Come in. You are a friend of Vilis's?'

He nodded. His facial expression gave nothing away.

'What is your name?'

'Georgs Vitols. I too am a trainee chef.'

Are you from Latvia as well, Georgs?'

'Yes, we came across together.'

'It appears that he has gone missing. Do you know why?'

'No. But Vilis wouldn't be involved in any crime. He is very good man. He has no violence in him.' Georgs spoke with a pronounced Eastern European accent.

'But why has he disappeared, Georgs?'

'I cannot say. He went out after breakfast for a walk. He buys a newspaper sometimes. He says it will improve his English. He did not come back.'

Does he have a mobile phone?'

Georgs shrugged.

'You've tried phoning him? No answer?'

This time there was a single nod.

'What was he wearing?'

'Blue clothes. He wears blue a lot. It is the colour of his favourite football team at home.'

'How old is he? About your age?'

The young man shook his head as if he didn't know.

'Where might he go, Georgs? Does he have a favourite spot? Maybe where he goes with Donna?'

He shrugged.

'Georgs, if I don't get your cooperation, you may find that your time here will soon be over. I think you do know where he could be. A word from me in the right ears, and you could be on an early flight back to Latvia. Now I'll ask again, where does he go on his walks?'

The answer was sullen. 'Sometimes just along the front. But they sometimes walk to the point.'

'And exactly how old is he?' asked Sophie.

'Twenty.'

'Right, thank you. You can go now, but you'll be interviewed fully by another officer later. And I'll expect you to be more helpful then. Stay in the building, please, and give me your mobile phone.'

'You can't do that.'

'This is a murder enquiry. Your phone has his contact number, and I don't want him warned. Hand it over or I'll arrest you for obstructing us in our inquiries.'

Vitols did as he was asked and left the room.

Sophie met Melsom in the foyer. A uniformed man was now stationed outside Berzins' room in the staff block at the rear of the hotel.

'When Barry arrives I want the two of you to start taking statements from the staff, Jimmy. He should be here soon. Did you get a description of Berzins from the chef?'

'Yes, ma'am. He's about five foot nine with short, dark hair. Clean-shaven. I've got a copy of the staff photo of him and it's a pretty clear one.'

'Good thinking, Jimmy. Get it sent down to the station for circulation as soon as you can. Apparently he likes to wear blue. And he walks along the seafront. Could you phone that across to the station and ask all teams to keep a lookout? Could you sort all that? I'm going to take Lydia with me to Donna's mother.'

She was about to leave, but stopped abruptly.

'Jimmy, were there any wet clothes in Berzins' room?'

'No, ma'am. Not as far as I could see.'

'Check again carefully, then have a look in other likely places in the hotel. If he was standing around waiting for Donna last night, he'd have got soaked. Oh, and when you speak to the staff find out who saw her last, just before she left. I want to know whether she had an umbrella with her.'

The other two detectives arrived. Sophie gave her orders and drove off with Pillay.

* * *

They were soon in Corfe and driving slowly along West Street to its far end. The house they were looking for stood back from the road along a short track. It was set apart from its neighbours, and not overlooked. Like many of the other houses in the village, it was a low, two storey cottage, made from the local Purbeck stone. They parked the car and made their way through the low, wooden gateway. There was a small flower garden in front of the building, although by this time of year there were no blooms left. The two detectives could make out the edges of a well-worked vegetable garden to the rear, as neat and tidy as the flower garden. They walked to the door and rang several times. There was no answer.

'Shall I have a look around the back?' asked Pillay.

'Yes. I'll check with the neighbours. There's someone in the last cottage on West Street. I spotted a woman at a window as we passed.'

The neighbour, an elderly woman leaning on a stick, expressed surprise that there was no answer at Brenda Goodenough's cottage, since she hadn't seen her going by her window that day. Brenda always drove past on her way to work as a cleaner in one of the local hotels. She had not done so this morning. Sophie began to feel a slight unease and asked the neighbour for the name of Mrs Goodenough's employer. She phoned the hotel and was dismayed to learn that she hadn't turned up for work that morning. Sophie walked back up the lane and found Pillay waiting at the door.

'No sign of life, ma'am. There's a back door, but it's locked. There's an insecure window just beside the door. I can give it a go if you want me to.'

'Yes. I'm worried about her. Have a look, if you can manage it. Put gloves on, Lydia.'

Pillay clambered on top of a nearby bin, and pulled at the window. It opened easily.

'I've got it open, ma'am. It wasn't really secured. Shall I go in?'

'I want to see how she is, so yes. Go ahead. But try not to disturb anything.'

Pillay was slim enough to slide easily through the window. She unlocked the rear door from the inside, and the two detectives passed through a small, neat kitchen into the hallway of the cottage. There was no answer to their calls, so they continued through the house. The other rooms on the ground floor consisted of a sitting room that had windows looking out onto both front and rear gardens, and a small dining room next to the kitchen. Both rooms had been kept clean, with polished furniture that gleamed in the late-afternoon light.

The stairs were old and creaked as they climbed. They found Donna's mother in bed, still in her nightclothes. Dead.

CHAPTER 3: The Working Girl

Early Tuesday Evening, Week 1

In the late-afternoon chill, Sophie leant against the cottage wall. The drizzly rain had stopped in the middle of the afternoon, the damp air-mass replaced by colder, drier air from the north. She was warm enough, in a fashionable but thick woollen coat, black trousers and boots. She warmed her hands on a cup of coffee from a flask she kept in the car. She looked back towards the village, where the sun was now sinking behind the striking ruins of the castle. The odd, brooding shapes of its walls and towers dominated the skyline, looking forbidding in the fading light. Perfect for a photograph, she thought. Martin, her husband, would drool over a shot like this.

It had been one of the busiest days Sophie could remember, and the pace showed no sign of slowing down. A forensic team had arrived soon after her phone call reporting the murder, to be quickly followed by Benny Goodall, the pathologist. The team were in the cottage now, taking photos, examining the surfaces with their ultraviolet scanners, looking for any evidence that the murderer might have left. Sophie held out no great hopes. He'd already proved to be very efficient at removing all identifying clues. The only possible exception had been the cigarette butts found beside the wall at Spring Hill, but Sophie was not optimistic that they would yield any evidence. What were the chances that a couple of sodden fag ends would even be connected to the murder, or yield any useful evidence?

'I'd better be off,' she said to Pillay. 'Find me when you get back, or call me earlier if they find anything you think I should know about. I'll be interviewing Berzins in about an hour, once I've digested all the facts.'

She was about to return to Swanage to interview Vilis Berzins. The young trainee chef had been picked up by a transport police officer at Bournemouth railway station, just as he was about to board a train for London. Sophie thanked her good fortune and the sharp eyes of the watchful policeman. If Berzins had managed to disappear into the London immigrant community, it would probably have been impossible to trace him again. Now they had their main suspect in custody. The problem with the case was going to be finding the evidence to convict him. The crime scenes suggested meticulous preparation. Like Donna's flat, each room in her mother's cottage had been thoroughly searched by the intruder. Just as in the flat, no diaries or address books had been found. This worried Sophie. It would make the job of tracing and interviewing friends, family and acquaintances much slower.

Above all, there was a nagging doubt in her mind that a twenty-year-old, particularly one from a foreign country, would be so ruthlessly efficient. A telephone call to the police in Latvia might prove to be useful, once she'd interviewed Berzins.

* * *

As soon as she met him, Sophie's doubts resurfaced. Vilis Berzins stood up as soon as she and Barry Marsh entered the interview room. No one had prompted him to do so. Sophie told the slim dark-haired young man to sit down.

'You are Vilis Berzins from Riga, Latvia?' she asked.

'Yes.' He seemed calm but wary.

'Currently working at the Ballard View Hotel as a trainee chef?'

'Yes.'

'I'm Detective Chief Inspector Sophie Allen from the Dorset police. This is DS Barry Marsh. You may be able to help us with our inquiries concerning a recent serious crime. We have been taking statements from all of the hotel staff. I understand that you weren't at work today. I also understand that when you were approached by the police officer at Bournemouth railway station, you were happy to accompany him. You came back here to Swanage quite voluntarily. Is that the case?'

'Yes. I am always happy to help the police. My older brother is a policeman in Riga.'

Sophie made a mental note of this fact. If he was the murderer and was familiar with police techniques, it might explain his apparent lack of apprehension.

'How old are you, Vilis?'

'I am twenty. I will be twenty-one in January.'

'Why were you in Bournemouth rather than at work today?'

'I received a phone call this morning just after breakfast. It was from the embassy in London. They said that there was a problem with my passport and work permit. I was to go to Bournemouth where one of the staff would bring me a new document to complete. This person would be travelling to Poole to get a ferry to France, so could meet me in Bournemouth before travelling on to catch the boat.'

'Why didn't you tell the hotel staff before you left?'

'I was told not to do so. He said that if the hotel suspected a problem with my permit, it would put my job at risk. It was better for them not to know.'

'And did you meet this man?'

'No. He didn't come. They told me this might happen, and if so, I was to get a train to London to collect some new papers from the embassy. I am now worried that it was all a trick. It is all too strange and I don't think there is a problem with my papers.'

'How did you travel to Bournemouth?'

'On the bus.'

'And how did you get to the bus terminus this morning?'

'I walked there. It is only a few minutes.'

'So you saw the police tape across Spring Hill when you went out?'

'Yes. I would go that way, but I saw a policeman there. I used the Town Hall Lane instead. What has happened?'

'A young woman was murdered in the lane last night, Vilis.'

'Oh.' He sounded surprised and perplexed. And then he suddenly turned pale.

'Not . . . Donna?' he whispered.

'The body hasn't been formally identified yet, but it is very likely.'

Berzins' breathing became fast and shallow, and tears ran down his colourless cheeks.

'She didn't deserve this. She was such a good person,' he finally said.

'She was your girlfriend, Vilis?'

He didn't answer. He held his head in his hands until his sobs began to subside.

'You think I did this?'

'We cannot say until we have more facts. We are not questioning you under caution at this time, Vilis. Now answer my question please. Was Donna your girlfriend?'

'Yes.' He looked hollow and empty. 'For the last two months, we have been seeing each other.'

'Have you slept together?'

'Yes.'

'Did you ever meet her mother?'

'Yes, about two or three times.'

'Vilis, I am going to terminate this interview now. We will contact the duty solicitor, unless you have your own that you wish to use?'

He shook his head.

Sophie continued. 'You are now a suspect, and you need legal guidance. Do you understand that?'

He nodded.

'Your English is very good, Vilis. Normally I would have to arrange an interpreter at this stage. Do you want one?'

'No. I studied English at college before coming here. Also my parents speak English well and taught me when I was growing up.'

'The Latvian embassy should be informed of your whereabouts. We will arrange for you to do that. Sergeant Marsh here will contact them shortly and explain the situation, but you must also speak to the embassy officials yourself. You must tell them where you are and how you are being treated. And now, have you eaten since breakfast, Vilis?'

He shook his head weakly.

'I will arrange for some food and drink to be brought in. You must remain here meanwhile. If you need to use the toilet, ask the constable at the door. I will be back later.'

The two detectives left the small interview room.

'This is a difficult one, Barry. There are no obvious clues in his demeanour, are there?'

'I have my doubts, ma'am. His reactions seemed very genuine. He'd have to be a really good actor to put all that on. He went as white as a sheet.'

'It can all be planned in advance, you know. I've heard of suspects who hide a tiny sachet of a drug in their mouth. They bite it open and go pale. It's staggering what people will do. What I do know is that we have precious little evidence at the moment. Nothing really, apart from those two or three cigarette butts.'

'Why didn't you keep questioning him for a while longer? Don't you think we could have got a bit more out of him while he was surprised?'

'If he is our man, then all that was just an act anyway. If he isn't, then we haven't lost anything. And I don't want to chance losing on a technicality later. He's a foreign national, Barry. Their embassy would have a field day if I broke the rules, and so would the CPS. He's our prime suspect, and he probably knows it. Next time I speak to him it will be under caution, with a brief present. By the way, when you put him through to the embassy, make sure that he speaks in English. Make that clear to him. It's not playing entirely by the rules, but I want you to listen in. He was brought in when? Three thirty? That gives us until mid-afternoon tomorrow to get some evidence. I'll chase up forensics about those stubs. If there is a DNA match, we'll have clinched it.'

* * *

Sophie sat in her office in the incident room. She hadn't revealed her own doubts to Marsh, but she agreed with his observations about Vilis. The young man seemed so mild-mannered. Was he capable of a hatred deep enough for murder? And even if he was, had he known Donna long enough for such a hatred to develop? But then seemingly random assaults of terrible ferocity occurred all the time. Sophie pondered her next moves. Jimmy Melsom came into the room, breaking her reverie.

'Finished getting all the statements?' she asked him.

He nodded. 'But I can't say that anything striking came out of them, ma'am.'

'What about the damp clothes I asked you to look for? Any sign?'

'No. We took another look at his room. Nothing wet. And nothing hidden anywhere. The place is a bit of a rabbit warren, but we did our best.'

'Jimmy, have you had experience with tracing mobile phone calls?'

'A bit. Mainly cyber-bullying with teenagers, but there was one assault case last year where we had to trace some calls.'

'Berzins claims that he got a call this morning on his mobile from the Latvian embassy in London, about a mix up in his papers. He says that's why he left Swanage. I've just been on to the embassy and they deny that any such call was made. Could you get on to his phone company and try to trace that call? His phone is on Barry's desk. I've got the embassy calling me back shortly when they've traced any records they have on him. If I'm out when you've finished, call me on my mobile.'

She contemplated the incident board for a moment, then called Melsom back. 'Jimmy, did you find out whether Donna had an umbrella with her last night when she left?'

'Yes, ma'am. The night porter was fairly sure she did have one. Apparently it's quite eye-catching. Lydia knows more about it than me. She stayed to ask Maria more about it.'

* * *

Just after six thirty that evening Sophie arrived at the county police headquarters at Winfrith for a meeting with her boss. She got on well with Superintendent Matt Silver, but she knew he had his limitations. He was a little unimaginative, and sometimes his decision-making was slow. But he always provided a sympathetic ear, and he was proud of Sophie's achievements since he'd appointed her a year earlier.

Silver stood up as she entered his office. He welcomed her, indicating a seat in his usual friendly manner. The other person in the room remained seated. She recognised Silver's own boss, Area Chief Superintendent Neil Dunnett. She had not expected him to be present. She was expecting an informal discussion, to bring Silver up to date on her thoughts.

Silver started by asking for a review of the day's events. Sophie sensed tension in the air as she recounted the details. It felt as if there had been some disagreement between the two men before she'd arrived. Dunnett was very new to his post. He was an unknown quantity, having been appointed from outside the county force. Sophie completed her summary, and Silver questioned her about the lack of evidence at the crime scenes.

Dunnett intervened. 'Are you sure everyone was looking hard enough?' He had sat silently up to now, watching Sophie as she spoke.

'With respect, sir, the forensic team here is one of the best I've ever worked with. They do everything meticulously.'

He looked at her coldly. 'No. I meant the detectives at each scene. I didn't mention forensics.'

So this was what he was like.

'We examined everything we could that wouldn't jeopardise forensics at each location,' she said.

'Your team were first on the scene at both houses, yet you spotted nothing. I find that difficult to understand. In almost every murder case I've been involved with something has been noticed at the scene. Murders of this type, of a mother and daughter, are usually not well planned. They're killed by family, a boyfriend or someone like that. They always leave clues.'

Sophie knew that Dunnett was arguing from a position of ignorance. When he'd been appointed, she had looked up his record, and had spotted his lack of experience in violent-crime cases. He'd come through an almost entirely administrative route to his current job.

She kept her voice calm and controlled. 'Sir, I have been involved in more violent-crime cases than anyone else currently serving with this force. I know this for a fact, but you might want to check. I learned my trade in my five years under Harry Turner at the Met, then with Archie Campbell in the West Midlands. You'll already know from my record that I have the highest clear-up rate for violent crime of any officer at my rank in the south west of England. I resent the implication that I don't know my job.'

She stared back at him, wishing that she could add a few choice words. There was a silence.

She turned to Silver. 'I'll need to be off, Matt. The ACC wanted me to pop in before I go back to Swanage. I'm interviewing Berzins later this evening, if you want to be there.'

Silver looked relieved. 'Yes, that's a good idea. I'll come back with you.'

As she left the room, she heard Silver saying, 'I warned you.'

* * *

'What the hell was that all about, Matt? And what did you warn him? And just for the record, I do apologise for swearing at my immediate superior officer. I don't make a habit of it.'

Silver had been lurking in the corridor, hands in pockets, as she came out of the assistant chief constable's office. They had walked to the car park in silence.

'I'm glad of that. It doesn't go with your ice-queen image, Sophie.'

'Oh, ha bloody ha.'

'I just warned him that you had a masters in psychology. You know, I think he might be a bit thick. I wonder if he took my comment to mean that you were an academic, head-in-the-clouds type. And I didn't mean that at all. I meant it as a warning that you were an expert at behaviour, and would use it on him.'

'Do I use it on you, then?'

'Well, I've never managed to outmanoeuvre you yet. So what does that tell you?'

She ignored the question. 'I think he's just an old fashioned misogynist. A throwback to the time when men were men and women weren't detective chief inspectors investigating murder. I've never come across anything quite so crass in my entire career, and that stretches back nearly twenty years. It's unbelievable. He can't have ever read my record to make those comments. Who the hell does he think he is?'

'Don't get angry now, Sophie. You kept your cool remarkably well back there and you may well have to continue doing so for a bit longer with him. By the way, what did our friend the ACC have to say? And I must say that was the perfect coup-de-grace. "The ACC just wants me to pop in before I go back." Ouch. I was watching you at the time, but I could almost hear his jaw drop.'

'It was genuine. He did call me this afternoon and ask me to see him. And I can tell you're dying to know, but I didn't mention that little difficulty with our moody friend. I don't want to start a feud. Anyway, the ACC asked the same kind of questions that you did. Did I have enough manpower, what were my thoughts on Berzins' story, et cetera. Reassuring, eh? You're both on the same wavelength.'

'Except that you were holding back on something, Sophie. Do you want to tell me?'

'Not yet, apart from the fact that there could be more to this than meets the eye. And that's all I'm willing to say, since it is more than likely that Berzins is the killer, and that we'll somehow get the evidence to prove it.'

Just then her mobile phone rang. 'Hello, Benny. What have you found?'

'Just to let you know that the detailed scan results of the young woman are here. In addition to the bruises that we saw, she had a healed fracture of the right shin bone. Consistent with a very hard kick, but there could be a number of other conceivable causes.'

'How long ago?'

'I'd guess nine to eighteen months. And I'm sticking with my guesses about the other marks on her body. They are consistent with physical abuse over a period of time, but it's difficult to be sure of when they happened. If they were mild injuries, then within the past few weeks. If they were more serious, they could date back several months. It's impossible to be certain since people heal at different rates.'

'That's terrific, Benny. Thanks. Let me know if anything else turns up, okay? Listen, I want to come over and look at that X-ray with you. Maybe tomorrow morning? I could call in first thing.'

She ended the call and they drove in silence for a while. Then Silver spoke. 'When do you expect news about the DNA check on those cigarette ends?'

'I've leaned on them to push it through as fast as they can. I'm expecting the result mid-morning tomorrow. Apparently they got something off them, which is amazing, considering they were out in the rain for hours. Our problem, Matt, is that we know absolutely nothing about Donna before she came to Swanage three months ago. But these previous injuries give us a start. We can trawl through the hospital records.'

'You still seem to be concentrating on the girl and not her mother. There are two murders, Sophie.'

'The girl is the key, I'm sure. I'd guess that her mother was killed because she knew something that would identify her daughter's killer. It's possible that they both knew him. Maybe he was a friend or family member. That's why all the address books and diaries have gone.'

'So you don't think it was Berzins?'

'It's still possible, if he knew her for longer than he says. This case is proving to be a real puzzle and some things don't add up yet. And something else has only just occurred to me: Why did this supposed call from the embassy this morning ask him to go to Bournemouth? If some official had to be in Poole to catch a ferry, then surely they'd have asked Berzins to meet him there? It's a shorter, easier bus trip for him from Swanage, and wouldn't require an extra stop for the official. It doesn't make sense.'

'That's my girl.'

'Shut up, you patronising pig.'

* * *

The interview room was bare and functional. No matter how attractive a police station was from outside, the interiors were all too often plain and characterless. Sophie wondered if a vase of flowers would make a difference to the atmosphere. No good, of course. The vase could be broken and used as a weapon. Would plastic flowers be practical . . . ? Her thoughts were wandering — she must concentrate. She'd been questioning Berzins about Donna, trying to build up a picture of what the young woman was like. She appeared to have been intelligent but slightly guarded and prickly. This tied in with what Maria Jones had said at the hotel.

There were more people in the room at this session. The duty solicitor was sitting beside Berzins, and Matt Silver sat next to Sophie, with his chair pulled back. He was present as an observer. Barry Marsh stood leaning against the back wall, next to the solitary uniformed constable.

'Tell me what you know about Donna's family background, Vilis.'

'She told me that her father was recently dead. I don't know how. You have asked me about her mother. I do not know much about her. Donna has an older brother. I think his name is David. She said that he lives in Birmingham. I never met her grandmother. She moved to Swanage many years ago and bought the flat. She left it to Donna when she died last year.'

Sophie scribbled on a notepad, tore off the page and handed it to Marsh, who glanced at it and left the room in order to follow up the information about a brother. The bodies had still not been formally identified.

'Tell me about her mother,' said Sophie.

'She seemed a nice woman. I met her the first time when Donna took me to tea at her house last month. She talked to me about Latvia. I think she was anxious in case we became serious and I wanted Donna to return to Latvia with me.'

'Did you ever discuss this with Donna?'

'No. We had not reached that stage yet. I really liked her, but I was not sure about her feelings for me. She seemed to like me, but there were times when she was cold to me.'

'When did you feel this coldness towards you?'

'It was the morning after we . . . slept together. I felt very happy, but she did not show that. She was more distant than cold. I tried to assure her of my love, but she just smiled, and the smile had no warmth.'

'How many more times did you sleep with her?'

'One more time. Last week. Again she was cold afterwards, even more than the first time.'

'Where did you sleep together?'

'In her flat. Not in my room at the hotel. Everyone would know of it there. We did not want that.'

'Vilis, did you ever hit Donna?'

'No, of course not.' He sounded sincere enough.

'She had bruises on her face and arms. Where did they come from?'

'I did not notice them at first, when she started working at the hotel. But that was because she would keep them covered. I saw them only recently. I don't know where they came from. She wouldn't tell me.'

'How many times did you ask about them?'

'Once only. She did not want to talk about it. I was frightened that if I kept asking she would stop seeing me, and I didn't want that.'

'How obvious were the bruises when you first saw them?'

'The ones on her face were not easily seen because she wore make-up over them. On her arms they were stronger, but she wore long sleeves so people didn't know about them. They are nearly faded now. I think she was happy about that.'

'And she gave you no idea at all about how she got them? Weren't you curious?'

'Of course. I felt sorry that she'd been hurt. But she clearly didn't want me to ask about it again, so I didn't.'

'Do you smoke, Vilis?'

He looked surprised.

'Yes, but I have been trying to give up. Donna didn't like it. I am down to just three or four cigarettes a day.'

What make of cigarette do you prefer?'

'Marlboro.'

'Did Donna say why she didn't like you smoking?'

'No, but last week she told me that I must give up if I wanted to stay with her. She gave me until Christmas. So I was determined to stop.'

'Show me your writing, Vilis. Would you write your name and address on this pad, please.'

Berzins wrote his Swanage address and his address in Riga with his right hand.

'You are right-handed?'

'Yes.'

'Can you write with your left hand, Vilis?'

'No. If I do it is untidy.'

'Do you drive?'

'I learned to drive back in Riga, but I do not drive in England. Driving on the left would worry me.'

'Did Donna drive?'

'Yes, but she didn't have a car. She was saving for one. She has not driven since I knew her.'

Just then, Pillay knocked and opened the door. 'Sorry to interrupt, ma'am. You need to see this.' She stepped back into the corridor.

Sophie followed her out and took the sheet of paper.

'Christ. That's unbelievable. And the times match. And surely that's only about half a mile from the station?'

'I think so.'

'How did you spot this?'

'I was just keeping my eye on messaging, and realised something was going on. I phoned Bob Thompson over in Bournemouth once I realised its importance. I asked him to email the details across.'

They went back into the interview room.

'We will terminate this interview now, Vilis. You will remain in custody overnight, while we continue to make enquiries.'

'Is that necessary?' asked the solicitor.

'I'm afraid so. This is a murder inquiry, and Mr Berzins is one of the chief suspects. It is getting late, and we have some further inquiries to make. I suggest that we continue the interview tomorrow.'

'You only have until three thirty to keep him without charging him,' said the solicitor.

'I'm aware of that. We'll meet tomorrow.'

The Duty Constable led Berzins out of the room, followed by the solicitor.

'Look at this.' Sophie handed the paper across to Silver.

'My God. Do you think it's linked?'

'What are the chances of it not being connected? I'll need to get across there to see. Want to come? I can drop you home afterwards.'

Marsh came back in. 'What's happened?' he said.

'Another murder. This time in Bournemouth. A young woman, a prostitute, was strangled, probably earlier today. Her room has been cleaned out of any personal or contact information, and there is no trace of a mobile phone.'

'Surely it's just a coincidence? Why do we think it's connected to this case?'

'It's in the red-light district. Which is only half a mile from the railway station. And Berzins was at the station for much of the morning, waiting for a supposed meeting with a non-existent embassy official.'

CHAPTER 4: Silk Umbrella

Late Tuesday Evening, Week 1

The four detectives drove north out of Swanage. It had been a long and stressful day, so Sophie had told Barry Marsh and Lydia Pillay that they needn't come, but they had both opted to.

'We don't want to miss this,' Pillay said. 'It could wrap the case up. It's just too much of a coincidence, surely, him being in the neighbourhood when this girl was killed?'

Sophie didn't reply. She was thinking hard about how the latest murder added so many complicating factors to the investigation, forcing her to rethink some of her tentative theories.

'Never assume anything,' replied Silver. 'You can easily make a fool of yourself if you jump to the wrong conclusions. Let's just say that, at the moment, it could be a very interesting development. But we need to wait to see what the facts are first. By the way, do we know who's in charge at Bournemouth?'

'Bob Thompson was the one I spoke to, sir. He's a DS,' replied Pillay. 'I think it's a DI McGreedie in charge.'

'I know Kevin McGreedie. You've worked with him, haven't you, Sophie?' Silver said.

'Yes. He's a good detective. It'll be done properly if he's in charge.'

'That's if he stays in charge. If it looks as if it is linked, I could ask the ACC to transfer the case to us. It would make sense. But let's wait and see.'

Sophie asked Pillay about the missing umbrella.

'Maria thinks that it was an expensive designer one. It was deep burgundy in colour with a pattern of small cream-coloured roses. She also said that, even though it was obviously pricey, Donna had said she needed a new one. Maria didn't know why.'

Outside the busy holiday season the ferry route to Bournemouth, across the mouth of Poole harbour, was quicker than the long drive around the huge inlet. On a chilly and damp November evening, the wait was non-existent. They drove straight onto the ferry and were across to the Bournemouth side within ten minutes.

They soon found the road they were looking for. It was in a rather down-at-heel area of Bournemouth. At the end of the street, close to the railway station, there was a mix of commercial premises and terraced houses, but these soon gave way to larger properties, some converted into guest houses and hotels. It was easy to spot the building they were seeking. Two squad cars were parked outside, and a uniformed policeman stood guard at the door. The paint was peeling from the window frames and doors. The house looked as if it had been subdivided into six flats, spread across three floors. Sophie couldn't help comparing the building to the neatly-kept block in Swanage where Donna had lived.

Inside, the décor was worn but clean. They were met by Kevin McGreedie, a tall plain-clothes officer. Sophie liked him. He'd been in the Dorset police longer than her, and knew the criminals who operated in the Bournemouth and Poole area better than any other detective.

'Evening, Kevin,' said Silver. 'I think you know Sophie Allen?'

'Of course, sir. Glad to see you both. You're very welcome, if that's a word I can use in a situation like this. I understand you're investigating a couple of murders over in Swanage that might be related to this one.'

'We're holding a suspect at the station, Kevin,' said Sophie. 'The murders took place last night, but our man spent this morning here in Bournemouth waiting at the station for a London train. He was here for a good couple of hours. Lydia heard about the death here, and contacted Bob for details. One of ours was a strangling. In both cases the homes were ransacked in an odd way, and from what we heard that was what happened here. Is that what you've found?'

'Yes. The girl was strangled and someone has searched the flat. It's really more of a glorified bedsit, really. Anyway, we can't find any communications, lists, diaries or phones. Even the landline phone has gone missing, although we're pretty sure there was one. Forensics have just about finished, and they haven't found a thing that can be used to positively identify our victim.'

'So you don't know who she is?' said Marsh.

'Oh, we do. Her name is Susie Pater. But that comes from her neighbours. There isn't anything here with her name on it. Bob and I are mystified.'

'Has her body been taken away yet?' asked Sophie.

'No. It's ready to go, but once I heard that you were on your way, I delayed things. She's still in the position she was found in.'

'Thanks, Kevin. Can we see it now?'

McGreedie led the way to the top floor and opened a door on the left side of the stairway. There were three doors off a small entrance hall, and Kevin took them into the room on the right. It was a small bedroom with a window looking out from the back of the house. The room had a deep red carpet and red curtains. The large bed had red satin sheets, and a matching duvet. The small, pale body lay like a doll on the bed, and the white skin contrasted with the dark hair cascading across the pillow. She was wearing a satin nightdress in deep blue. A matching negligee lay untidily across the bottom of the bed, its sleeves falling almost to the floor. On a chair beside the bed were some daytime clothes — a pair of jeans, a jumper, and a matching set of bra and pants. A pair of trainers had been kicked under the chair.

Sophie looked closely at the woman's upper torso and neck. 'Can I move her head?'

McGreedie nodded. She put on a pair of latex gloves and gently turned the neck to get a better look at the ligature pattern.

'Yes,' she said. 'The marks are similar to those on Donna's mother. With her we think it was some kind of thick cord. Have a look, Lydia. You saw the marks on her. Do they look similarly placed to you? Sorry, but I need you to check.'

Pillay bent over the body.

'I think so, ma'am. The scarring looks quite precise, just like at Corfe, and in about the same position. As if whoever it was knew what he was doing.'

Sophie turned to McGreedie.

'Well, you have our thoughts, Kevin. We think it could be the same guy, and he was no novice at strangulation. Beyond that, I can't add anything. I'm totally mystified as to why she needed to die, other than that maybe she knew something that he didn't want let out. That's if there is a reason.'

There was a short silence.

'You think it might have been done for the sake of it? No other reason? He could be a psychopath killing at random?' asked Silver.

'I don't think that's the case, but we have to consider it. Nothing can be ruled out at this stage. What are your thoughts, Kevin?'

'I don't disagree with you, Sophie. Thank God you've got someone in custody already, because three murders inside twenty-four hours would just be too terrible to contemplate if he was still on the loose. But it worries me that there are no leads here, nothing substantial to go on. Let's follow the MOM principle, shall we? Means? He was prepared and had the cord with him. Opportunity? Early morning is quiet in this area, particularly mid-week. Either she knew him and let him in, or he'd booked a session with her. Motive? Well, that's the unknown, as Sophie has said. We've already started to take statements from the other flat occupants, and the neighbours. We know her name was Susie Pater, that she was twenty-four, and that she came from Exeter. We're trying to trace her family now.'

'So where do we go from here?' asked Silver.

'If you're asking what I think you are, Matt, then I'm quite happy to let Kevin deal with this end of things,' said Sophie. 'Particularly since he's made such a good start. But if it is what we think, the work of the same man, then it has to form part of the same investigation. I'd like Kevin to report everything to me. That's if you're happy with that, Kevin?'

He nodded. 'Fine by me. It makes sense.'

'I'm sure we'll work together well. If we keep each other informed of everything we discover, then we can bounce ideas off each other. And you know this locality and the residents in it better than anyone else on the force. It would be pointless for us to muscle in and take over completely. In fact, do you want to come over and see our man for yourself tomorrow morning? I'm waiting for the results of some forensic evidence, and may end up charging him late morning.'

'Absolutely. I'd like to see this guy, but I'm due in court tomorrow. Maybe Thursday?'

'Fine. Has anyone put a time on her murder? Even a rough idea?' Sophie said.

'Forensics won't commit at the moment. But the body temperature gave them something to go on and, as a rough estimate, they think it was somewhere between eight this morning and noon,' said McGreedie.

'If that does get confirmed, then it fits the time frame for when our man was hanging around at the station. He was there from mid-morning until two, when he was spotted by a transport officer.'

'That was pretty stupid. Why on earth didn't he just hop on the first train out?'

'It's complicated, Kevin. By the way, who found the body here?'

'A friend of hers called Bernice Halley. I think she's another working girl. Apparently they were due to meet for lunch at one, and when Susie didn't turn up her friend got worried. Susie was always prompt. She wasn't answering her mobile, and that was unusual. Her friend called by and found the door locked, yet a couple of windows were open. That was also unusual. She had a spare key, and our victim had one for her place. A sort of mutual safety plan in case of trouble, although it didn't work in this case. She found things as you see them, had a screaming fit and then called us in.'

'I wonder if she'd already been up and about, dressed in those clothes on the chair. They're the kind of things she might have put on for breakfast and a visit to the shops. Any evidence that she'd been out?'

'No. We don't think she had. No one else in the building had heard her go out, although I expect that there are plenty of comings and goings here. But the local shops hadn't seen her this morning.'

'Thanks. I'll just have a quick look round, if that's okay. Barry, you're with me on this.'

Sophie opened a small wardrobe that occupied a corner of the bedroom. Hanging inside were several glitzy dresses, a couple of tight skirts and three faux-fur jackets. Pairs of high heels were neatly aligned on the floor, along with several pairs of boots. On the top shelf stood a row of wigs, all on individual stands, and some ornate masks.

The dressing table unit contained a range of make-up, and two drawers of colourful lingerie. Another drawer had a neatly stacked pile of silk and satin blouses and strappy tops, while a fourth held some shiny, vinyl clothes.

'It's all well-organised, Barry. A lot cleaner and tidier than similar places I've seen. What do you think?'

'Her outfits are the kind of stuff I'd expect. As for neatness, all I can say is that it's better than my place. Makes me a bit ashamed.'

Sophie left the bedroom and walked slowly through the rest of the small flat, with Marsh following. There was a small toilet and shower room, decorated in white tiles with a pale yellow pattern. The room, too small for a bath, had a tiny washbasin fitted into one corner. She opened the cabinet, and looked at the bottles of pills and medicines on the shelves. There was nothing out of the ordinary — painkillers, birth control pills, vitamin pills and several packets of condoms, along with a toothbrush and toothpaste. The other shelves contained cotton wool, cleansing creams and hair products.

A small window looked out over the front garden to the road. The top fanlight window was open on the latch. This must have been the one that her friend had spotted. Most people wouldn't bother closing an upper-floor window as small and as invulnerable as this when leaving the house for a short time. Yet, according to her friend, Susie always secured all of her windows before going out.

The tiny kitchen was also decorated in pale yellow. A fabric-block print of sunflowers hung on one wall. A table was pushed close against one of the other walls with two chairs beneath it. There was a sink under the window, with a small worktop beside it. Fitted against a third wall was a small electric stove, with a fridge and a tiny microwave oven nearby. Sophie opened the cupboards and peered inside at the few packets and tins of food on the shelves.

The sparse collection of cooking utensils didn't look as if they were used much. The fridge contained some milk, cheese, butter and some salad vegetables, but little else. The window faced out over the front of the house and, just like the bathroom, had a small top section open slightly.

'Could you see yourself living here, Barry?'

'No. Grubby neighbourhood,' he said.

'I mean in this flat. Forget where it is.'

'Possibly. It would be okay for one person. A bit poky, but I could cope fine.'

'What about the food that's here? Any thoughts?'

'Well, she was obviously into salads. The microwave is fine. I eat a lot of ready meals. She doesn't seem to have any. I'd put a TV onto the worktop over there. You could sit and watch while eating your dinner. She doesn't seem to have a telly.'

Sophie didn't reply. The flat didn't feel right to her, but she was too tired to work out why.

'Time to go,' she said.

They returned to the hallway and Sophie turned to speak to McGreedie, who was standing and waiting for them. Three coat hooks hung from the wall beside his head, empty except for a brown leather jacket which didn't seem to be hanging straight. Sophie reached out and moved the jacket aside. Then she stood still, looking at the long, slender umbrella that was now exposed to view. It was deep burgundy, patterned with tiny, ornate roses. She turned to smile at McGreedie, put on a pair of latex gloves from her bag, and carefully lifted the umbrella into a plastic evidence bag.

'A connection. I don't know how it links them, or what it means, but this is it. A silk designer umbrella in burgundy with a flower pattern. Donna had this last night when she left the hotel.'

* * *

Sophie was curled up on the couch in her lounge, sipping coffee after the light supper that Martin had prepared. She'd changed into slacks and a cashmere jumper after a quick shower.

'Are you sure you've had enough to eat?' he asked.

'Yes, thanks. It was lovely. I've been snacking during the day, so I wasn't totally famished. And you're a genius with pasta. I don't know how you do it.'

'Sheer talent,' he said. 'Coupled with the fact that the chicken was on special offer in the supermarket, as was that jar of posh sauce. Couldn't go wrong. I got Jade to pop into the shops on her way home from school. She knows what you like.'

Sophie glanced at their teenage daughter who was sitting in the corner of the room reading a geography text-book. 'Thanks, sweetheart.'

Jade yawned. 'I'm off to bed. That hockey practice has worn me out.'

She waved to her parents as she left the room. The TV was on, but Sophie paid little attention to it. She flicked through a small pile of photos that she'd taken out of her bag. This was the third time she'd looked at them. She was frowning slightly.

'Something worrying you?'

'Possibly, but I'm most likely being paranoid. I'm about to get the results of a DNA test on a couple of cigarette butts that still had a tiny amount of saliva on them. I was astonished that it hadn't been washed off by the rain. It was pouring down for most of last night, and they must have been lying there for several hours.'

She handed Martin the photos.

'It looks as though they've been protected from the rain,' he said. 'I can see two butts, lying under a couple of leaves. A sort of umbrella effect? I'd say you've been really lucky. If that hadn't happened, I wouldn't have thought there'd have been any saliva traces left. But then, I'm no expert. Maybe it doesn't get washed off by rain as much as I'd have expected.'

'What's the leaf?' she asked. 'What type of tree?'

'Looks like a sycamore.'

'That's what I thought. There are a couple of sycamores in nearby gardens.'

He examined the photos more closely. 'Sophie, look at those fag ends again. They're almost touching, probably about a centimetre apart. What are the chances of a smoker dropping two butts, and them falling that close together, and then a leaf or two blowing over them and staying there, keeping them dry?'

'Well, if they are that close together, then it increases the chances of a leaf covering them, I suppose. But I do see what you mean.'

'You know, that leaf doesn't seem to be lying quite naturally on the ground. There's something odd about its position. Maybe it's just the photo. What do your colleagues think?'

'Haven't told them. There are a few things I haven't mentioned. I just need some thinking time, and that hasn't happened yet. It's been non-stop today, and tomorrow won't be any different. It'll probably be even busier.'

'Well, I could say that I'll be thinking of you tomorrow, but it wouldn't be true. Most of my thoughts will be on 11C's maths mock exam results.'

Sophie laughed. 'As they should be. Though I do hope you think of me sometimes during your working day.'

'Yes, but it tends to be only when I see that tall sixth-former who looks like you from the back. Sorry!'

'And I'm really sorry that there are no tall sixth-formers who look like me from the front. The wrinkles and drying skin haven't hit them yet.'

'I'd take your face over theirs any day. Listen, I'm whacked and need to get to bed. And I think you need to as well.'

'Yes, boss. This can all wait until tomorrow . . .'

Sophie stopped talking and stared into space.

'Sophie? Are you alright?' Martin said.

'Her face. I think I've seen it before somewhere. And quite recently.'

'Whose face?'

'Susie Pater. The young woman who was killed today. It was you mentioning faces just now. I knew something was niggling away at the back of my mind. Now where could it have been?'

CHAPTER 5: Scars and Bruises

Wednesday Morning, Week 1

It was a bright and sunny morning with a fresh breeze blowing in from the sea. Sophie had sent a message to the incident room, listing the tasks she wanted done in the first half of the morning. Meanwhile she visited Benny Goodall at his lab in the hospital in Dorchester.

As soon as he saw her walk in, Benny said, 'I always see you and think 'here's trouble!' You look as fresh as ever, though I expect you were up half the night.'

'It's all down to the careful application of cosmetics, Benny. Though careful is maybe not the word I should have chosen on this particular morning. Just don't examine me too closely under a strong light.'

They stood in front of a flat screen in his office.

'Here are the results of the scans I had done,' said Goodall.

He clipped an X-ray to the screen and turned on the backlight.

'What am I looking at?'

'It shows her left leg below the knee. If you look carefully you can see the residual marks from a hairline fracture mid-fibula and lying just to the outside of centre. Here.'

He pointed to the scan, where a slight, thin shadow lay across the thinner of the two shin bones.

'Now if you look closely with this magnifying glass, you'll also see a slight darkening on the surface of the tibia. It wasn't broken, but it does have a residual bruise scar.'

'So?'

The most common explanation for this type of scarring is a kick. It's why footballers wear shin-pads. A hard kick in the middle of the shin can slide off the stronger tibia. It catches in the gap and causes the fibula to break. In this case it wasn't a complete break, just a hairline crack. But it's there, as clear as day.'

'Can you be sure that it was caused by a kick?'

'No, not totally. There could be other reasons. But it is likely.'

'Okay . . . Could you face me, Benny? I want to act this out. It's your right leg, and I'm standing opposite you. I kick out like so.'

She moved her right leg so that the toe of her boot touched his shin, and then slid across the leg towards the outside.

'That doesn't seem right. Let me try the left.'

This time she stood with her right leg taking her weight, and acted out a kick with the left.

'That seems more like it. The toe-cap area is more front-on to the tibia, and catches the gap more forcefully. I think the chances are that he was left-footed. Wouldn't you kick out with your stronger foot?'

'Almost always. But we are dealing in probabilities here, not absolutes. The scarring was probably caused by a hard kick. It was probably from a left foot. This means that the perpetrator was probably left-footed. They're all probables.'

'Benny, what I do is always built on probabilities. And I've got even more ifs than you. After all, she may have been playing hockey or football and the break may have nothing whatsoever to do with the case. But there are the other marks that you spotted, and taken together it all tends to point one way, doesn't it?'

'I'm not an expert on domestic violence, Sophie. But I have seen plenty of evidence for it over the years. And I have to say that this bone-scarring, coupled with the skin marks, does tend to point that way. They seem to fit the pattern. Here are the photos for you.'

Sophie looked at the close-up images of the marks on Donna's arms and face.

'Do you think that the faint marks on her neck could have been due to attempted strangulation?'

'Well, I did wonder that yesterday when I first spotted them. And nothing in the close-up images would count against it. But they are almost healed, so it's difficult to be sure.'

'How do they match up with the position and marks on her mother's neck? You haven't started her autopsy yet, have you?'

'No, it's scheduled for mid-morning. But there are close-up photos of her injuries. I had them taken when her body was brought in yesterday evening. I haven't had a close look yet.'

They moved to his desk, and he opened a file of digital images on his computer. He placed a set of ruler guides on the screen, and took measurements. When they returned to the photos of Donna and compared the relative positions of the marks, there was little variation.

'Looks similar,' Goodall concluded. 'But then it could be argued that there won't be much of a variation in position, no matter who the strangler was. The pressure points are pretty localised.'

'Even so. There was a strangling of a young woman yesterday in Bournemouth, over by the railway station. It might be the same guy. Her post-mortem will be late today at the infirmary, I expect. I wonder if it's possible for you to have a word with whoever does it about getting really accurate measurements for the neck marks, and some close-up images? We could then compare all three.'

She looked again at the photos of Donna's mother on the computer screen.

'Is it possible to make any conclusions about the ligature used?'

'Not from the girl, no. The marks are too faint to be certain. But we might be able to from the marks on her mother's neck. My guess is some kind of cord, but I'll do some measurements during the examination.'

'Fine. Any information is better than nothing.' She pointed to the X-ray still clipped to the backlit screen. 'Did she have treatment for that fracture? Can you tell from the scan?'

'It would have been very painful, and would have induced swelling. Most people would have got it checked out. Standard treatment would have been a cast for three or four weeks to allow a clean knitting of the bone tissue. A hairline fracture like that would probably have healed cleanly if she'd strapped it up tightly herself and kept off her feet for a couple of weeks. But how likely is that? My guess is that she had it treated. Most people would because of the pain.'

'That means there must be hospital records somewhere. Can you be any more definite about a possible date for the injury?'

'Not really. I'm sticking my neck out a bit with the guess I've given you. Don't take it as gospel, and be prepared to go for dates before or after.'

'Look, I'd better be getting back to Swanage. The team have been chasing up some loose ends, and I want to see how they are getting on. And the DNA results should be coming in soon.'

'By the way, Sophie, there were no signs of recent sexual activity. And there's something you need to know about the knife injury. It didn't do nearly as much damage as the doctor at the scene thought.'

'What does that mean?'

'She may not have died instantly. There's a distinct possibility that she bled to death, maybe taking up to ten minutes or so.'

'Would she have been conscious?'

'Unlikely. At best she would have been drifting in and out of consciousness, and that only for the first few minutes. The main cause of death would have been blood loss.'

'That's given me something to think about. Thanks.'

She shook his hand and turned to leave.

'I was hoping for a goodbye kiss,' he said.

'You'll wait a long time for that, young man,' she laughed. 'Any more cheek and I'll set my six-foot-four, rugby-playing husband onto you.'

'Is this someone new? Martin is a five-foot-ten maths teacher who shares my hobby of birdwatching. He hasn't played rugby since we were at school together, and he hated it then. But thank you for the "young man" compliment.'

'You're most welcome. Bye, Benny.'

* * *

Sophie was back in Swanage by ten. The incident room was busy, with all of the detectives either inspecting documents or making telephone calls. Barry Marsh looked up as she came in, and raised a finger. She crossed the room to his desk.

'Morning, Barry. Something useful?'

'Yes, ma'am. The street light on Spring Hill was out because someone had cut some of the internal wiring. I went across this morning with an electrician called by the council.'

'So does that imply someone with electrical knowledge? Isn't it difficult to get inside those things?'

'No. Apparently it's fairly simple. All you need is a triangular key to get the cover-plate off, and some insulated wire-cutters to snip the wires inside. Job done.'

'How easy is it to get these keys? Are they common?'

'If you didn't have one, a small wrench would do the job perfectly. So our man didn't need any special skill. It would only take a minute or two at the most.'

'Did you check the inside fittings for prints?'

'Nothing came up. He must have been wearing gloves,' said Barry.

'It was all meticulously planned and carried out. He left nothing to chance. That's just for you and me, by the way.'

'But what about the cigarette butts? Isn't the DNA match due in later? If they do match, that'll have been a serious slip-up. Maybe luck will be on our side after all,' Barry said.

'Maybe. The results should be in any time now. Any luck tracing Donna's brother?'

'Not yet, but I'm hopeful. There are three of us working through the lists. It would have been near-impossible if we didn't know his name was David. But there are still an awful lot of David Goodenoughs in the Midlands, or even ones with an initial D.'

'Keep at it. We need to get a family member to identify the bodies. And the knife?'

'Not yet. We've got people combing the immediate area. They've searched all the obvious places, including the brook, and nothing's turned up. Maybe we'll never find it.'

'That wouldn't surprise me, Barry. It all looks so well planned that I'd expect him to have thought of disposal in advance. I don't think our guy would just throw it away hurriedly. It'll be somewhere where we're unlikely to find it. Either that or he's still got it as a trophy. That might be more in line with the kind of person he is. And the umbrella puzzles me. Turning up the way it did in Susie's flat confirms the link between her murder and Donna's. But why would the killer take it there and then partly hide it behind a jacket? I just don't get it.'

'As far as we can tell it is the same one. Maria described it in detail. But like you, I can't see why he would want to take it. The knife I can understand. He wouldn't want it left at the scene, but an umbrella? Strange.'

'By the way, Barry, I had the strangest feeling last night that I'd seen Susie Pater's face before. My husband happened to mention something about faces and it suddenly occurred to me. Maybe it was down to my tiredness, but I was convinced there was something familiar about it.'

'Can't say I spotted anything, ma'am, but I'll give it some thought.'

Sophie nodded and crossed to Lydia Pillay's desk.

'How's the hospital search going?'

'Good, ma'am. I started here in Swanage at the local cottage hospital, and with the local health centre, but found nothing. Same with Poole, but I struck it lucky in Bournemouth, and got a positive right away. I can go across and see them tomorrow morning. Is that alright?'

'Absolutely. If we're in luck someone might remember her. Maybe someone discussed the injury with her.'

'It would have been so much easier if she'd been registered with one of the local doctors. They'd have had her records to hand. I wonder why she didn't?'

'Maybe she just didn't get around to it. But she must be registered somewhere.'

Sophie walked to the centre of the room and addressed the whole team.

'Listen, everybody! We'll have a full meeting at one thirty sharp, directly after lunch. I'd like a verbal report from everyone on progress so far. By then we should know the DNA results. Let's keep our fingers crossed.'

* * *

She was sipping a coffee in the corridor when her mobile rang. It was the forensic office at county headquarters. She listened intently, and then went to find the senior station officer.

'The DNA analysis has come back from forensics, and it's positive. I'd like Berzins charged at one thirty. Could you put someone on to getting his solicitor back in?'

'That's brilliant news. You must be pleased. Do you think you can find enough evidence to charge him with the other two murders?'

'We'll do our best, Tom. By the way, I've arranged for someone to come in and observe while we charge him. She's DI Wendy Blacklock from the Met's domestic violence unit. She should be arriving sometime soon, but if she is late we hold back on the charge until she's here. Okay?'

She returned to the incident room, called the team together and told them the news about the DNA match. There were one or two whoops and cheers.

'Don't get carried away. We still need all of this backup evidence. If anything, it's even more important now. And we need to trace the brother. So keep at it.'

She spoke quietly to Marsh.

'Barry, we'll charge him at one thirty. His solicitor is being contacted. I've arranged for someone from the Met to be present as an observer, just so that you know. I want you there as well.'

* * *

Wendy Blacklock had been second in command of the Met's domestic violence unit for three years. She was considered to be one of the foremost experts on assaults within relationships. Sophie had met Wendy while attending several training courses that Wendy had run, and they had stayed in contact. She was shorter than Sophie, dark-haired and with none of Sophie's sharp dress sense, but they got on well. Both were dedicated and shrewd, and well respected professionally. Wendy had travelled from London to Wareham after Sophie's phone call the previous evening.

'I can do my paperwork on the train, so it won't be a problem,' she'd said. 'It will be good to get out of London for a day, particularly to the seaside.'

Berzins had been brought up from the cells, and was sitting in the interview room with the solicitor. Sophie sat down opposite him. Barry Marsh and Wendy Blacklock stood against the wall, just inside the door. Berzins looked tired and pale.

'Good afternoon, Vilis. Have you been treated well since I saw you last?'

The young man nodded.

'Is there anything you wish to change in the statement you made yesterday?'

'No. I told you what I know.'

'Is there anything that you wish to add? Maybe you've thought of something else, something that you forgot to tell us?'

'I do not think so.'

'We didn't really talk much about what you did while you were at the railway station in Bournemouth. Did you leave the station at any time?'

'No. I took a book with me and sat reading it while I was waiting. I sat for most of the time in the waiting room where it was warmer than outside on the platforms.'

'What book was it?'

'*A Tale of Two Cities*. I am trying to read some of Dickens' novels.'

'Where is the book now?'

'In the cell. It was taken from me when I was first brought here, with my phone and other things. But I asked for it to be returned yesterday evening so that I could read more.'

Sophie turned and looked at Marsh, indicating that he should fetch the book.

'So you didn't leave the station? Were there others in the waiting room with you?'

'Yes. People came and went. Most didn't stay long, just to wait for their trains to arrive.'

'Did you talk to anyone? Would any other travellers be able to verify that you were there?'

'I don't think so. I sat reading all of the time. I don't remember speaking to anyone.'

'Have you been to Bournemouth before, Vilis?'

'Yes. I went several times with Donna to visit the shops.'

'How did you travel there?'

'On the bus. Across the ferry. We got on the bus at the station.'

'Where did you get off in Bournemouth?'

'In the town centre. Where the big shops are. We had lunch there too. It was on our days off.'

'Where did you have lunch?'

'Donna liked the big pub beside the square. You can use the upstairs bar and look out over the gardens.'

'Did you go to the area near the station on any of these visits?'

'No. Yesterday was the first time I went there. The other times we stayed in the shopping area. What information do you want from me? I don't understand.'

'A serious crime happened yesterday only a few minutes' walk away from the station, Vilis. It seems to have occurred at about the time you were there. Also, we found the body of Donna's mother yesterday in her house. She had been strangled.'

He dropped his head onto his arms and sobbed quietly. Finally he raised his head and looked at Sophie through tear-filled eyes.

'I didn't do any of these terrible things. I could never hurt anyone that way. Please believe me.'

Marsh returned and handed a paperback book to Sophie. She opened it and read the inscription: 'Happy Birthday, Vilis. Love from Donna.'

'So Donna bought this for you as a gift? How long ago?'

'It was for my last birthday, in September. Before we were seeing each other. She knew I liked reading, and I had read two other Dickens' books. She gave me this, and told me I would enjoy it. She said it was a novel about liberation and sacrifice. She said that it meant a lot to her.'

'Do you know what she meant by that?'

'No. I told you that she didn't talk about her past. Even when I asked her. And this was before we were together.'

Sophie opened the novel at a bookmark. 'So where have you reached?'

Berzins sounded weary. 'To where Sidney Carton has visited Darnay in prison and has taken his place.'

Sophie nodded. 'Why do you think he did that?'

'Because he loves Lucy. He wants her safe and secure and have a happy life.' He paused. 'That is what we all want. That is what I would have wanted for Donna.'

Sophie remembered Wendy Blacklock's suggestion that she should ask questions about his family, particularly the female members.

'Do you have any sisters, Vilis?'

'Yes. I have twin sisters still in Riga. They are sixteen.'

'Did you help your parents out when they were growing up?'

'Of course. My mother was often working in the café. I would read to my sisters on many evenings. I even started to read to them in English. They are doing well at school. They want to be doctors. I think they will do so. They are both clever, and study hard.'

'Did you help in the café sometimes?'

'Yes, we all did on busy holidays. It was expected, because my parents came from poor backgrounds and worked hard to make the café popular. They wanted it to be in the family.' Berzins almost smiled as he spoke about his family.

'How do you get on with your mother, Vilis?'

'Why are you asking me this? I love her of course. She means much to me. My parents have worked so hard to build up the café. It started small. I remember as a small boy that they had to struggle. Now it is one of Riga's most popular restaurants. I am very proud of my parents. And my mother is very proud of us all, me and my brother and my sisters.'

'What did you think of Donna's mother?'

'She was a nice lady, I think, but she was not warm like my own mother. I felt that she didn't trust me. But I don't think it was just me. From her talk with Donna I think she was probably the same with other men. She did not seem very close even to Donna. Not like my mother is with her children.'

'Can you explain, Vilis, how we came to find her dead yesterday in her cottage?'

'I cannot believe it. It cannot all be true. How can such terrible things happen? I do not understand any of this. Not any of it.'

'Vilis Berzins, we have a positive match for your DNA at the scene of Donna's murder. You will now be charged with committing that murder.'

Berzins shrank in his seat, looking bewildered. Sophie turned and nodded to the custody officer. He came forward, read out the charges, and handed the sheet to the solicitor.

* * *

Sophie and Wendy Blacklock walked along the corridor.

'What do you think, Wendy?'

'He's a puzzle. I must say he didn't ring any alarm bells. He didn't show any sign of being a violent man. His reactions all seemed genuine. But he is speaking to us in what to him is a foreign tongue. His English is very good, but there was always a fractional delay in responding to questions. He had to pick his words — quite naturally. So he didn't answer your questions instantly. And he is obviously very intelligent. How many of us could discuss a Dickens novel like that?' She turned to Marsh. 'Could you?'

'No. Haven't even heard of it. The only one I know about is Oliver Twist, and that's only because I saw the film.'

'Yet he was quite able to talk about it. He's mentally sharp. Physically he doesn't fit either, but the stereotype is too often wrong. Wife abusers come in all shapes and sizes, and from all classes.'

'Aren't you getting too hung-up on the abuse side of things?' asked Marsh. 'You are implying that the abuser is also the murderer. But the signs of abuse are old. They are probably from a relationship that was over some time ago. That doesn't mean that Berzins didn't commit the murder, just that he may not have caused the scarring on her body. Isn't it the case that some women seem to be attracted to potentially violent men? They leave one but somehow manage to find another almost as bad, or maybe even worse? Maybe she's had a string of troubled relationships, and without realising it she found herself in another one with Berzins.'

'Donna's friend Maria described Berzins as totally placid. She said that he wouldn't harm a fly,' said Sophie.

'That doesn't mean a thing, Sophie,' answered Blacklock. 'Maria was on the outside. Many domineering men are adept at hiding their real nature from even their closest friends. That's why so many women are bewildered by the abuse that they suffer, and why people often don't believe them. Friends and other family members think that the man couldn't possibly be violent or abusive, so the woman must be partly to blame. The wife or partner can even come to believe that herself. She starts to think "It's only with me that he is like this, so I must set it off somehow. It must be my fault." This line of thinking is very common, but it's completely wrong. The abusive man chooses to be abusive. He doesn't choose to abuse his friends, sisters or neighbours, otherwise they would know. It's almost always a rational decision, and he keeps the abuse within a single relationship at any one time. That's what I was looking for in Berzins, those signs of a controlling nature. I didn't spot it, so I don't think he was the abuser, but I can't be sure.'

* * *

They assembled in the incident room where the rest of the team were waiting. Sophie called the group together.

'You all need to know that Vilis Berzins has just been charged with the murder of Donna Goodenough.'

There were loud sighs of relief.

'But there is still a massive amount of work to be done. There are too many loose ends, and we still lack a clear motive. Really, the only thing that has allowed us to charge him is the DNA on the cigarette butts found at the scene. Without that, we would be nowhere. It makes me very uneasy, I have to tell you. We did think that the motive was linked to the old scars found on her body. But the time frames don't match, and DI Blacklock here doubts that he had an abusive relationship with Donna. Barry has suggested that the two may not be linked at all. Donna was in an abusive relationship but it ended. Berzins was the new partner. He was not abusive but he did murder her. We have to follow all of these leads until each is wrapped up neatly, and we still have to find the motive for this murder — and that of her mother.' She looked at Wendy Blacklock. 'Is there anything else you want to add about your observation of Berzins?'

'Not a great deal. Just be aware that he is very intelligent. It would be foolish to underestimate him as a typical young incomer from Eastern Europe, working at a low-level hotel job. He comes from a high-achieving family, and he is here for a clear purpose. His parents started with a small café, have turned it into a successful restaurant and have plans for a hotel. That's why he is here. He's no fool. If he is your man, then he is clever enough to have thought all of this through. From what I've heard, it will be difficult to get more evidence from him to support the case.'

'Anything else to report, people?'

'I think I've traced her brother,' Melsom said. 'In Walsall. I phoned and a cleaner answered. Apparently she comes in to do his cleaning and laundry twice a week. She confirmed that his name was David and that he has a family connection to Swanage. He gets in from work at about six thirty. He works for a small delivery company.'

'We need to pay him a visit. Jimmy, do you think you could contact the local police and tell them? See if they know anything about the brother. I'll go this evening if they agree. Do you want to come?'

Melsom looked surprised. 'Me? Oh, yes. I'd love to.' Then he added, 'ma'am. Thank you. Ma'am.'

Sophie turned to Marsh, and winked.

He smiled back. 'Good move, ma'am,' he whispered.

'We'll set off in an hour or so, and drop Wendy off at Wareham station on the way. By the way, Jimmy, has there been any progress on the supposed phone call to Berzins' mobile?'

'I contacted his phone company, ma'am, and they're doing a trace back. They said it might take a couple of days.'

'Follow it up again tomorrow. If you feel they're not pulling out all the stops, threaten them with me. Tell whoever it is that I'll go direct to the top and give them a roasting.'

Sophie turned back to Marsh. 'Barry, I'd hoped to see Kevin McGreedie in Bournemouth this afternoon. That's impossible now. How would you feel about going instead?

It'll mainly involve keeping him up to date on what we are doing, and finding out anything new from him. And the initial post-mortem reports should be coming in from Benny Goodall later. Could you keep me posted? Phone me with any news.'

'I'd be pleased to, ma'am. Things are really beginning to hum now, aren't they?'

CHAPTER 6: Brotherly Love

Wednesday Evening, Week 1

Sophie, Melsom and a local police officer were on the second floor of a four-storey block of apartments. When they rang, a tall man in his late twenties came to the door. He had curly fair hair and was wearing jeans with a blue shirt open at the neck. He didn't look anything like his sister.

'Yes?'

Sophie held up her warrant card. 'I'm DCI Sophie Allen, from Dorset police. This is my colleague, DC Jimmy Melsom. Constable Angel is from the local Walsall force. Are you David Goodenough?'

Goodenough nodded. 'Yes, I am.'

'May we come in?'

He looked puzzled. 'Yeah. I've only just got in myself. Come through.'

He led Sophie through a small hallway to the living room. It was on the small side, but was neat and tidy. Sophie noticed a well-filled shelf of DVDs along one wall.

'You can sit down. I've only just put the kettle on, so it should be ready in a mo if you want some tea.'

'That would be lovely, Mr Goodenough.'

Sophie and the local officer sat on the sofa. Jimmy remained standing just inside the doorway from the hall. Goodenough came through from the kitchen and stood beside a coffee table in the middle of the room.

'Why do you want to see me? It must be something to do with Donna or my mum if you're from Dorset. Are they okay?'

'You need to sit down, Mr Goodenough.'

His eyes didn't leave her as he sat.

'I have very bad news for you, and I'm finding it difficult to find a gentle way in. I don't think that there is an easy way. I have to tell you that your sister was found dead two nights ago. She had been stabbed. We had difficulty in tracing your mother despite the fact that she lived close. When we did so yesterday afternoon, I found her dead also. She had been strangled. We think that the two murders occurred within a couple of hours of each other.'

He sat absolutely still, his face a rigid mask of disbelief. 'Surely there's a mistake? Both of them? It can't be,' he whispered. 'No.'

'We are certain that there is no mistake, Mr Goodenough. We are positive that the victims are, as I said, your mother and sister. We are all most dreadfully sorry about it.'

'How can you be sure?' His voice shook.

'There hasn't been a formal identification yet, which is why we've been trying to trace you. But we do have a photo from your sister's flat. And descriptions given by Donna's workmates, and your mother's neighbour. We have little doubt.'

'Who could have done it? And why?'

'We have someone in custody at the moment. The motive is unclear but I'm sure we'll discover it. They weren't random killings.'

'I heard about some murders in Dorset on the news this morning. But they didn't give any details. I was going to phone Mum tonight to check up on her. And now . . .'

'When did you last see them?'

He screwed up his eyes. His face looked crumpled, suddenly older.

'In the summer. Late August. It was Mum's birthday. I went to stay with Donna for the weekend. She was just moving in to her flat.'

'You stayed with Donna rather than your mother?'

'Yes. We were close. Mum's a bit reclusive and doesn't like her routine changed. We took her out a couple of times, and I visited the cottage. But I rarely stayed with her. Neither did Donna.'

Sophie looked across at Jimmy and mouthed the word 'tea,' but Liz Angel spoke up.

'It's okay. I'll get tea for everyone. Are there some biscuits, sir?'

Goodenough nodded.

'I don't think we should talk about the details, Mr Goodenough. You've had a terrible shock, one that few people will ever have to face. What I'd like to do now is arrange with you a time when you can visit Dorset and carry out the official identification. It would be really helpful if you could make it as soon as possible.'

'Whenever suits. Work is a bit thin at the moment, and the boss can handle it okay without me. When are you going back?'

'This evening. But don't think that you have to come with us. We can send someone for you anytime in the next couple of days.'

'No, that's fine.' He sounded very tired. 'I won't sleep tonight if I stay here. I may as well come with you. I feel slightly distant, as though I'm no longer part of the world. Is that normal?'

'Yes, and it's absolutely to be expected. You're in shock. Let's have some tea and a couple of biscuits. You need something inside of you. I'll arrange for a doctor to be available for when we arrive in case you feel worse. DC Melsom here can arrange somewhere for you to stay. Maybe a local hotel or guest house.'

'Oh, I suppose I can't use either of their houses?'

'No. They are both crime scenes. But I'd like you to take us through both properties at some stage just to check for anything unusual. Would you be able to stay for a few days? We can contact your work for you if necessary.'

* * *

Jimmy drove on the journey south. He'd just completed the police forces' advanced driving course and obviously enjoyed the feel of the smooth, high-powered saloon. Sophie sat in the back with David Goodenough.

'Donna's flat has obviously been searched by someone. Forensics have finished with it, and it would be useful for you to tell us if anything obvious is missing. There's a photo of Donna in the lounge. It shows her on a beach somewhere. Probably abroad?' Sophie said.

'I know the one you mean. I think it was the summer before last. She went to Greece with a friend. She had it on the shelf beside the one of the three of us — her, me and Mum.'

'The photo of Donna was the only one we found. It had dropped behind a chair. There were no others anywhere in the flat. And no address books, diaries or anything else that could help us trace her family and friends.'

'That's odd. She had quite a few photos, and she should have an address book.'

'Who was the friend she went on holiday with?'

'I don't know. No one close. It might have been someone she was working with. She had part-time jobs while she was at university.'

'We know nothing about your father, David. Is he still alive?'

His face seemed to harden slightly. 'No. He died in a car accident in August. But he and Mum had been apart for years, and we never saw him. He wasn't our favourite person. I don't really want to talk about him at the moment. Donna and I hated him. If he'd still been alive he's the first person I would have pointed you towards. So can we change the subject?'

He had become quite agitated, so Sophie asked him about his job. He was worried about the effect of the economic downturn on the delivery company he worked for. As for his personal life, he wasn't currently in a relationship. He had broken up with his last girlfriend when she returned to her home in Norway. Apparently neither of them was unduly upset.

'Did you know about Donna's leg fracture?' Sophie asked.

'Mum told me about it. I think it was last winter. It was just a normal fracture, that's what she said. And that she did it playing hockey.'

'Was this before she moved to Swanage?'

'Yes. I think she was living in Bournemouth at the time. I hadn't seen her for ages. Mum said she appeared on her doorstep without any warning, hobbling on a crutch and with her leg in plaster. She said that she'd been in a lot of pain. She was in a cast for a few weeks.'

'Do you know where she was treated? Was it in Bournemouth?'

He shook his head. 'No idea. She hadn't registered with a doctor there. She was still with our old family doctor up here.'

'Yet she'd been living in Bournemouth for some time?'

'More than a year, I think. I didn't see her for a long time. She almost dropped out of our lives, and that includes Mum, who didn't live far away.'

'Do you know why?'

'It was a bit odd. I thought that the three of us would stay in touch, even though I was still in Birmingham. I still saw Mum when I could, but it was as if Donna had gone into hiding. The only other time I've seen her was when I stayed in August. I hoped that we could start to get close again, just like when we were growing up.'

'What about your father? I know you said that you didn't want to talk about him, but at some time I will need to find out from you where he fits into all of this. If you really want to leave it until tomorrow, I'll understand.'

'You may as well know. He was a bastard. He was the cause of it all. He used to beat my mother up. And he used to knock us about, too. I put up with it until I was about seventeen and about to leave home after I got a job. Then I thumped him back, and walked out. I never saw him again, I'm glad to say. Mum left soon after. It was harder for Donna. She was the apple of his eye when he was sober, but he used to hit her when he was drunk. They were bad times. Thank God they're over.'

He suddenly realised what he'd said, and looked shocked. 'I didn't mean that. Oh God, what a mess.'

'Don't worry. Your reaction is very understandable, and maybe I pushed you a bit hard. Would you like us to stop for a coffee or food? I think there's a service area a few miles ahead.'

He nodded.

* * *

'This must be a difficult thing for you to have to do,' Goodenough said as they sipped their coffees. 'I mean this part of your job. Visiting relatives of victims, and breaking bad news to them.'

'It's not easy, as you say. But it helps us to build up a picture of the person's background.' She took another sip. 'This has been particularly difficult, with the double murder of your closest relatives. I really feel for you. I felt like I was walking on glass when I first broke the news to you. It must have been heart-rending to hear it.'

'I still can't take it in. I still think that you must have made a mistake somewhere, that it won't be them, or maybe not both of them. But I know that's not likely. I think you've handled it the best you could.'

Sophie nodded her thanks. She checked her mobile phone for messages. Barry Marsh reported that the meeting with McGreedie had been fairly routine, with no new information. Lydia Pillay's message said that she had managed to arrange her visit to Bournemouth in the morning to interview hospital staff. She hoped to be back by midday. Sophie walked a short way from the table and phoned McGreedie.

'Hi, Kevin. Listen, can we meet sometime tomorrow, fairly urgently?' There was a pause. 'Mid-morning would be fine. Yes, come across to us in Swanage if you like. There are a couple of things that have been niggling me. It would also give you an opportunity to see Berzins, our suspect. I'd like your views on him. See you then.'

* * *

It was late evening by the time they arrived back in Swanage. Marsh was waiting for them outside Donna's flat.

'Do you have a key?' Sophie asked.

Goodenough shook his head. Marsh unlocked the door and Donna's brother went in, moving slowly through to the lounge. The two detectives followed him.

'It seems as if it's lost its soul,' he said.

'Everything is pretty much as we found it. DS Marsh here can get a doctor across if you think you need one. You'll still be in shock.'

Goodenough shook his head.

'Okay, but could you do a really quick check of the photos, just to confirm what's missing?'

He made his way through the silent rooms. 'Family portraits,' he said. 'A couple in each room.'

'But why would they have gone missing?' asked Sophie. 'I'm puzzled. I can only suppose they might have helped us trace you earlier.'

'Donna always wrote on the back of her photos. She'd list the people, and the date and where it was taken.'

Sophie spoke quietly to Marsh. 'That's probably why all of the photos are gone. Maybe our man was worried that he was named on the back of a picture somewhere. He didn't have time to check them all so he took the lot. He must have had a holdall or something with him. Yet the neighbours didn't hear or see anything?'

'No. The top-floor flat is a holiday home, apparently. They're not in it very often once the summer is over.'

'We'll get Jimmy to trace them tomorrow, Barry. Just in case they were here, and saw something. It would be stupid not to check. If we could just find a clue as to what time it was ransacked, it would help a lot.'

'Why's that, ma'am?'

'Berzins finished work at ten thirty and apparently didn't hurry out. Donna finished at eleven sharp. If Berzins killed her, he would have had to search the flat after the murder. There just wasn't time before, particularly with the need to get that street lamp sabotaged — and smoke two cigarettes while waiting on the path. If we find it was searched before the murder, then it wasn't him, and we're barking up the wrong tree.'

They dropped David Goodenough at a nearby guest house. They arranged with him to carry out a similar inspection of the cottage at Corfe sometime the following day. Then they discussed the initial post-mortem findings on Brenda Goodenough and Susie Pater. Apart from the obvious marks left by the strangulation, neither showed any other signs of physical abuse. There had been no signs of recent sexual activity in either case, but Brenda did have traces of an anti-depressant in her blood-stream. She also showed signs of cirrhosis of the liver, something that is consistent with long-term alcohol abuse.

CHAPTER 7: More Puzzles

Thursday Morning, Week 1

Martin was drawing back the bedroom curtains. He'd already deposited a mug of tea on her bedside table, but she hadn't woken until the sound of his voice and the scraping of the curtain-rings filtered through her dreams.

He gave her a kiss on the cheek.

'Come on, sweetheart. Time to wake up.'

'Oh, Martin, I didn't even know you'd got up. I was sound asleep.'

'No need to tell me. I had noticed, you know. It's nearly eight, so I need to be off. I left you to lie in a little longer than you asked. You're in danger of wearing yourself out.'

'No, I'm okay. Really. I'd tell you if it was getting to me. But thanks anyway, you're a star.' She sipped the tea. 'Busy day today?' she asked.

'Moderate, but maybe not by your standards.'

'Well I'm usually only dealing with one or two people at a time, not a roomful of resentful teenagers. And your life is consistently busy. Mine veers between the frenetic and the very calm. I'll try to be in for dinner tonight. Okay?'

'Lovely. I'll get something tasty on the go for us. Phone me when you're setting out. Bye!'

He blew her a kiss from the doorway. Sophie finished her tea, and left the house, heading to the police station before collecting David Goodenough.

* * *

The pathologist had emailed through a copy of his full post-mortem report on Donna Goodenough. Sophie quickly skimmed through the long text, picking out the main points. She decided not to share these with the rest of the team for the time being. There were one or two details that required careful thought, and a couple of the items needed checking with Kevin McGreedie.

She walked through to the main incident room to check for new information. Lydia Pillay had already left for her visit to the hospital in Bournemouth where Donna had been treated for her leg injury. She wasn't expected back until late in the day. Sophie had asked her to drive to the Midlands in order to visit Donna's GP in Walsall once she'd finished at the hospital. Jimmy Melsom was on the phone to Berzins' mobile network provider, trying to extract information about the call made on the morning of the murder. Sophie couldn't hear exactly what he was saying, but his voice sounded rather more forceful than on the previous day. Maybe he'd make better headway today. Other people were cross-checking details against data held in the police central system or writing up reports on the house-to-house inquiries. The room had a satisfying bustle. Barry Marsh walked in.

'Morning, Barry. The place is a hive of activity. How are you?'

'Fine, ma'am. I've got a couple of people following up on the owners of the other flats in Donna's block. We've got a name and address for the top-floor people, so we should be able to talk to them soon. I've put a team out on a house-to-house in Gilbert Road. When you mentioned how important the time was, it occurred to me that other neighbours might have seen or heard something. They can be a bit of a nosey lot round here, you know.'

'Good idea. God knows where the police would be if it wasn't for nosey neighbours. Well, it's probably time we were off to collect David Goodenough. I'd like to know your thoughts about him, so stay watchful please.'

'You think he could be involved somehow?'

'Look how much he has to gain. He'll presumably pick up the proceeds from the sale of the two properties. The total value can't be much less than half a million, given house prices in this area. Something to think about, isn't it? We should check the details of the father's death in that car accident. It must be on record somewhere. Could you set one of the local people onto it?'

* * *

The two detectives had another short tour of the flat before collecting Donna's brother, this time checking the views from the windows. The kitchen and lounge at the rear of the apartment looked over houses in nearby streets, but from the windows of the main bedroom at the front Sophie was able to see over the station and clinic rooftops, beyond to the Spring Hill path.

'Barry, I can see the top section of the path from these windows. The lower section is hidden by the station roof and the health clinic. It may not be important, but it's worth noting.'

Marsh came over to have a look. The back of the old hotel building where Donna had worked could be seen on the skyline, looming over the top of the Spring Hill footpath.

'You'd need good eyesight or a pair of binoculars, even in daylight, to see any detail. At night you wouldn't be able to see anything. But it must have been convenient for her, easy to get to and from the hotel for her shifts.'

'Did you get the impression that Goodenough was holding back on something when we were here last night? It was when I asked about the photos.'

'Not really, ma'am. But then I'd only met him a few minutes previously. You and Jimmy were with him all evening.'

They walked the two hundred yards to Goodenough's hotel. He looked much better than he had the previous evening.

'We were just admiring the view from Donna's flat,' said Sophie. 'It's lovely in the front rooms. They must get the sun all day.'

'Yes. Donna was thinking of rearranging the rooms, but hadn't got around to making a start. It's broadly just left the way Gran had it. The kitchen has been decorated, but that's as far as Donna got. Apparently she did chuck out a lot of Gran's old furniture, and other stuff that was cluttering up the place.'

'Didn't it bother you that Donna was left the flat when your grandmother died?'

'Not really. She left me some money, and Donna promised me to even up the amounts when Mum's cottage was left to us.'

'That wouldn't have been for some time, surely?'

'Mum wasn't a well woman, Chief Inspector. She developed a heart weakness some years ago.'

'Mr Goodenough, is there anything else that I should know about the family? Anything at all that could shed light on these awful events?'

He shook his head.

'Apart from the situation with your father, the rest of you had normal relationships — where you supported each other?'

'Yes. That's a good way of describing it.'

They set off for Dorchester. Sophie drove, with Goodenough sitting in the passenger seat. Marsh sat in the back seat behind Sophie, to observe Donna's brother during the forty minute drive.

'I know it's not an ideal time to ask, David, but it would be really helpful if you could tell us anything else you remember about Donna's relationship with your father, particularly over the past year or so. Did you talk about him at all when you saw her earlier in the year?'

'Not in terms of Donna seeing him. As I said, he died in August. We did talk about what he'd left us, but it was almost nothing. He went to pieces after Mum left him, and drank away his money, as far as we could tell.'

'Wasn't there any property left?'

'Mum left after Donna went to university, and the house was sold. They split the money and Mum put her share towards the cottage in Corfe. As far as I know, he ended up living in and out of hostels for the homeless once he'd drunk and gambled his way through his share.'

'In Birmingham?'

'I can't tell you where. I never bothered to find out. He was out of our lives by then, I'm glad to say.'

'Was there a funeral?'

'I suppose there must have been one, but we didn't find out in time. We had no idea where he was and, quite honestly, didn't want to know.'

'So he died a few months after the time Donna was nursing her leg injury?'

'Yes. She had her leg in a cast until mid-April, as far as I can remember.'

'How did you find out about his death?' Sophie said.

'We had a letter from someone who knew him. Apparently he'd been knocked down while living on the streets. By then he was a raving alcoholic and homeless, as I said. Look, can we change the subject?'

'Of course. The reason I've asked about this is because of the scars that Donna had. We could see that she'd been the victim of abuse. But I'm sorry if my questions have upset you.'

'I didn't think she was still in touch with him. I thought it was all over years ago, when she left for university.'

'Where was that?'

'She went to Bournemouth. She told me that her school felt she could have done better and studied economics at one of the top places, but she decided to stay close to her family. I suppose I did the same sort of thing when I got a job in the Midlands when I left school. Mum was still at home then. Donna was always close to Gran, so going to Bournemouth made sense. She could pop across to Swanage on the bus for the day if she felt like it.'

'Donna didn't complete her degree, did she? Do you know the reason?'

'I never found out, and neither did Mum. Donna refused to talk about it. She would just walk out of the room if we asked too much. But I do know that there was a long period when she disappeared from our lives completely. For more than a year she only spoke to Mum on the phone. They never met up.'

'Wasn't your mum worried?'

'It all went over her head a bit, as far as I remember. She was on tranquillisers. She had a breakdown after she left dad, probably as a result of the build-up of tension after all the years of abuse.'

'It figures. How did you get into your line of work?'

'My uncle. He started the business. I joined after I left school, and stayed on under my cousin when his dad died a couple of years ago. It's Micky that owns the business now. There's just the two of us and an office lady.'

'Did you feel that Donna was the one with the brains?'

'I suppose you could say that.'

'Did your mother move to Dorset to be close to her own mother?'

'Yes.' He closed his eyes and seemed to doze off.

Sophie decided to let him rest if he wanted. Maybe he hadn't slept well.

* * *

As expected, the identification was a formality. Goodenough nodded slightly as each body was uncovered. Once it was over, Sophie left him with Marsh while she sought out Benny Goodall. He was in his office and welcomed her inside.

'Good to see you again, Sophie. Was the identification okay?'

'Fine, as far as these things can be. And thanks for the report on Donna. There are a few interesting items that you found, but I haven't followed them up yet. Benny, when you carried out the post-mortem on her mother, were there any signs of heart defects? The son told me that was the case, and implied that she probably wouldn't be living to a ripe old age.'

'Possibly some minor damage. But that doesn't mean much. I would have only seen physical signs, such as clogging up of the arteries or really severe deterioration and there wasn't much sign of that. But a lot of heart trouble can be caused by problems inside the heart with the wiring, as it were. Nerve damage. The best evidence would have shown up on an ECG carried out while she was alive. Why not speak to her GP?'

'That's already in hand. Did anything else show up that I ought to know about?'

'I don't think so. I've already told you about the liver damage, haven't I? By the way, I've been in touch with my opposite number in Bournemouth. She's going to send across detailed photos of the ligature marks on that young woman who was strangled. I can compare them with the ones I've taken here and let you know in the next couple of days. Alright?'

'Fine. Thanks, Benny.'

* * *

'Let's get a coffee in the town before we visit the cottage in Corfe,' Sophie said to the two men. 'It'll help to take your mind off all of this, David. By the way, I have to ask you this question for obvious reasons. Can you recall where you were on Monday night?'

'I was doing a delivery to Bath late in the afternoon. It's in the company records.'

'And after that?'

'I drove back to Walsall. I got back mid-evening.'

'Are there any witnesses who can confirm the time you got back?'

'No. Sorry. It was late because of a hold-up on the motorway. Our secretary, Gail, finishes at five thirty and Micky had gone home earlier.'

'Micky's your cousin?'

He nodded.

'What's his surname?'

'Spencer. The company's called Spencer Express.'

Goodenough found nothing amiss at his mother's cottage, apart from the missing address books. No photos had been removed, for the simple reason that she hadn't had any on display.

Once they were outside the cottage, Sophie asked him for his keys. 'We need all the keys for both properties at the moment, Mr Goodenough. I'm sure you understand. You'll get them all back once we've finished with them as crime scenes.'

He took a small fob from his pocket, prised a single key from it and handed it over.

'I don't have a key for Donna's flat.'

They were back in Swanage by late morning and dropped Goodenough back at the hotel. He'd closed his eyes and appeared to sleep for most of the return journey. Sophie had already asked all she needed to for the moment. She did request that he remain in Swanage for a few days more, but this fitted in with his plans anyway.

He'd already decided that there was no hurry to return to Walsall.

* * *

Jimmy Melsom's boyish face was unable to hide his enthusiasm. Sophie smiled at him.

'Good news, Jimmy?'

'Yes, ma'am. Partly, anyway. Two lots. The phone company got back to me. They confirmed that an incoming call was made to Berzins' mobile on Tuesday morning, just after eight. It came from another mobile. They are still trying to trace the route the call took through the networks, but apparently it didn't originate from London. They are pretty sure that it was local to Dorset. There's been no response when I've called the number they gave me. It doesn't ring, as if it's switched off.'

'Well, it's better than nothing. And the other news?'

'Bournemouth University have confirmed that Donna was a student there, doing a business degree. She dropped out about Easter of her second year, despite being one of the top students on the course. They never saw her again. That would have been a year and a half ago.'

'Well done, Jimmy. Get back on to the university and find out if there are students still around that were on the course with her. If so, get their names. Plus staff who knew her. We'll try to pay them a visit tomorrow, so find out when the best time would be. I then want you to find out about an RTA death in August in the Walsall area. Donna's father was killed. See what you can dig up.'

* * *

It was late morning when Kevin McGreedie arrived at the station. He made a brief visit to Berzins with Sophie, and came out looking thoughtful.

'Don't say anything just now,' she said. 'Wait until this afternoon. I've a few things to show you, but we'll have some lunch first. I want to take you to the scene of the first murder, and get your thoughts. I'll get Barry to come with us, since he was there with me on Monday night. By the way, have you found out Susie Pater's mobile number?'

He nodded, and opened his notebook.

'Well, I'll be damned,' Sophie said when she saw the number.

* * *

The three detectives walked up the Spring Hill path. It was still closed off to the public, and Sophie had resisted a request from the council for it to be reopened. A forensic tent still covered the place where Donna's body had been found. They stopped there.

'I want us to work through a re-enactment, if you'll bear with me,' said Sophie.

She took a ruler out of her shoulder bag. 'I've chopped the final two inches off, so it's now ten inches long. That's probably a realistic length for the kind of kitchen knife that was the likely murder weapon. I'm the same height as Donna, and I've got two inch heels on, the same as she had on her boots.'

She handed the ruler to Marsh, and moved him into a slight alcove behind the lamp post.

'When I reach this point I want you to step out and swing the ruler towards me, as if you were trying to stab me in the heart.'

Sophie walked up the path several yards, then turned and came back down. Marsh swung out from his hiding place and tried to swing the short length of plastic towards her chest.

'Can we try again?' he asked. 'I didn't get a good angle.'

They repeated the exercise twice more, but Marsh was still not satisfied that he could get the supposed knife to hit her torso straight-on.

'I'd have to step out a second or two earlier, so that I was facing her,' he said. 'I can't swing out and stab in one motion, and get the approach of the knife right. Have we got the forensic report yet? Do we know the angle of entry that the knife made in her chest?'

Sophie nodded. 'Yes, it came in this morning. But I'm not telling you until we've finished this little trial.'

McGreedie spoke at this point. 'Move it to your left hand.'

Marsh did so, and another attempt was made. This time, he could swing round and stab with the ruler in one fluid motion with no delay needed to align his body angle.

'We'll repeat that again,' Sophie said. 'This time, Kevin, can you watch the angle that the ruler makes against my body? I want to check it against the angle of the wound in Donna's body.'

They repeated the simulated attack several times until they were sure of the motion that produced both the most natural movement and the strongest force.

'Well?' asked Marsh. 'Don't keep us on tenterhooks. How does it match up?'

'I'm not saying until Kevin has a go. So can you swap places, please? Sorry about this, Kevin, but you'll see the reason if you'll just indulge me for a minute or two longer.'

The whole exercise was repeated several times with McGreedie first using his more natural right hand, then his left. Because of his greater height, the ruler's angle of approach to Sophie's body was higher, giving a near-horizontal entry line.

'I wouldn't have found it at all easy to produce a fatal stabbing motion. The path is still quite steep here, and with the extra height that your heels give you, you are way too tall. Realistically, I'd have to swing you round then stab you when you are level with me or lower. But that would mean that Donna's body would have to be slightly lower down the path from where we found it. The inspector's extra height means he can do it much easier. How does it all match up, ma'am?'

'You're about the same height as Berzins, Barry. He's not a tall man, and he's right-handed. He told me so, and I double-checked with the chef at the hotel. The post-mortem report shows an entry wound that dips slightly downwards.'

'So that means it wasn't Berzins?'

'I'm not going as far as that. It would tend to point to a six-footer, or maybe someone even taller. But we don't know what actually happened here. Maybe it was Berzins and he managed to turn her slightly so he was above her on the slope before stabbing her. Maybe he walked forward a yard or two to speak to her, then stabbed her, so she fell slightly further up, then pulled her down, although I can't see why. But it puts doubt in my mind. What do you think, Kevin?'

'I agree. This little exercise doesn't prove anything, but it was worth doing. Is there any room for doubt in the DNA evidence? Could it be re-checked?'

'No, there wasn't enough. We were incredibly lucky to find a spot of saliva on one of the cigarette butts.' She paused. 'But that brings me to the second reason for dragging you along here this morning.'

She walked the yard or two down the tarmac path to where a narrow grassy area left it at right angles. She took a set of photos from her shoulder bag and handed one each to Marsh and McGreedie. They stood looking, orienting themselves with the features shown in the set of photos.

'The forensics team have told me that the area was left undisturbed. I'm looking for the place where the butts were found.'

'But surely that's unrealistic, ma'am, to expect it all to be the same? We're talking about nearly three days ago. There's been more rain, some wind. And don't forget animals. We might have had the path sealed off from people, but dogs and foxes will still have got through.'

'I know, Barry. In fact, it would be a bit suspicious if we found that things were exactly as they were on Monday night, wouldn't it?'

She crouched down, using the broken ruler to move a few bits of fresh debris aside. She held the photo of the partly hidden cigarette butts in front of her.

'Okay, this looks like the set of leaves. Would you agree?'

Her two companions compared it with the photos.

'That's the right leaf there. It's quite a large one,' said McGreedie. 'It's exactly the same shape and is in the same position.'

'I wonder why? You'd think it would have blown around a bit since Monday, given the windy weather we've had. Barry, have a closer look. Try to move it aside, but don't force it.'

Marsh did so, finding that the brittle, dry leaf could only be moved around a fixed point.

'There's a tiny bit of broken twig pushed through it at the back, pinning it to the ground. It's hardly noticeable. That's incredible! How did you know?'

'I can't claim the credit for it, I'm afraid. I thought it was a bit odd, the way that the two butts ended up so close together. It was my husband who thought the leaf didn't look right the way it was lying. I managed to speak to the forensic chap who found the butts and took the photos. He had thought it slightly unusual, but not important enough to report. I don't think he'd spotted that it was pinned in place.'

Sophie took a small, digital camera from her bag.

'Take some photos, Barry. This time showing the twig that's pinning it in place. There's a macro button on the camera.'

Marsh took pictures from different angles. They looked at the images closely, to make sure the securing twig was visible. Then they walked down to Kings Road.

'Where does this leave us, Sophie?' asked McGreedie.

'I think it just confirms what we already suspected. I think we both thought that it wasn't Berzins. I've thought so for some time, you since you saw him earlier. I got

Wendy Blacklock, from the Met's domestic violence unit, to observe while I interviewed him yesterday. She was not convinced that he had the right personality to commit these acts. He did receive a phone call on Tuesday morning soon after eight, but it didn't come from the embassy in London. It was made from a mobile. His phone company gave us the number, and guess what? It was Susie Pater's. I think Berzins was a convenient fall guy, very cleverly set up.'

'But what about the other two murders? Surely he's still in the frame for Susie Pater? He could have made that phone call himself if he had her phone,' Marsh said.

'The times don't match. He wasn't in Bournemouth when the call was made. And that's where the call originated.'

'I have my doubts, just like you,' said McGreedie. 'But we also need to consider the possibility that he was working with someone else.'

'You're right, Kevin. We do need to consider all other options. It would be really useful if the CCTV footage from Bournemouth station could be checked to see if he shows up on it. His claims of when he travelled to Bournemouth do check out. They've been verified by the bus driver.'

'I've got someone on to that already. He should have spent the morning on it. Give me a moment.'

McGreedie phoned back to the Bournemouth incident room.

'He didn't leave the railway station,' he reported after he'd hung up.

'What?'

'The CCTV shows him sitting in the waiting area. The only time it loses him is when he bought a coffee and a sandwich, and when he visited the toilet. A couple of minutes at most in each case. He happened to be sitting directly in view of a camera. Bob went across to the station to double-check, and a couple of the staff remember him.

They wondered what he was doing, waiting there so long. Apparently they asked him if he was okay and he said he was waiting for someone. He did keep looking at his watch.'

'What did he do all the time?'

'He was reading. He had a thick book.'

'*A Tale of Two Cities*. Well, it helps to put him in the clear, doesn't it? My guess is that we're looking for someone who's planned all this meticulously. Tall, probably fairly powerfully built, left-handed and very aggressive. He probably caused the bruising on Donna's body. Possibly even the leg fracture. And whoever it is also knew Susie Pater, killed her and used her phone. By the way, Kevin, there is another Bournemouth connection. Donna went to university there, although she dropped out midway through her degree. Apparently that was about a year and a half ago. That means that there is a missing year in her life that ended when she came here to Swanage. She didn't see her family during that time. According to her brother, she only spoke to them on the phone.'

'You're very focussed on the girl, and not her mother. Are you so sure that she's the more important one?'

'Yes. In fact I'd guess that she's the key to all three murders. The subsequent two were only done to cover the murderer's tracks. Donna's mother and Susie Pater both knew something that could have identified him. He knew that, so he killed them. I think they were all murdered in cold blood, premeditated. He's evil, Kevin. Anyway, talking about Susie Pater brings me to the other reason why I wanted us to have a chat today. And I want your views on this as well, Barry.'

'Fine. Fire away.'

'I don't think that Susie's flat was her main living place. Think about the lack of food and utensils in the kitchen, and the lack of everyday clothes in the bedroom. And there was nothing personal there, nothing that made it her home. I think it was just used for her working life. It was rented, wasn't it?'

McGreedie nodded. 'From a rather shady character who owns a lot of properties in that area.'

'My guess is that she had another place, probably in Bournemouth somewhere, that was her real home. With a well-stocked fridge and food in the kitchen cupboards. With ordinary clothes in the bedroom drawers. With books, magazines, DVDs and everyday things scattered around. That flat was wrong. It was all for show. No woman could have lived in that place all of the time, believe me.' She paused. 'Well?'

McGreedie nodded. 'Sounds likely.'

Marsh said, 'Don't ask me. I'm useless at home life. As long as there's a telly, a chair and a microwave, I'm okay.'

'You're a sad case, Barry. But seriously, do you agree?'

'I suppose so, yes. My mum, my sister or my girlfriend would have a fit about the way that flat was arranged. I suppose we just hadn't thought of it, being blokes.'

'Makes sense,' said McGreedie. 'We've another interview with her friend Bernice Halley tomorrow. I'll see if she knows of another place.'

Sophie looked at Marsh with a perplexed expression. 'Barry, I'm a bit worried about the order in which you listed the important women in your life. Mum first and girlfriend last? Where are your priorities, for God's sake?'

CHAPTER 8: Nervous Neighbours

Thursday Afternoon, Week 1

Soon after McGreedie set off back to Bournemouth, Sophie and Marsh drove north to Corfe Castle. The picturesque village, its buildings largely built of the local Purbeck stone with its soft grey tone, looked beautiful in the low afternoon sun. The ruined castle loomed over them as Marsh turned Sophie's car from the village square into West Street and drove down the narrow lane to the cottage.

A team of officers had been carrying out house-to-house enquiries, but Sophie wanted to visit Mrs Goodenough's immediate neighbours herself. They might have remembered something else since her last visit. She also wanted to talk to her employers at the hotel.

None of the neighbours had anything to add to their previous accounts. She and Marsh interviewed the occupants of each of the cottages, but no one could remember being disturbed during the night of the murder. It was obvious that the local community had been traumatised by the murder.

'Are we safe?' asked one elderly lady. 'You've arrested someone, haven't you?'

'Yes, we have. And you are safe. We're convinced that the murder was premeditated. Whoever did it knew Mrs Goodenough. You are in no more danger now than you were before. And remember that Dorset is one of the safest counties in the country. There really is no need to worry, as long as you take sensible precautions to safeguard your home.'

The woman hadn't look convinced. They heard the sound of several bolts being engaged as they walked back down the path.

'It doesn't make sense, Barry. Surely someone heard something? As soon as our car came down here you could see the curtains twitching. I know the murder happened at night, but the lane is so quiet that someone must have heard a vehicle, surely.'

They returned to the car and drove the final few yards along the lane to the turning circle at the end of the cul-de-sac. Open farmland stretched in front of them, rising towards the high ground of the coastal ridge three miles away to the south. Sophie idly took in the view from the passenger seat as Marsh turned the car.

'Barry, there's a footpath heading off from here. Do you know where it goes? Stop the car a minute.'

'I'd guess that it leads to East Street. That's the main road coming up from Swanage. The two roads join together back at the square, but here they must be about half a mile or so apart.'

She got out of the car and walked across to the start of the grassy pathway. Marsh joined her.

'I'd guess from the angle of the sun that it heads south east,' he said. 'That would take it towards the end of East Street, maybe at the edge of the village, but I can't be sure. It may even miss it completely and come out on the Kingston Road.'

'Let's go and see. I've got an OS map in the car.'

The map confirmed Marsh's guess. The path crossed an area of Corfe Common to finish on the B-grade road to Kingston.

'Might need sturdier boots, ma'am,' said Marsh, looking at her shiny leather boots and grey pencil skirt. 'Could ruin your clothes if you slipped. It looks pretty muddy.'

'Okay, if you say so. I'll get my wellies from the boot. My husband wouldn't be best pleased if I ruined this jacket. It was my birthday present.'

'Very stylish, ma'am.'

'The way to a woman's heart. Take her out and buy her some nice clothes. Take my word for it.'

'If you say so, ma'am.'

She extracted her pair of pink wellingtons from the boot. Marsh couldn't help grinning.

'Barry, when you've got children of your own, and they remember your birthday, let alone get you a card and a present, you'll be grateful. So don't smirk. They're two years old, bought by my younger daughter, Jade, when she was thirteen. She thought they were the height of fashion at the time, and who was I to argue? And see, they've come in really useful. I've got nothing for you to put on,' she said, looking at his shoes. 'The best I can do is to offer you a rag to wipe the mud off once we get back. But then, you're probably tough enough to cope, aren't you? Not like us weak girls.'

'I'll be fine, thanks,' muttered Marsh. 'I'm a country copper at heart and dress for it. I ruined enough shoes in muddy lanes in my early years.'

They walked along the path past a group of grazing horses. Through a second gate, the way forward opened up across a wide expanse of common. The line of the path was still clear in front of them, although wet and slippery in places from the recent rain. Marsh guessed that the path would be popular with walkers. They soon noticed the half dozen or so detached houses on Townsend Mead appear to their left on the edge of the village. Within ten minutes they were approaching a gate that opened onto the quiet country road that connected Corfe with the village of Kingston, some three miles south.

'There's a pull-in area just in front of the gate,' said Marsh. 'Enough room for one car, I'd guess.' He looked at his watch. 'Twelve minutes. He could have come this way, and walked back across the heath afterwards.'

'Someone in one of these houses may have seen something suspicious. They'll need to be interviewed,' said Sophie.

She phoned Melsom to request for a unit to come out and tape off the lay-by and look for tyre prints. He was to come up with a small team to interview the occupants of the half-dozen houses in Townsend Mead. Melsom passed on the latest news from the house-to-house inquiries in the vicinity of Donna's flat.

'What was the other news, ma'am?' Marsh said.

'Someone from one of the neighbouring houses saw a tall figure get out of a small car and go into Donna's building mid-evening. That was when Berzins was still at work.'

'He could have been visiting one of the other flats, ma'am.'

'Yes, Barry. But it's still a possible lead.'

* * *

The manager of the hotel where Brenda Goodenough had been employed was away on holiday for the week. His deputy had been on the staff for less than a month and was unable to add much to their picture of Donna's mother. He said that she kept herself to herself much of the time. She came in punctually, did her cleaning job with the minimum of supervision, and left promptly. He'd heard that the only staff social event she attended was the annual Christmas party, and even there she tended to stay in the shadows. She rarely talked about her private life, although other staff members did know that her daughter had moved to the area recently. Sophie found it a little odd that none of her workmates knew that her mother had lived as close as Swanage. They didn't know about the death of her ex-husband either.

They returned to the car.

'I'm not surprised she didn't bother much when her husband died,' said Marsh. 'She was probably still getting over the death of her mother. It was probably only a few weeks beforehand. And if he was the nasty waster that her son described, you can understand her not wanting to get involved.'

'There's an "if" there, isn't there, Barry?' Sophie said.

Marsh walked around the car to get into the driver's door. 'Did you go to university, ma'am?' he asked as he started the engine.

'Yes.'

'Where was that?'

'Oxford.'

'What did you study?'

'Law, and I also have a masters in criminal psychology. But don't worry, Barry, I'm still human.'

'They must be wary of you up at headquarters, ma'am.' He chuckled. 'You must scare some of those plonkers to death.'

'That's no way to talk of your elders and betters, Barry,' she said with a wink.

* * *

The meeting at Winfrith was once again tense. The chief superintendent, Neil Dunnett, was less confrontational at first. Matt Silver was his normal calm self. He expressed some surprise over Sophie's plans for Berzins. Barry Marsh looked nervous and said little.

'You want to keep him in custody? But you said you don't think he did it,' said Silver.

'While he's in custody the real culprit will think his scheme is working. If we release him, we couldn't keep it from the press and that would put our murderer on his guard. I'd really like to put Berzins into a safe house.'

Dunnett interrupted. 'We've had notification that his brother is to come across and visit. Apparently he's a policeman in Latvia. Did you know?'

'About his brother being in the police? Yes, sir. Berzins told me. And it doesn't surprise me that he's decided to give us a visit. Wouldn't we all try to do the same? In some ways I'm surprised it's taken this long, but I don't know how the Latvian police work. Maybe he's been on a case.' She paused. 'I don't want him told in advance about our decision not to press charges. We could see what he's like, and if he seems okay get him to stay in the safe house with Berzins. He'd be doing something useful and reduce our manpower needs. When does his brother want to come across?'

'His flight was due this afternoon. He should be landing about now. I've sent a car to Heathrow to pick him up. That might smooth difficult waters.'

Sophie wondered how long Dunnett had known about the brother's visit, and why she hadn't been informed earlier. She decided not to press the point.

'Good idea, sir. Are we in contact with whoever is picking him up? It's just that I'd prefer it if the case wasn't discussed on the journey, before I've had a chance to weigh him up. Is that okay?'

Dunnett merely nodded.

'So who are your suspects?' asked Silver.

'It might be Donna's brother. He stands to inherit almost half a million in property. He's tall enough and quite powerfully built. If the father was still alive I'd also put him in the frame, going on his son's description of him as a violent bully. I've no reason to doubt the son's word, but I have put someone on to checking death certificates just to make sure that the father really is dead. We only have the son's say-so, and he has no direct evidence, by his own admission. But we are looking into the lost year in her life. Between the date she dropped out of university and when she surfaced again last spring with a broken leg. We know nothing about her during that year. We don't know where she lived and who she met. My guess is that she remained in Bournemouth, because there has to be a link with Susie Pater. And I'd also guess that she either knew Susie directly, or our murderer formed the common link between the two of them.'

'So you think it was someone who hasn't entered into our reckoning yet?' said Silver.

'Someone who's covered his tracks really well. But we're chipping away at the edges, and I'm beginning to get a feel for him. Nothing more definite than that at the moment.'

'How well do you think Kevin McGreedie is handling the Pater case?' asked Dunnett.

'It couldn't be in better hands. He's meticulous.'

'Good. You know, I'm not convinced about the link with your cases now that Berzins is not a suspect. After all, he was the connection, with his morning at the railway station at the same time as Pater's murder. Now he's out of the frame it could be treated independently, and handled just by McGreedie, leaving you to concentrate on the Swanage end,' said Dunnett.

Silver stiffened slightly. Had this already been discussed between the two of them, with Silver arguing for Sophie's wish to keep the cases together? Or hadn't it been discussed at all?

'Please don't, sir, not at this stage, anyway. Kevin and I work well together. I know I can leave him to manage all of the Bournemouth inquiries about Susie Pater, but we're both convinced of the connection. I know there'll be a lot more house-to-house visits and personal interviews in an area like that, and he knows it like the back of his hand, but I need to keep a handle on it. We speak every day, either on the phone or in person. He was across with me earlier today, and I'll be at Bournemouth University tomorrow, so will see him after that. It really is better left as it is.'

'We'll leave it as it is for now, then,' Dunnett said and left the room.

* * *

Sophie sent Marsh out of the office while she tackled Silver. 'Matt, why wasn't I told about Berzins' brother coming across? And why is he trying to split the inquiry?' Sophie was angry. They should all be working together, pooling ideas and keeping each other informed. That was the way to set about a complex case like this, not this political infighting.

'I didn't know, believe me. It was as much a surprise to me as it was to you,' said Silver.

'Can you please contact the driver and ensure that he doesn't speak to Berzins' brother about the case? I don't trust Dunnett to do it. I would have sent one of my own people to Heathrow if I'd known. Do we know where the brother will be staying? And for how long? This is awful. I can't work properly if things are going on behind my back. What does that man think he's doing?'

'Okay, leave it with me. I'll chase it up right now, and I'll have another word with him. Tactfully, of course, since he's the boss. And I'd already told him of our decision to keep Kevin in charge of the Pater case, so that was a surprise as well,' said Silver.

'Dunnett might be the chief super, but it's my case and I should make all the tactical decisions. It's not as though I don't consult you both. He's trying to become part of the investigation for his own pet reasons. He'll end up mucking it up unless we're careful. I'll go over his head if I think that's going to happen.' She didn't wait for a reply.

Before joining Marsh at the car, Sophie called through to the forensics team leader.

* * *

Berzins' brother appeared in the incident room shortly before seven. Matt Silver himself had driven him down from HQ. Sophie called the team together just before they packed up for the evening, and told them of the day's developments. She and Marsh were the only officers still there when the two men entered.

The brother looked to be about five years older than Vilis Berzins. Nicolajs was taller and broader than his sibling, but had the same dark hair and clear blue eyes. His greeting was wary. He shook her hand and watched her carefully.

'How was your journey?'

'It was as expected. I cannot say that I enjoyed it. It was necessary because of Vilis. I wish to see him as soon as possible.' He spoke with a much more pronounced accent than his brother. 'I have a letter of introduction for you from my chief officer, and my police ID card.'

He handed over an envelope. Inside was a single sheet of official paper from the office of the Riga chief of police, and apparently signed by him. It described Nicolajs Berzins as an outstanding young policeman, and the Berzins family as being upright citizens. Sophie glanced briefly at Silver, who nodded. He'd obviously checked its authenticity back at headquarters.

'Thank you, Nicolajs. The letter reflects well on you and your family. Your brother is in the interview room with the duty solicitor, waiting for us. I have already explained to the solicitor what I am about to say and do, so he is prepared. I want you to know that we have your brother's best interests at heart.'

Vilis looked up as his brother entered the interview room, gasped and stood up to hug Nicolajs. He started to sob, as if the days of tension were finally being released. Barry Marsh appeared with a tray of coffee and biscuits, then took up his position by the door.

Once Vilis calmed down, Silver motioned everyone to sit. 'I'm handing over to Detective Chief Inspector Allen, who is in charge of the investigation into the murders of Donna Goodenough and her mother, Brenda. She will explain the purpose of this meeting.'

Nicolajs looked puzzled and opened his mouth to speak, but Sophie held her finger to her lips. She turned to the younger brother.

'Vilis, you were charged with the murder of Donna because traces of your salivary DNA were found on some cigarette butts recovered at the crime scene after the discovery of her body. However, the positioning of the butts appears to be highly suspicious and artificial, and we are now convinced that they were planted there by the murderer to divert suspicion to you. Other factors that have come to light also lead us to believe that Donna's murder was carried out by someone else. We are therefore planning to withdraw the charges against you. Do you understand?'

Both brothers looked shaken. There was a silence.

'Do you understand?' Sophie repeated.

'Yes, I think we both do,' said Nicolajs. 'But—'

'Let me explain, please,' she went on. 'I have a favour to ask of you both that will help our investigation. The real murderer will know that Vilis has been charged. This would have been part of his plan. He will be feeling safe. If we release the news to the press that Vilis is to be freed, it will put him on his guard. So I would like you to agree to Vilis remaining under police supervision while we continue with the investigation. We would like you both to stay in one of our safe houses, with Vilis out of view so that the press do not find out that he has been released.' She turned to Nicolajs. 'You are a respected policeman, and we can use your experience to help us in this. If you agree, you would be free to come and go, but Vilis must remain out of view. He must still appear to be in custody for a few days longer.'

'If we don't agree to do this? What will happen?' asked Nicolajs.

'I will have to officially drop the charges in several days' time, and release him. But I won't try to hide him from the press.' She turned to Vilis. 'If you want to see Donna's killer brought to justice, and I believe you do, you will do as I ask.'

'Of course I do. And we will help you, won't we, Nicolajs?'

Nicolajs said, 'Someone in the chief's office in Riga knew of you from a talk you gave in Geneva. He said, if you see Inspector Allen, she is worthy of respect. I will agree to your request, but I can only be here for five more days. Then I must fly back.'

'Thank you, Officer Berzins. Now, we can't get the safe house ready until tomorrow morning. Vilis will need to remain here overnight, but you are welcome to stay at my house tonight. Too many questions will be asked if you stay at a hotel here in Swanage. I think your parents deserve to know what is happening. You can phone them from my house, but they must not tell anyone else.'

Sophie wondered how her husband and daughter would react when she brought a handsome young Latvian policeman home with her. She collected a wad of papers from her in-tray before they left the office. She was intrigued by the message Melsom had left for her.

CHAPTER 9: Student Days

Friday Morning, Week 1

The safe house was in a quiet cul-de-sac on the northern edge of Wareham. Sophie took Nicolajs Berzins to inspect it before they set off for the police station in Swanage. It was a small end-of-terrace property, built in the seventies. It was basic but comfortable. It had no garage but a driveway ran alongside the house. This meant that a car could be parked off the road, unlike the houses in the rest of the terrace, whose owners clearly had to jostle for parking places on the street.

'This is fine,' said the elder Berzins brother. 'We will be comfortable here. It is better than would be provided in Latvia.'

'You and the duty officer should take the first-floor bedrooms, and we'll put Vilis in the loft room. It has sloping skylight windows. I don't want any chance of him being seen from outside, so he should keep away from the windows.'

'I will take care of him. And thank you again for allowing me to stay last night. You have a lovely home and family.'

The early morning sunshine was beginning to break through the mist. A few yellowing leaves remained on the trees, and the woodland areas looked stunning with frosty halos of ice crystals clinging to the foliage.

'You are lucky to live in such a beautiful area, I think,' said Berzins. 'It is bad that such crimes can happen in such a place.'

'Murder is unusual here, but it happens. I sometimes wish that my job didn't have to exist. But to be honest, I enjoy my work. I love the challenge.'

'Are you getting close to the real murderer in this case, Chief Inspector?'

'No comment, Nicolajs. I'm sure you were expecting that answer.'

He smiled.

* * *

Sophie drove into the car park at the rear of the police station, and took her car as close to the back entrance of the building as possible. A gaggle of reporters and press photographers were still occupying the area outside the front entrance.

Once inside, Berzins' brother was shown to a small interview office. Sophie made her way to the main incident room to catch up on the latest developments.

Lydia Pillay reported on her visit to the Bournemouth Hospital the previous day. The medical staff had found the records relating to Donna's visit and could confirm the nature of the injury. They were unable at first to provide any further information, but with some help from one of the doctors, Pillay managed to trace a nurse who had interviewed Donna during her visit. The nurse was suspicious about the cause of the break, but Donna had insisted it was a sports injury. She had other noticeable bruises and marks on her body, some of them quite severe.

Pillay had left the hospital mid-morning and had driven to Walsall in order to pay a visit to the family GP. The doctor had been worried by some of the comments in the report from the hospital. She had been unable to trace Donna for any follow-up treatment. The address she held for the young woman was the family home in Walsall, but the family were no longer living there, so it hadn't been possible to contact her. Pillay spent some time with the doctor, talking through the family's medical history.

'Where did she get the plaster taken off?' asked Sophie.

'She had a follow-up appointment at Bournemouth for removal after six weeks. She turned up, but there's nothing added to the notes made at her first visit.'

'You know, Lydia, her behaviour shows all of the classic signs of her being in a very controlled and violent relationship. The secrecy, the lying to cover up injuries, the gradual withdrawal from previous friendships and family ties. I think the poor girl was being beaten by a psychopathic bully. I wonder if she ended the relationship when she moved to Swanage, but he found her and these murders are the result. What about the other things I asked you to check? Her parents?'

Pillay told Sophie what she had found out from her inquiries.

'It just doesn't add up, Lydia. We have to follow it up.'

Melsom reported that he'd spoken to the owners of the flat above Donna's. Apparently they'd been at the flat on the evening of the murder, as they had visited for the weekend and stayed over until late on Monday. They reported that they were sure someone was in Donna's flat when they left at ten. They'd heard a bump, as if something had been dropped, as they passed the door on their way down the stairs.

'We need a statement from them, Jimmy. Can you contact them to arrange a time? Try to pin them down on exactly what they heard. And well done for that information about the father's death. It's intriguing, isn't it?'

Sophie decided to accompany Tom Rose, the station's senior officer, to the front of the police station when he made his daily statement to the press in the middle of the morning. It would give her an opportunity to gauge how much interest there was. They were outside for less than five minutes. Sophie was obliged to make a short statement in response to an unexpected question from one of the reporters. She felt uneasy about it, and tucked the memory away, hoping that it wouldn't get lost in the logjam of her mind.

* * *

It proved fairly straightforward to get Vilis Berzins out of the station and into her car, helped by his elder brother and Jimmy Melsom. Vilis still seemed bemused by the sudden turnaround of events.

'I have been thinking of your questions about the cigarettes,' he said when they were safely on the road. 'There was a man who spoke to me last week while I was outside one of the bars. I had forgotten about it, because of all the other thoughts about Donna. I only remembered last night. I had not seen him before. I was in the garden at the back, lighting my cigarette. I think he had come out after me.'

'Was Donna there with you?'

'No. Each Tuesday she had the evening off and often visited her mother. I went out with Georgs after we finished work. We did this each Tuesday if I wasn't seeing Donna.'

'Can you remember the conversation?'

'Not clearly. I think he asked where I was from. He saw I was not English.'

'If he is the person we are looking for, he must have got hold of your cigarettes after you had finished smoking them. How could he have done that?'

'There is a small tray for butts on one of the outdoor tables. I think he cleaned it as we were there. I think he said it was too full, so he emptied it into a bin. I was going in after the cigarette, but he asked me to stay for another. He said that he wanted to visit Riga sometime, and needed to know the best places to visit in the city.'

'Was Georgs still there?'

'Georgs doesn't smoke. He likes to think he is a tough guy, but he isn't really. He doesn't drink much either, and only comes out to keep me company. He was in the bar talking to other people.'

'So what did this man look like?'

'He was taller than me. He had begun a beard.'

'What was he wearing?'

'Jeans, I think. He had on a hooded jacket.'

'Did he tell you his name?'

'I think he did, but I don't remember. He talked about the visit to Latvia he was planning.'

'Was he by himself?'

'It is hard to remember. I think he left soon after I went back in. Someone may have followed him out, but the pub was busy that night. People were coming in and going out.'

'Keep trying to remember, Vilis. I'll bring up an identity expert as soon as I can, and we'll see if we can create a likeness that might stir your memory.'

* * *

Jimmy Melsom had volunteered to carry out the first overnight duty at the safe house. Meanwhile, once the Berzins brothers had been dropped off and their belongings unloaded, he and Sophie drove on to Bournemouth University.

Jimmy had traced two members of staff who had known Donna fairly well, and had asked them to be available. David Bell had been her economics tutor in her first year at university and had seen her regularly for monitoring and progress interviews. He was now approaching retirement age. He said that Donna's attitude to her work had impressed him. She had a considered and mature approach to her studies, and he guessed that this would also have been true of her life in general. But she sometimes seemed troubled.

'Can you be more specific?' asked Sophie.

'Well, she was the same age as the other students but was not quite one of them, if that makes sense. She seemed older. She took her work more seriously. She was less relaxed, particularly as the year went on. If someone cracked a joke during a group tutorial, she'd smile but would rarely laugh. She mixed with the other students, but didn't seem to fit in with them. I got the feeling that she was a bit of a loner.'

'What about in her second year? Were you still in touch with her?' Sophie asked.

'I was no longer her tutor then. I only saw her during a short series of lectures that I gave in the autumn term. If anything, she seemed even more remote, but that could have been my imagination. I seem to remember the lectures being first thing in the morning, so that might explain it. Some of the students didn't even bother coming.'

'Were you surprised when you heard that she'd dropped out?'

'Yes, and very disappointed. I tried to contact her, but none of her contact details seemed to be correct. She was no longer at the address we had on record, and we got no response from any of her phone numbers. I put one of the welfare officers onto tracing her, but she didn't get any further than I had. It was even impossible to trace her parents. We gave up after a while. We could only guess that she didn't want to be found.'

'Did you ever notice any marks on her body? On her face or arms?' said Sophie.

'Oh, goodness. Don't tell me she was being abused. That makes me feel terrible. We should have been looking after her if that was the case. But no, I don't recall any. But if I remember rightly, she always wore long-sleeved tops and trousers, so I wouldn't have seen any marks. I'll do what I can to find some of her fellow students. Some are back on campus if they did a year out in industry. Those that were on a normal degree finished in the summer, I'm afraid.'

'Do you know why she opted for Bournemouth?'

'It's on her record, from when she was first interviewed. Apparently it was because her gran lived somewhere near, and they were very close.'

'That's all been very helpful, Dr Bell. If you do remember anything else that might be relevant, please let us know. We'd like to interview other students who were on her course, so a list would be useful. Do you have group photos taken at the start of your degree courses?'

'No, not officially. The only ones we organise are the graduation shots. But no doubt the students take lots of photos at the different events.'

'What about at freshers' week? Would there be photos of balls or discos, do you think?'

'It's possible. I'll get onto the student committee and see if there were any official photos for when Donna started.'

'And any other social events for her first year here. I'd really like to see who she was with,' said Sophie.

'Of course. It may take a day or two, but I'll get the department secretary onto it. Now, if you'd like to use my office, I'll round up the others that you wanted to see. Mary Porter was her tutor for her second year, and there are a couple of students still here that might fill in some details. I asked them to be available.'

Donna's second year tutor was less helpful. She appeared to be a cold, unemotional woman and gave the impression that she resented giving up her working time. She admitted that she had failed to act when Donna started to miss her tutorials. She'd thought that the problem was temporary. Donna was still attending some lectures, although somewhat irregularly. Sophie formed the impression that this woman didn't bother to get to know her students very well. But she was able to supply one vital item of information. Sometime before she dropped out completely, Donna had appeared with several bruises on her face.

'Did you ask her about it?' said Sophie.

'I didn't have an opportunity, since she wasn't attending my tutorials. One of the other students said she'd heard that it was a sports injury.'

'Didn't you check?'

'I can't possibly check every incident of that type. There just aren't enough hours in the day.'

'But surely that is the job of a student's personal tutor, isn't it? These were classic signs of a student in distress, weren't they, Dr Porter? A pattern of absences building up, along with signs of injury?'

'You seem to be judging me against your school teachers, if I may say so. We couldn't possibly offer that degree of personal guidance to our students. Since you've probably never been to university, you are in all likelihood speaking from a position of ignorance, Inspector.'

'I think I can see the problem that Donna faced with you as her tutor, Dr Porter. You jump to conclusions far too readily. I am a chief inspector, by the way, and I did go to university. I have a degree in law. Moreover I remember that all of my university tutors took their roles very seriously. I think we're finished for now, but if you do remember anything else about Donna, please let us know.'

She turned to Melsom before the pink-faced Porter could respond.

'Jimmy, could you show Dr Porter out, please, and round up those students?'

The students' recollections of Donna were vague. Sophie knew how quickly friendships come and go during early adulthood, but she was nonetheless surprised. She interviewed them in a group, hoping that the memories of one might trigger others. No such luck. The only man, Alan Mathieson, was worse than useless, and at first seemed to resent being interviewed. The two female students did realise the enormity of the crime that was being investigated, but couldn't add anything to what the police already knew.

Sophie sighed and sent Jimmy out for a tray of tea and biscuits. Mathieson, who had a hairstyle that seemed to have been shaped with a hedge trimmer, mellowed after his fifth chocolate biscuit.

'Was she still seeing that guy?' he suddenly asked.

'What guy?' Sophie said.

'Oh well, maybe it was nothing.'

'Please tell me. Anything might be helpful.'

'I was going out with a girl from the town for a while. Went to a pub near where she lived a couple of times. I saw Donna there with a bloke.'

'When was this?'

'How do you expect me to remember that?'

'Was it a year ago? Two years ago? Six months ago?'

He looked blank.

'Well, how long ago was it that you went out with the local girl?'

'We hung around together for a couple of months. We broke up last Christmas, because I didn't fancy visiting her family over the holiday. Boring or what?'

'And when did you start seeing her?'

'At the Autumn Ball. She blagged a ticket from somewhere, even though she wasn't a student. Cracking figure.'

The two women students rolled their eyes. Sophie just about succeeded in keeping a straight face. Even Jimmy Melsom looked amused.

'So you went out with her for about four months? From September until Christmas?'

'Sounds about right.'

'So we're talking about this time last year?'

He nodded. 'Suppose so.'

'And how many times do you remember seeing Donna in this pub?'

'Only twice. I hadn't realised she'd dropped out. I tried to have a quick chat. That was the second time. The first I just saw her in the corner of the bar. Didn't speak.'

'And what did she say when you spoke to her?'

'Not much. I only had a chance to say hi, and then this tall guy comes back from the bar with some drinks. He gave me the evil eye and says for me to push off, but not as politely as that. And I was only trying to be friendly. Anyway, I wasn't gonna argue. He had a bit of a nasty look about him. You know, confrontational. So I just waited for my bird to come out the loo and we left. I didn't like the place anyway.'

'Did Donna say anything at all?'

'Not to me. She didn't get a chance. As I backed away, I heard her say something like, "It's fine, Andy, it's okay."'

'Andy? Are you sure?'

'Yeah, pretty sure. My memory's pretty good, you know.' He grinned.

Sophie smiled politely. 'And what about the pub? What was its name?'

'Haven't a clue. But I could take you there.'

'Whereabouts is it?'

'Near the station.'

Jimmy Melsom's eyes widened.

'Can you take us now, please?' said Sophie.
'No problem.'

* * *

They drove around the station area for several minutes before Mathieson got his bearings. He then took them almost a mile away to a pub in a quiet residential area.

'I thought you said it was near the station,' Melsom said. 'We're a good fifteen minute walk away.'

'Sorry. We used to come from the other direction when I was with Carol. And I was often a bit pissed.'

'Are you sure this is the pub?' Melsom said.

'Sure as sure.'

Sophie knew why Melsom was tetchy. Like her, he had probably thought that the pub might tie in with the Susie Pater murder. It turned out to be in a relatively well-heeled part of town. Sophie introduced herself to the landlord and showed him a photo of Donna. He gave it no more than a glance.

'Sorry, we're new in the pub. We've only been here since the summer, so we can't help you.'

'What about your other staff? Are there any who might have been here a year ago?'

'No. We didn't keep any of the old staff very long. The pub didn't pay its way, which is why the brewery got rid of the last licensee. I run it with my wife and son, and we try to keep the overheads low. That way, we just about make a profit.'

'Can you find a list of the staff who were here then?'

'I think there's one in the office, but they were a dozy lot, to be frank. Don't bank too much on coming up with any useful information.'

'What about your customers? Were some of them regulars last year?' asked Melsom.

'Worth a try, but our midday crowd are very different from the evening one. If she was here in the evening, then you'll need to visit then.'

'Can you make it this evening? Say about eight thirty?' Sophie said to Mathieson.

'Oh yeah, no problem.'

Back at the campus, Sophie phoned Kevin McGreedie. He agreed to join her for the evening visit to the pub.

* * *

Barry Marsh was dispirited. He'd revisited the houses that lined the eastern side of Townsend Mead shortly after eight that morning. He'd thought that the top-floor windows of the houses would have unbroken views across to the footpath that crossed the open grassland. But no one had seen anything. One houseowner had even taken him up to look out from a first-floor window to show how unlikely it would have been. The view towards the road, where they suspected the car had been left, was obstructed by low, grassy hillocks dotting the common. And even in broad daylight, it was difficult to pick out the features of the few people walking the footpath because of the branches from the trees lining the other side of their own lane. At night, anyone on the common would have been well-nigh invisible.

He left the last house. He turned and bumped into a plump woman bustling up the path, causing her to stumble and drop her bag. He apologised and helped her to pick it up. She told him she was the cleaner for the house he'd just left. He told her the reason for his visit.

'In that case, you'd better come back inside. My Harry saw a car parked there on Monday night.'

Marsh apologised to the householders, and asked for a few minutes alone with the cleaner, a Mrs Jones. His day had just got a lot better. He guessed that Harry Jones was a bit of a rogue, since his wife was deliberately vague about what her husband had been up to late on Monday night. But she did remember how angry Harry had been about a driver trying to turn in the narrow lane just as he drove down the hill in his pick-up.

'Crazy, that's what Harry said. It was a wonder they didn't crash.'

'Did he say anything about the car?' asked Marsh.

She didn't know any further details, but told Marsh where he could find her husband. Marsh visited him at work.

'An old Ford Fiesta. I think it was a red colour, but it was muddy.'

'Did you get the registration?' Marsh asked hopefully.

'I think it was an 02, but the rest was too grubby to see clearly. I tried, but it was too dark. And they raced off like a blue-arsed fly, down to Corfe. I did notice that the car turned left at the junction with the main road at the bottom of the hill.'

'You said "they," Mr Jones. Was there more than one person in the car?'

'I can't be sure. It was all so quick, and the car scarpered sharpish, like. And it was a bit filthy. But there might have been another face. I couldn't swear, though. It might have been a reflection. I can't be sure, but I might have seen a car a bit like it filling up in the local petrol station a couple of times.'

Marsh thanked him and shook his hand. Harry stood watching him as he left, looking somewhat bemused — and relieved.

Harry Jones was lucky his pick-up hadn't been inspected. It still contained some of the lead he'd stolen from the roof of the local manor house's outbuildings on Monday night.

CHAPTER 10: Split Lip

Friday, Week 1

'Is press work always like this?'

The reporter turned to the tall, heavily built man standing beside him. 'What, the hours of standing in the freezing cold getting bored to death, followed by a couple of minutes of frenzied activity? Haven't you got used to it by now? Or are you new? Weren't you here a couple of days ago?'

'I was only passing. Like today. Just thought I'd catch up on what's happening. Not much by the look of it. I'm not with the press.'

'Oh, there's more going on than meets the eye.' The reporter, Bill Rogers, thrust his hands more deeply into the pockets of his threadbare coat and stamped his feet.

'Haven't they already charged someone? It all looks pretty quiet to me.' The onlooker hunched his shoulders and pulled up the hood of his jacket.

'They need the evidence for it to stand up in court, even if they've got the killer. They sound confident enough when they come out to give us the press summary, but the official statements at this front entrance are only for show. Everything is set up for the telly nowadays. The main entrance here is very photogenic. It's just the right place for them to come out and make reassuring statements. Joe Public will see, and think that it's all under control. But the people doing the real dirty work go in and out by the side entrance to the car park. And they're still hard at work, judging by all the comings and goings. Did you see the car that went in a few minutes ago? The silver Honda Accord? That was the boss, Detective Chief Inspector Sophie Allen.'

'What do you mean?' said the man.

'She's in charge of the investigation.'

'I thought it was a bloke with a beard. He was on the news a couple of days ago.'

'That'll be the superintendent. Silver's his name. He's only the public face. His rank and above spend their time behind a desk. No, it's her that's the real boss, even though she's only a chief inspector. All the murders get passed over to her. They even lend her out to other counties, she's that good apparently. I got in her way once and, boy, didn't I know it. I still bear the mental scars. I had to beg the paper to keep me on. Even then, it's taken me a year to get back some of my editor's faith in me. Apparently she went in to see him with the paper's owner, and I was lucky to keep my job. One hard, clever cookie.'

'Don't papers have lawyers to deal with police pressure?'

'Yeah, but they didn't get a chance. Apparently she's got a top law degree herself. She's one of those really dangerous things, a clever cop. Shouldn't be allowed.'

A pressman standing in front of them turned and spoke. 'Couldn't help overhearing you,' he said. 'Apparently they're looking for a small, red car. No idea why.'

'How did you find that out, Les?' asked Rogers.

'My brother-in-law runs a petrol station up the road. He just had a visit from a copper asking about any small red hatchbacks that might have been in. They asked him to keep quiet about it.'

'So he phoned you, and now you're telling us?' Rogers said.

'Well, what's to lose? Maybe don't spread it any further, though. Just in case.'

Just then a group of police officers came out onto the steps at the front entrance. Rogers nudged the man beside him.

'The local boss, Tom Rose. He's been giving us the press briefings. And look who's behind him. Wonders never cease. She's actually deigned to appear for the news update.'

'Good morning, ladies and gentlemen. Just a few minutes to give you a copy of this morning's press statement. There have been few new developments. We are still holding Mr Vilis Berzins for questioning at this stage, and are happy with the progress we are making in our enquiries. Members of the public can rest assured that these are not random killings, and so their safety is not at risk. Are there any questions?'

There were several queries about Berzins. Rose explained that no details could be given out while the investigations were still ongoing.

'Are you looking for a car that might somehow be involved?' This came from Rogers.

Tom Rose paused before replying, 'I have no further comments to make.'

Sophie Allen looked at the reporter and her glance flickered across the small group surrounding him. She spoke to Rogers directly.

'We have several loose ends to tie up, Mr Rogers, that's all. I'm sure you'd expect us to carry out a thorough investigation into a series of crimes as horrific as these. We would be failing in our duty if we did otherwise. Thank you for your interest.'

She directed a bleak smile at Bill Rogers. Then she turned and followed Tom Rose back into the building.

* * *

Shaz Fellows had a simple view of life. It was crap, and that went for most of the people in it. If you didn't look after yourself then no one else would give a rat's arse. They'd just dump on you instead. It was happening again, here and now, in the small Bournemouth café where she worked as a waitress.

'Oh Christ, Vince. Why me? I've worked all fucking week, and now you want me to do the evening shift as well? I'm knackered.'

'Paula's just phoned in sick, and I need you to do the early evening cover. There's no one else. And don't swear at me. I'm your employer, for God's sake.'

Vince's reprimand sounded weak. Shaz knew that Paula, her fellow weekday waitress was pregnant, and was often too sick to do all her shifts. Vince needed her.

'Please, Shaz. I'll pay you time and a half, but with the extra as cash-in-hand. No tax on it. Okay?'

'Yeah, okay. But I'm out of here at eight on the dot. And I'm not doing any cleaning. You'll have to do that yourself.'

She flounced off to the staff toilet. She'd told Vince it was a cold sore, but her cut lip was difficult to hide. Once inside, Shaz began to sob. She looked in the mirror again, and dabbed a little more make-up onto the bruise on her right cheek. It was nearly invisible with its covering of concealer, but not so the cut lip. How had it all happened? She was completely confused. Admittedly she'd had a few drinks, but they'd been in the pub after all. What were pubs for if not to get a bit pissed in? And have a few laughs with your mates? Whatever she'd done to offend her current boyfriend, it hadn't been bad enough to warrant those blows to her face.

She glanced again at the sorry-looking reflection in the mirror. Swollen lip, bruised cheeks and eyes puffy from crying. Was that really her? Well, it wouldn't happen again. They'd only been together a couple of months, and if he thought that she felt enough for him to stay after he'd thumped her like that, then he was stupid as well as a complete tosser. She'd go home, put a few of her things into a bag and cadge a bed from one of her friends for the night. Tomorrow she'd get the landlord to change the locks on the flat, and that would be goodbye to Mister Bullyboy Bighead. The flat was rented in her name, for fuck's sake. She'd had it for nearly two years. He'd only moved in a month ago, and had already started lording it over her as if he owned the place. He'd soon find out who was boss, the stupid wanker.

She dabbed at her eyes and took a couple of deep breaths. The mirror showed her the tattoo on her shoulder, the heart with his name inside it. How much would it cost to get it changed or removed? One thing was for certain: it was going.

CHAPTER 11: A New Romance

Friday Night, Week 1

Lauren Duke was going to have an evening out and enjoy herself. She'd parted from her last boyfriend earlier in the week, having discovered that he'd been two-timing her. It wasn't a great loss. He was an immature, self-centred idiot who liked drink rather too much and her company rather too little. Definitely not someone to settle down with. She'd met up with a fellow student from Southampton University and, after a drink in a city centre pub, they had decided to go clubbing. So here she was, on a crowded dance floor, her slender legs keeping perfect time to the beat. Her friend Kirsten had vanished with a young man she'd had her eye on for weeks. Lauren smiled at the tall figure who'd moved into the vacant spot opposite her. He looked cute.

* * *

She awoke the next morning in a slight daze, always the sign of a good night out. She turned onto her side and found herself looking into dark brown eyes. She smiled shyly, and he smiled back.

‘Hi,’ he said.

Her smile widened. ‘Thank you for a lovely time last night. You were very thoughtful, not like most of the boys I’ve met. They just seem to want to get it over with once we’re in bed.’

‘Well, there’s the thing. I’m not a boy, so I do know how to treat a lovely lady like you. And I must thank you as well. You’re a gorgeous person to be with. The least I can do is to offer you breakfast. I don’t really want to share it with your student housemates, so how about coming out to a great café that I know? I’m starving. I don’t think it’s more than five minutes’ walk, if I’ve got your place situated right.’

‘That would be lovely. I don’t usually do breakfast, but I’m hungry as well. You can tell me about yourself while we’re eating. We seemed to spend all of our time last night talking about me. I’ll go for a shower, if one of my housemates hasn’t got there first.’

She self-consciously slipped on a baggy T-shirt and went to the door.

‘Can I join you if it's free?’ he suggested. ‘I do a fantastic back scrub.’

She gave him a soft smile that seemed to open up her face.

‘Oh, of course!’

Then she became embarrassed as she realised she’d responded to his suggestion rather too enthusiastically. The T-shirt revealed the flawless skin of her shoulders, a delicate pale-pink colour. She held out her hand.

* * *

The café breakfast was the best Lauren had tasted since she’d left home. Perfectly cooked eggs, bacon and mushrooms, followed by toast and marmalade and several cups of hot tea. She looked at him over the top of her teacup as she answered his questions about what she wanted to do after uni.

'That's still ages away yet. I've only just started my second year. But geographers do all kinds of things. Many don't even use their degrees directly, but work in other areas.'

'Like?'

'Well, the tourist industry, journalism, the environment, general management, even law, if you do a conversion course after graduating.'

'You added that last one deliberately. Why was that?'

'It's what my dad wants me to do.'

'And are his plans for you important?'

'Yes, because I love my dad. But I don't want to go into law. It's just not for me. I'd be happy working for the environment in some way.'

'Is he a lawyer?'

'Goodness, no. He's a dock worker in Poole. Or he was until he retired last year. He's only ever wanted the best for me. I've always been the apple of his eye, you see. My brothers are both brawny types, one's a car-mechanic and the other a plumber. My dad has always said that I must have fallen out of the sky as a baby angel because I'm so different from the rest of the family.'

'That's very sweet.'

'But it isn't true.'

He laughed. 'No, even I don't believe in angels.'

She looked mildly irritated. 'No, I don't mean that, obviously. I do take after someone, an aunt on my mother's side. She was a petite blonde, and went to university, when few women did. She became a doctor, did missionary work in Africa and got killed during an uprising. That was when I was a baby, so I never really met her.'

He reached out and put his hand on top of hers as it lay on the table-top.

'I'm sorry. I did understand what you meant.'

Her face turned pink. 'I always take things that people say too literally. My friends at school used to tease me about it, saying I was much too gullible. That may be so, but I was the only one of my friends to make it to university. Some of them got pregnant before they were eighteen. My dad always says, who are the gullible ones now?' She paused. 'Anyway, tell me about your last girlfriend. When did you break up with her?'

'Shaz? She was a waitress in a café, which is where I met her. And I broke up with her some time ago. Why do you want to know about her?'

'No reason. It's just nice looking at you while you talk.' She hesitated. 'I really like you. Shall we go back?'

Despite her shy nature she looked him steadily in the eye while she made her suggestion. Was she being a bit too forward? Maybe, but she didn't really care. She was enjoying herself after weeks of arguments with her previous boyfriend. Why not let go a little? Or maybe a lot?

* * *

That afternoon Lauren walked hand-in-hand with her new man through the local park, laughing at the antics of some children trying to get a kite airborne. They weren't having much success.

'Maybe you should help them,' Lauren suggested. 'You have a definite height advantage.'

'Well, that might be true, but it still wouldn't work. There just isn't enough wind today, even up at my head-height.'

'So the climate's no different up there in Andy-land?'

He looked at her and laughed. She was dressed in tight jeans, trainers and a pink fleecy jacket. A pink woolly hat was pulled down as far as her ears, with her blonde hair showing below.

'Did you love your last girlfriend?' Lauren suddenly asked.

He frowned. 'What, Shaz? No, not really. She was a convenient person to have around for a while, and I liked her a lot. But no, I didn't love her.'

'So you weren't too upset when it finished?'

He shook his head. 'It was a bit of a relief to be honest. I think we both felt the same.'

'Have you ever been really in love with someone?'

He stopped walking. His face darkened and he didn't answer.

'So the answer's yes?' she continued.

Finally he nodded. 'Sorry, I wasn't expecting that. Yes, there was someone really special. She broke my heart when she left me. I'm only just beginning to get over it. In fact, meeting you has been the best thing that could have happened to me.'

Her smile returned, lighting up her features.

'That was a lovely thing to say. Do you want to talk about her? I wouldn't mind.'

'No. I don't want to talk. It's just something that I want to bury now. It's over, and I can't go back and undo what's been done. And anyway, now that I've met you, I wouldn't want to.'

She clung onto his arm even more tightly. 'It's funny, but I feel really safe when I'm with you. You have such a protective aura about you, did you realise that? I'm such a small person that I notice these things. You make me feel so secure. Maybe it's because you're that bit older than my previous boyfriends. They were all about my age, and I suppose it showed in their attitude to me. They weren't as mature and thoughtful as you. I can just sense that you really want to look after me, that somehow you take that gentlemanly protective role quite seriously.'

'Maybe,' he replied, then shrugged his shoulders. 'Do you go back to Poole during the holidays?' he asked.

'Yes. It's so convenient for me. I always take up the same job at a local travel agent. I've been working there since I was at school. I suppose it might explain my love of geography, all those trips to exciting and exotic places on the covers of the brochures. I work on one of the desks, selling holidays.'

'Are you in a uniform?'

'Yes, I am. And I've been told I look really good in it. Why? Would you fancy me in a tight, blue, office-dress and high heels?'

'I'd fancy you in anything, but it does sound appealing.'

She suddenly looked more serious. 'Going home also gives me the chance to look after Dad properly. My mum died when I was twelve and although he's sort of got over it, I still worry about him. He doesn't bother very much with decent food when I'm not there, and my brothers, who both live quite close to him, aren't the cooking types. They live on takeaways and microwave ready meals most of the time. When I'm home I try to cook him healthier stuff. I go home some weekends during term time just to make sure that he's okay, and that there's stuff in the freezer for him. You ought to meet him sometime. You'd like him.'

'I'm sure I would like anyone who had a hand in producing you. But maybe not just yet.'

She laughed. 'I'm not sure that hands had a major part to play in it, you silly.'

She slipped her hand out of his, reached up to his neck and pulled his head down to hers, kissing him softly on his lips. Her fingers played with his dark, curly hair.

They had dinner in a local pub. Lauren managed to consume a pile of roast potatoes and vegetables, three Yorkshire puddings, and several thick-cut slices of beef. Then she'd finished off the uneaten vegetables in the serving dish, followed by the leftovers on his plate. This was followed by a sizable dish of sticky-toffee pudding for dessert.

'How can you eat so much and stay so slim?' he asked.

'I always eat like this,' she giggled. 'I'm one of the lucky few. And sex makes me even hungrier.'

CHAPTER 12: Holiday Snaps

Saturday Morning, Week 1

First thing on Saturday morning the team members waited quietly for the briefing to start. They were all now aware that there would be no quick breakthrough in the case. Sophie Allen watched her detectives assemble and cluster into small groups, all looking serious as they chatted among themselves. Finally Kevin McGreedie came in, accompanied by Tom Rose, the station's commanding officer. Sophie walked to the front of the large office and stood beside the display board as the room fell silent.

'Good morning, everybody. I hope that you'll all manage some time off over the weekend, because there is unlikely to be any let-up next week. It'll probably be only a couple of days before we start to get awkward questions from the press about the charges against Vilis Berzins. His cooperation has bought us some time, but some of the more canny reporters will soon start to realise that all is not what it seems. There were some stirrings at yesterday's press release, I understand. You were out there, Lydia. Could you tell everyone what you heard?'

Pillay had positioned herself in the middle of the small knot of reporters for Friday's short press briefing. 'Nothing definite, ma'am. Mainly the weekend's football fixtures, but there were a few murmurs about the lack of any news since we announced that we were charging Berzins. But the news about the search for the red hatchback had reached them somehow.'

Sophie said, 'I do want to say that Barry did exactly the right thing in the circumstances. The witness who'd seen the car doing a turn in the lane late last Monday night said it was an old 02 reg even though he couldn't read the rest of the number plate. He also said that he'd seen it before, possibly at the local petrol station. That's why Barry went down there. If they had been able to identify it, it could have saved us days of work, so it was worth a try. Unfortunately the manager chose to release the fact that we were looking for the car to someone from the press. I called in to see him late yesterday to tell him exactly what I thought of this. Anything else that the team should know about, Lydia?'

'Not really, ma'am. It was the usual mix of press and local people. The locals are still shocked by the murders.'

'You all know that there is a parallel investigation going on in Bournemouth, headed up by DI McGreedie here. He's agreed to visit us this morning to summarise progress so far. Over to you, Kevin.'

McGreedie spoke quietly in his soft Borders accent. 'There's a summary of the victim's details on your own board here, so I'm sure you're aware of them. Susie Pater was a twenty-two-year-old, and worked out of a small flat in the red-light district close to Bournemouth station. She wasn't a street girl. She worked from phone appointments and tended to stick with clients that she knew. That's why she hadn't been picked up on our radar. She's never been in trouble with us, and, as far as I can tell, none of the help agencies knew of her. Yet from what her friend said, she's been working in Bournemouth for at least three years, and has built up quite a reputation. This all tends to indicate that her killer was probably known to her. We haven't found any evidence yet that she knew Donna Goodenough, but it is possible that their paths crossed, since Donna lived in Bournemouth when she was at university.'

He took a sip of water. 'Susie worked out of a small studio flat that she rented, but she also owned a property somewhere else in the town. There were no clues as to its whereabouts in her working flat, but one of her friends remembered some comments that Susie made about having a flat of her own near the central gardens. We found it early this morning and have a forensic team there at the moment carrying out a search. Like you, we were desperate to find some names and addresses since there were none in her working flat, and we're in luck. They've just turned up an address book and a couple of notebooks. We're also examining a laptop computer that was there, so our computer expert will be looking for emails and anything else that might prove useful. We're hopeful that this stuff can help us, since it's likely that the murderer didn't know of the flat's existence. We're going over to have a look at the flat once this briefing has finished.'

'Thanks, Kevin,' said Sophie. 'Yesterday evening Barry, Bob Thompson and I paid a visit to a pub in Bournemouth that Donna had been seen in after dropping out of university. We didn't hold out much hope. The student who claimed he had seen Donna there with a man seems to have a memory that's all over the place. But we struck lucky, after a fashion, and a couple of people there remembered her. But that was as far as it went. They didn't know names, and couldn't remember much about the man she was with, apart from the fact that he was tall. What intrigues us is why they went to that pub. Was it their local? Was one of them, or both of them, living nearby? It's not an especially attractive place, so it's not likely to pull people in from a wide area. We plan to start house-to-house enquiries in the area later today, trying to jog a few memories with a photo of Donna. But more and more, we wonder if this tall man is the one we're after. It's our only lead, so we have to make the most of it. The student who gave it to us thinks he was older than Donna, and a bit aggressive.'

Barry Marsh interrupted. 'How close is the pub to Susie's flat? The one that's been discovered? It could provide the link between Susie and Donna.'

McGreedie answered. 'Ten minutes' walk, maybe. We'll certainly follow it up.'

'We started to look for similarities with other domestic assaults in the records. Do we have anything yet?' said Sophie.

Melsom answered. 'There are some similar assaults in the records, none in this area, but a lot in Bournemouth and Poole. We're wading through them all, but it's slow and nothing has shown up yet.'

Sophie continued. 'There's usually a fairly long past history to an abuser like this, and the behaviour does tend to show itself sooner or later in any relationship he has. It's a trap, really, that too many vulnerable women fall into. It usually starts with a sense that he's protecting the woman. It's reassuring, giving them a feeling of being looked after. But then it slowly mutates into control and, sometimes, aggression. What we are looking at is a worst-case. Only a tiny minority of abusive men take it this far — to murder. Even then, most of the murders are done in a fit of temper at the point of break-up or soon after, and that makes the job easy for us. This one is very different. I think it's probable that we have a psychopath here, someone who has no empathy for others and who can blank them out of his mind totally. He has probably planned this over a matter of weeks or even months. We're dealing with someone who is violent without scruple. He is far beyond the type of petty criminal that we deal with for most of our working lives. I'm not even sure how he fits into the spectrum of psychopathic behaviour, because of the amount of premeditation.'

'What, even the murder of Brenda, the mother, was planned well in advance?' interrupted Melsom.

'Yes, and there are two possible motives for that. There's the obvious one that she'd met him or knew who he was. But let's look at the other. The son has told us that his mother was a beaten wife herself, knocked about by a drunken husband. And she'd put up with it for years before she finally left. Then, all these years later, her daughter starts to show signs of the same kind of partner abuse. What's she going to say to Donna? Dump him. Dump him immediately, now. Get out, now. And if he got to hear of that somehow, he'd view her as the person who made Donna leave him. It's striking how many wife-murders of this type also involve the mother. Most mothers will fight for their daughters until their dying breath. The maternal instinct never leaves us, Jimmy, and our daughters are precious beyond description. To see a daughter tortured by a man who should be loving and cherishing her would cause us such anguish that we couldn't fail to get closely involved. Such a man would see the two women conspiring against him. No wonder that both are killed, if it gets as far as that. As we think it did on this occasion. The need for revenge is very powerful in such men.'

'And Susie Pater? How does she fit in?' asked Pillay.

'It's possible she was only killed to help throw suspicion onto Berzins, Donna's boyfriend. Again, another aspect of this type of personality is that vengeance must be handed out to all those who've played a part. Berzins has to pay for his relationship with Donna. What better than this elaborate construction that sets him up as the killer? And Susie's murder puts him so perfectly into the frame, since he was nearby at the time. Our man must have been on cloud nine when he thought it all up. It must have seemed perfect and it all seemed to go so well. But it was just too elaborate to hold together once we picked up on a couple of flaws. But to get back to Susie, I wonder why she was chosen. It was unlikely that she was a random choice since she didn't work the streets. She was picky and only saw her clients by arrangement. It tends to point to her knowing her killer. So was he one of her regulars? Again, we wonder if her murder solved two problems. It provided another nail in the coffin for Berzins, but it also removed someone who knew the murderer well enough to finger him.'

'Did her body show any signs of physical abuse?' asked Marsh.

McGreedie replied. 'No. There were none of the scars or marks that you found on Donna's body. But that doesn't surprise us. She wasn't a street girl. She used the flat where she was found, but also worked the upmarket hotels in the area. She didn't have to put up with anything heavy from her punters. And I'd guess that whatever relationship she had with our man was the same. According to her friend who found the body, Susie would have walked away from anything even remotely violent.'

'Are there any more thoughts about the umbrella that was found in her flat?' asked Pillay.

Sophie said, 'we think it was left there to provide the link. To ensure that we'd make the connection that whoever killed Donna also killed Susie. That worked fine when we thought that Berzins was our man, but it's a double-edged sword. We don't think that Berzins killed Donna, and he definitely didn't kill Susie. But the two deaths are linked by the umbrella.' She paused. 'As I said, I want everyone to get some sort of a break during the weekend, however short. Jimmy, you can have the rest of today off since you did the overnight stint at the house. By the way, did Berzins remember anything else?'

'Didn't get an opportunity to ask him, ma'am. He slept all the time I was there. I don't think he got much kip while he was here in the cells.'

'Okay, I'm seeing him later so I'll check then. Lydia, can you follow up on the domestic violence records? We're looking for a pattern of bruising on arms, legs and face, with possible strangulation attempts. Anyone else spare can help you. There's also a chance that he's called Andy, Andrew or similar, if he is the guy that the student talked about. See what comes up. Then take tomorrow off, and get a break from all of this. I want you feeling fresh on Monday. Barry, you go home this afternoon. Meanwhile are you going to keep digging for information about the car? Is there any CCTV that might have caught it on its travels? And all of you, make sure that we can contact you if needed. And phone me if you find anything that I need to know about, particularly the knife. Okay, everyone? Everything goes through me, unless it's only Bournemouth-related. Then it goes to DI McGreedie. Right, let's get cracking.'

* * *

An hour later, Sophie, with McGreedie and Thompson, entered a two-bedroomed, luxury apartment in a quiet residential area of Bournemouth. Sophie looked out from the lounge window over the flower beds and shrubs of the central gardens. 'This is worth a bit, surely?'

'Close to three hundred thousand, we think. You have to hand it to her, there are not many who manage to stay clear of drugs and pimps to bank that much,' said McGreedie.

'But she is dead, Kevin. Despite all her care in picking her punters, the total compartmentalising of her life, the tight control she exercised, she couldn't escape it in the end. She was gambling with her future when she started this life, and she probably knew it. Poor girl. And the place hasn't been ransacked in any way?'

'No signs,' said Bob Thompson. 'Everything was pretty well as you'd expect. We found address books in the telephone desk, a wall calendar with birthdays and anniversaries marked on it, bills, receipts and everything else you'd see in a normal home. The only difference is that it's almost too perfect, as you can see. It doesn't really look lived-in.'

'Maybe she only spent a day or two a week here. Either that or she was obsessive about cleanliness and tidiness. That wouldn't be surprising would it? Anything of interest in the address book?' Sophie asked.

Yes. Family members, addresses, phone numbers. And we found an Andy.'

He handed her the address book, opened at the letter R.

'Andy, but no surname. It is under the letter R, though. That must be significant, surely? It's just a mobile number with no address. Even so, that's brilliant. It might give us a better handle on him,' said Sophie.

'There's more.'

He took the book back and turned back to an earlier section. Under the letter G was written the name Donna Goodenough.

'So they did know each other. I wonder how?'

'You might also be interested in this.'

He passed over a wall calendar, open at the month of August. There was an entry for the twenty-fifth, with simply the name Andy.

'Probably his birthday? Shame it doesn't show his age. Still, it's better than nothing. I'll phone this through to Lydia. She's searching the records on domestic abuse. When will you start to work through the phone numbers?'

'I'll contact family as soon as I get back to the office. We'll then work our way through the others once we've got the family informed,' said Thompson.

They continued to explore the apartment. It was everything that the other flat had not been. Comfortable, spacious, decorated in pastel shades with matching furniture and fittings. Food in the kitchen cupboards, the fridge and the freezer. Cookbooks. Normal clothes in the wardrobe. Books and CDs on the shelves. Magazines in a rack in the lounge. Yes, thought Sophie. I could be at home here, though maybe it's just a bit too much like a show-apartment.

'Do her friends know how much time she spent here?'

'The ones we've spoken to don't know about this place in any detail. They wondered if she had somewhere else, but didn't know where it was. Like you, I'd guess at two or three days a week, but we might be totally wrong. We still can't find any accurate details about her life. She came and went quietly. Her neighbours rarely saw her, apart from an occasional greeting on the stairs or in the lift.'

'Bob, the fact that the name Andy actually appears in her address book and on her calendar is significant, if he is our man.'

'Absolutely. He wasn't just an everyday punter. He was someone closer to her than that. But then again it might be someone entirely different, a cousin or a close friend. We just don't know. We're still probing as hard as we can, but it's a slow business. There's an address for someone we think might be her mother. It's in Exeter, but the phone isn't being answered, and the local police say that there's no one in the house. The neighbours say that the owners are abroad on holiday. Which I can fully understand, given the weather we were getting last week. It's bloody frustrating for us, though. The squad back at the station are going through every phone contact in the address book. The ones we've been able to speak to so far haven't been very helpful. Just old friends who send Christmas cards, but don't stay in contact much more than that.'

Kevin said, 'Apparently, the team pick up a kind of reserve from many of them. They tell us how they knew Susie. Many of them were school friends. I'd guess that they had suspicions about what she did, and have become distant.'

'Is there anything else I should know about? What about photos?' Sophie said.

'We're trying to match them up to names. We've got a copy of your photo of Donna pinned up on the board, just in case she appears in any of the shots.'

Sophie had one last walk around the flat, looking in each of the rooms, in the vain hope that something would provide a lead. Nothing did. She rejoined McGreedie and Thompson in the hall. They were leaning against the wall, one on either side of the coatrack.

'Okay, I've seen enough,' she said.

The two Bournemouth detectives moved towards the door. Above the coat hooks hung a framed photo of Susie sitting on a beach. Sophie almost stopped breathing. 'These moments are few and far between, but they are worth savouring,' she said.

She lifted the photo down from the wall. 'I knew I'd seen her face before. She's the girl in the background of the photo of Donna that we found in her flat on Tuesday. It's the same scene as this one. They must have been on holiday together.'

CHAPTER 13: The Face on the Screen

Saturday Afternoon, Week 1

Sophie was sitting on a bench in the gardens by the old Victorian pier at Swanage, with Barry Marsh and Lydia Pillay. They'd decided to come out for some fish and chips, and were eating them in the weak November sunshine, looking out across the open sea to the chalk cliffs on the opposite side of the bay. The sunshine glinted on the waves gently rolling towards the sandy beach. A few families were braving the chilly air and bundled-up children were building sandcastles.

'It's the only way to eat fish and chips, ma'am. It's just got to be outside, in the sun, with a sea view. Trust me, I'm an expert.' Marsh popped another chip into his mouth.

Sophie laughed. 'I hope your weight doesn't end up doubling, Barry, if you're such an expert. Women like a toned man, don't they, Lydia?'

'Oh yes. Preferably one who's got some muscles on him, you know, just like that Diet Coke ad. Jeans, a white vest and well-developed pecs. Dark stubble. The moody, mysterious, Mediterranean look. That's what I go for.'

'There you go, Barry. You now know what turns the girls on, so go easy with the fish and chips. But I must say these are really tasty. Just what I remember from going on holiday with my mum as a child. It was always one of the high spots of our annual holiday. Fish and chips on the Friday night before we came home.'

'But I thought—' said Marsh.

'You thought what, Barry?'

He hesitated for a moment. 'Well, it's just after what you told me a couple of days ago, about going to Oxford and that. I was just a bit surprised that you came to places like this for your holidays.'

His face was pink with embarrassment.

'Oh no, this kind of place was a bit expensive for us. It was always a caravan in Weston-super-Mare or Portishead. I grew up in a council flat in Bristol. And it was just me and my mum. She was a single parent. I've never met my father. He disappeared before my mother knew she was pregnant. She was sixteen at the time. Things are not always as they seem, Barry, when it comes to people. Are you a bit disappointed now?'

'No, ma'am, not at all. The opposite. I'm even more impressed than I was. To think that you've done all you have, and come from an absolutely ordinary background like that. It's amazing. I always thought that you were from a posh family.'

'My mother was a bit of a rebel. She was — is — a very intelligent woman. But when she was a teenager and fell pregnant with me, her parents threw her out. She's never forgiven them and neither have I. She never spoke to them again. But I kept in touch, partly to try to understand why they did what they did. Though I've never managed to, not on an emotional level. It's kind of understandable when you put it into the context of those times, but whenever I think about the actual act of locking the doors against a pregnant daughter, I lose it. It wasn't as if she was on drugs or drank too much, or was a criminal. She was an intelligent kid with a bright future who made a mistake.'

'But it wasn't a mistake, was it, ma'am?' Pillay said.

'What do you mean?'

'It produced you. How could that possibly be a mistake? Your mother must be so proud of you and what you've done with your life.'

Sophie reached across and squeezed Pillay's arm. 'I'm going to get all choked up in a minute, the way this conversation is going. Bless you, Lydia. But now, can we get back on track? Have we all finished eating? Barry, summarise for us. What do we know, and where do we go from here?'

'The knife that killed Donna. Why haven't we found it yet?'

'We keep looking. What else?'

'We go on looking for signs of him in past cases. He won't have got this violent all at once. He'll have built up to it, so there'll be a record somewhere. Maybe there was teenage violence, or minor assaults, or cases that didn't make it to court. Or something.'

'What do we know about him already?'

'His name might be Andy. His surname might start with the letter R. Bournemouth CID are following up on a possible mobile phone number. We think he was older than Donna, maybe in his late twenties, even thirties. He's fairly tall, possibly heavily built. He's strong, probably a bit confrontational. He reacts aggressively, even in public places.'

Pillay joined in. 'He's not stupid, not to have planned and carried this out. It would have taken a lot of thought to have set up something so complicated. One thing is sure. He's not your average murderer, is he?'

'Which makes me more certain that he's got history,' said Sophie. 'We need to keep trawling through those records. I take it nothing's shown up this morning, Lydia?'

'Well, I'm only part way through. I managed to create a list of the cases where the name Andy or Andrew appears, all with a surname beginning with R. There are about twenty within thirty miles, going back over ten years. But I haven't started on the ones where there was a strangulation attempt yet. Or leg fractures from kicks.'

'Well, maybe something will surface this afternoon. Barry, can you temporarily shelve the search for the car if we need more time on the database? Or put someone else onto it? I'll leave a message if I'm not in tomorrow. I'm going back to visit Berzins this afternoon, and taking a photofit boffin with me. According to HQ she wants to try out some new software.'

* * *

Lydia Pillay continued to work through the criminal records. It was slow, laborious work, but at last she felt she was making some progress. She finally narrowed down the last search option and generated another list, this time of men who'd caused leg injuries to their partners. There were more than fifty, scattered across East Dorset and West Hampshire. She was horrified by how many there were. The list showed that violence seemed to be commonplace within some homes, almost a routine part of daily life. And it didn't occur in one particular group. It seemed to spread across all social strata. There was a lawyer, and a bank manager, both guilty of striking their wives in outbursts of seemingly pent-up fury. And there was a female shop owner who'd kicked her husband in the face several times with only minor 'provocation.' What was the world coming to?

* * *

Meanwhile, Sophie had driven to police headquarters to collect the facial artist who had co-developed new image-producing software. Sophie had expected a nondescript-looking computer geek, but was pleasantly surprised to find a vibrantly-dressed black woman, called Louisa Mugomba. Sophie drove Louisa to the safe house in Wareham. The artist spent an hour with Vilis Berzins, attempting to build an image from his rather vague recollection of the stranger in the pub. Neither he nor Sophie held out much hope, but Louisa managed to put exactly the right suggestions to Berzins about particular features. Once he saw them on the screen he could then ask for minor alterations until they arrived at a likeness.

'How do we manage to employ someone with your level of skill?' asked Sophie. 'I didn't know we had you until Matt Silver told me.'

'You don't. I'm on secondment from Southampton University, just while we develop the software. My team was funded by the Home Office. What you see is a prototype at the moment, but it's come a long way over the past two years, and we hope to have it ready for release before the summer. Mr Silver helped to draw up the original specification, and that's how I was asked to help you out on this case. It's an ideal test. But don't expect miracles, please. You can see that what I've produced still has to rely on a person's memory, so it can never be better than what he or she recalls. But it's kind of dynamic, and responds quickly to their inputs. And the fact that it's three-dimensional is a real leap forward.'

'It's very impressive. How quickly can you make prints available?'

'I can email an image to you this afternoon, once I'm back in my office. You can then print it off. But it is better viewed on screen, with the 3D effect. I'll create a guest login for you onto our system so that you can view the 3D image from your office.'

'I'll look forward to it, and thanks for your help. By the way, please don't talk about this case with anybody, even the other people in your team. Everything you have seen, heard and talked about this afternoon is extremely confidential. We haven't gone public on this yet, and I can't afford for even the merest whisper to leak out. I'll be brutal if I find you've talked, even to a family member, and you'll find yourself under charge without a job. Sorry to labour the point, but you'll already have guessed the significance while talking to our guest here. We might have a serial killer on our hands, and we're all treading on eggshells at the moment because we're trying to keep it out of the press. Do you understand?'

'Absolutely.'

Once Louisa had left the room, Sophie turned to Berzins.

'So that's him, Vilis? As far as you can remember?' She looked at the face on the screen. It was a face that would blend in anywhere. But something about it seemed familiar to Sophie.

'That is the best I can do, Chief Inspector. I only talked to him for a few minutes.'

'What about his voice? Can you remember how he spoke?'

'It was a deeper voice than many. He spoke carefully, but I think that was because he knew I wasn't English, and he wanted me to understand. But I do remember that he didn't smoke his cigarette. He lit one but he just held it in his fingers. He didn't once put it to his mouth while I was talking to him. It makes me think that his only purpose in being there was to talk to me, not to smoke.'

'You may be right. And are you sure that you hadn't seen him before? He hadn't visited the hotel, or spoken to Donna as far as you were aware?'

'No. He was new to me. And Donna never spoke of a man talking to her.'

'Did Donna ever talk of a holiday she took in Greece with a friend, sometime in the last year or two?'

'No.'

'That's all I have to ask, Vilis. Is there anything you want to talk about?'

He shook his head.

'In that case, I'll get back. I'll see you again in a few days. I hope you won't have to be here for very much longer. I'll keep you and your brother informed of our progress.'

Sophie drove Louisa back to Winfrith. She went to see Matt Silver and gave him a quick report.

'Tired?' he asked.

'A bit. The usual reason. I haven't been sleeping as well as I normally do, what with all the thoughts whirling round in my head.'

'Don't think that you've got to do it all alone, Sophie. If you need more help, just let me know. This is the first triple murder we've had for years. We can afford to give you all the resources you want for this one.'

'It's okay at present, Matt. I've got Kevin to talk to if I need someone. And I trust my team. Is you-know-who breathing down your neck?'

'Nothing that I can't handle. At the moment, that is. But you'll get to the bottom of it all. I have faith in you. And finding Susie's second flat was a real breakthrough. Kevin phoned me an hour ago to bring me up to date about the holiday photos. It looks as though you were right and the two of them were on holiday together. It'll be interesting to find out how they met.' He paused. 'By the way, there's a CCTV camera covering the slipway on the Poole side of the ferry. Apparently it went up a couple of weeks ago. I'll get the recordings for Monday and Tuesday, shall I?'

'Make it all week, Matt. I'll just have to find someone to plough through them. It'll help trace the car if we're lucky.'

'So what are your plans for next week?'

'I'll get someone to visit the owners of the flat above Donna's. Apparently they heard something on Monday evening. Someone else claims they saw a person entering or leaving the building, also on Monday evening. We'll need to get a statement from them. Kevin will start to contact the entries in Susie Pater's phone book, so I'll keep track of that.'

'You look troubled.'

'There's something niggling me about the facial image that the photofit generated. But I don't know what it is.'

* * *

McGreedie had little new to report other than some communication with Susie's family. They had tried to contact the number that had been listed in Susie's address book for Andy, but the mobile had been switched off.

'Listen, Kevin. Can you leave that number for the moment? I don't think we should do anything that might warn him off. If he gets suspicious, he'll ditch the phone, start to cover his tracks and we'll be facing another blind alley. Wait until Monday. We'll get some tracking equipment and the phone companies involved, and we'll try it then. I'll come across, if that's okay.'

She returned to Pillay's desk to see how she was getting on with the search. The young detective had several printouts spread across the desk in front of her, and was looking puzzled.

'It's odd, ma'am. This left list shows cases where there's been a strangulation attempt, although none of them caused death. There's an Andrew on the list, with the surname Rule. This second list is for cases of leg injuries, mostly from kicks. There's an Andy on that list, but with the surname Ridgeway. You'd think they were different, but look at the birth dates. Both have the same day and month, but with the year of birth differing by one.'

'August the twenty-fifth. That's the date that was marked on Susie's calendar. Did either of these cases result in a conviction?'

'No. Didn't come to court. In each case the woman dropped charges after the initial complaint. Then there's this one.'

She pointed to an entry on the third list. 'It lacks detail, but an assault case was started. It was dropped and soon after the woman just vanished totally. Apparently she couldn't be traced, although whoever was in charge of the investigation didn't consider it suspicious.'

'Whereabouts did these happen?'

'The first one was in Poole. The second in Bournemouth. The third one, with the woman who vanished, was earlier than the others. It was in Southampton.'

'What were you searching for in this third one?'

'Bruising around the throat.'

'Get the full details printed out for each one. Put a concise summary on the incident board. I'm just going to call someone I know in Hampshire CID.'

Sophie found the number. 'Hi Jack, it's Sophie Allen. Yes, you're right, I am on that case, and no, I can't tell you what's happening. Listen, some seven years ago in Southampton a young woman called Debbie Martinez started an assault case against her boyfriend. She had bruising around her throat. The case was dropped, and she disappeared soon afterwards. Can you find out the details for me? Do a bit of digging? I'll be eternally grateful. Okay, call me when you can. And keep quiet about it, will you? I can't afford for the press to get hold of this.'

She returned to Pillay's desk.

'We need to follow up these cases. What are the names?'

'Tracy Beck in Poole in 2005. Sasha Purfleet in Bournemouth a year later.'

'See if you can find any contact details for them. Barry can call them tomorrow. And well done, Lydia. All the time you and the others have put in will pay off in the end.'

Then Sophie's phone rang. When it finished she turned again to Pillay. 'Well, that was interesting. That was David Bell, Donna's first-year tutor at university. He must have really put some time in, because he's managed to organise a batch of photos from a variety of social events that Donna attended, many taken by her fellow students. He's willing to help us identify people in the shots. He also said that the university reported Donna's disappearance to the local police. If so, it will still be on record somewhere.'

'Are the photos likely to help that much, ma'am?'

'There's always the chance that this boyfriend, Andy, is in one of the shots. He wasn't a student as far as we know, but maybe he came to one or two of the parties. And if we can eliminate most of the bona fide students, there might just be a chance that her boyfriend is left as an unknown. We match it up against Berzins' photofit and who knows? That reminds me, the artist promised to email me this afternoon with the photofit image. I'll just check.'

Within a few moments she had the image on screen and a photo-quality picture en-route to the printer. Pillay picked up the image and looked at it intently.

'I've seen that face somewhere, ma'am. I'm sure of it.'

'That's what I keep telling myself too. But it's only a vague, fleeting recognition, so I wondered if it was just my overstretched imagination. So where could we both have seen him? We were at Corfe on Tuesday when we found Brenda Goodenough. Was it there?'

Pillay kept looking at the image on the screen as Sophie pinned the paper copy onto the incident board.

'Remember he's tall, at least six foot. And Berzins reminded me earlier about the grey hoodie he was wearing.'

Pillay rolled her finger over the touch pad and rotated the image. She walked to the window which looked out onto Argyle Road. The area in front of the station was empty. All the reporters and photographers had gone home for the weekend. A few bits of litter blew around in the breeze.

'It was out here. He was in the crowd yesterday. I stood almost beside him. He was talking to a reporter.'

Sophie came across to join her. 'Of course. That's why he seemed familiar. I looked past him when that reporter asked about the car. Shit. That means he heard. It could mean that he suspects his scheme might not be working.'

'Not necessarily, ma'am. We could just be covering all angles, as far as he's concerned. But it will make him cautious.'

'Can you remember what he did when we finished?'

'Someone left the crowd and walked across Kings Road. I think it might have been him, but I can't be sure.'

'I wonder if there's any CCTV that we could check?'

'Not this far away from the town centre. I remember asking Barry about it, and he said that it's all down at the seafront area. If I remember rightly, the reporter this man was chatting to was the one who asked you about the car.'

'So I now face a real problem. That man works for the local press and I've had a run-in with him before. If I ask him about the conversation he had, he'll smell a rat. Hmmm. I'll think about it overnight. And we'll need to find a way of getting this photofit out without arousing too much suspicion. Monday, I'll get Jimmy to go across to the campus and see David Bell. He thinks he'll have the photos ready for checking by then. I want them examined there so he and the students can identify people.'

She looked at the clock. 'I think we're getting closer to him, Lydia. Time to go home. You need a break, so I don't want to see you in tomorrow. Barry and Jimmy can take over from you.'

'What about you, ma'am?'

'I'll take some time off tomorrow. Hannah, my elder daughter, is home from drama college for the weekend. We're planning to have lunch out, and I don't want that spoiled. I'll pop in first thing to check things out, then maybe head off mid-morning. But on Monday I want the whole team back and working at top speed.'

CHAPTER 14: The Hidden Daughter

Sunday, Week 1

'Do you recognise him, Barry?'

They were looking at the 3D image, based upon Berzins' recollection of a ten minute conversation that had taken place two weeks prior to the murder.

'How can he be so sure?' Marsh said. 'I doubt if I could remember the details of a face from that long ago.'

'Your girlfriend hasn't been murdered. I think that might help to concentrate the mind a little, don't you?'

'But that's part of my difficulty, ma'am. How much is wishful thinking? He's probably been thinking about nothing else for days.'

'I'd agree with you, except both Lydia and I recognised that face, and it was someone we think we saw, out front on Friday.'

'But with all due respect, ma'am, it might be some perfectly innocent local man Berzins once saw in the pub and who happened to stop by for the press briefing. There were lots of locals out there.'

'Well, we won't know until he's identified. Maybe we'll discover that what you say is true, but at the moment we have to assume that the image is probably the man we want. If we find that he has nothing to do with the case, then we'll move to a different tack. But at the moment we assume some degree of accuracy. Okay?'

Although it was useful to have a sceptic on the team, it could also have a demotivating effect. Sophie was slightly annoyed.

'I didn't mean to snap at you, Barry. You know how high the pressure is on this one, particularly since I let Berzins go. I wanted you to look at the image to see if you recognised him, since you're a local. I know that there's a chance we were mistaken. So you can't place him here?'

'No, no one I know, ma'am, and I do know most of the local press guys. He's not one of them.'

'Okay. Now, these three possible earlier victims Lydia picked up yesterday. That's what I want you to concentrate on, and Jimmy when he comes in later. I'd like them traced so that we can talk to them. Can you make a start on that? Then take a break this afternoon and do something to relax. We'll all need a clear head this coming week. I don't know how far this thing is going to extend. We started off on Monday night with what appeared to be a single murder. Now we have at least three, with two earlier assaults and a possible disappearance. I can't believe that this guy hasn't shown up on our radar before. If it is the same person, then he's a meticulous planner, and we can't afford to underestimate him. And what do we know about him? Nothing. What do we suspect about him? His name's Andy. His surname might be Rule or Ridgeway. He's tall and strong. He looks like that.' She pointed to the image. 'It looks as though his birthday's on the twenty-fifth of August. It's not much, is it?'

Marsh didn't answer.

'Barry, it would be useful to find a way of talking to that reporter without raising his suspicions. Bill Rogers is his name. I can't do it. I had a run-in with him a couple of years ago in Birmingham when he crossed me, and I went to town on him and his editor. He might not be eager to help me. Can you think of a way of questioning him without making it obvious? Give it some thought.'

'Of course. One thing, ma'am. It's too easy for a bloke like that to fool everyone completely by shaving his beard off. We could do with another picture of what he'd look like without a beard. Does that fancy software do that?'

'Brilliant. I'll phone Louisa and ask. By the way, when Donna dropped out of her degree course and the university couldn't contact her, they reported her disappearance to the local police. I'd like to know what they did about it. Would you ask Jimmy to follow it up when he comes in?'

* * *

It was well past noon when Sophie finally arrived home. She was worried that she was late. But Hannah, her elder daughter, had overslept and wasn't ready. Sophie took the opportunity to catch up on the news in the Sunday papers. Martin sat opposite her in their lounge.

'Are you okay, sweetheart?'

'Oh, you know, things could be better. A lot better, actually. We're running out of time, you see. The public think that we've already got the killer under lock and key, but we haven't. And sooner or later it's bound to come out that we've dropped charges against Berzins. Then all hell will be let loose, believe me. The press will be after blood. They don't like being strung along, which is what we've been doing with them since Thursday night. But there isn't an alternative. We have to make the real killer think that he's got away with it so he lowers his guard. That's the plan, anyway. Meanwhile we've got dozens of people doing house-to-house inquiries, searching records, interviewing contacts, but trying to keep it all away from public view. We are making headway, but it's hard work.

He's a clever bastard. That's the trouble with some of these psychos. They plan everything so carefully. We saw through his first false trail, but has he laid others? Is he working on one now, as we speak? I keep thinking, what's he doing now? Because he won't be sitting idly by, twiddling his thumbs, not this guy. He's too much of a schemer. And I'm his main opponent.'

'Would he know that you're heading up the investigation?'

'I don't know. Matt's done most of the media stuff and Tom Rose has dealt with the press releases. But if our guy has been doing his groundwork, he'll know. We think he might have been outside the station for several of the briefings and, if so, he'll have spotted me coming and going, and talking to the team. But that's one of the reasons we've kept up the pretence about Berzins.'

'Do you think he really believes that you've fallen for it?'

'No. Not in my heart of hearts. He must guess that at some stage his whole scheme will fall apart. It was just too good to be true. I'd bet that was why he was there on Friday, to see if we'd seen through it all. It will only take one or two details to get out, and he'll switch to an alternative plan that he's got ready.'

'And that might be?'

'It doesn't bear thinking about. He's already killed three women that we know of, maybe more. We're trying to trace some of his possible other victims who are still alive, and he'd guess that. It'll be a race to see who finds them first, and their lives will depend on us being the winners. I've told you more than I should have done. But I need your understanding on this case, Martin. Maybe more than most of the others I've worked on since we came here.'

He reached across and stroked her hand. 'I'm glad you told me.'

Just then Hannah and Jade came into the room.

Sophie looked at her two daughters. 'You both look beautiful,' she said. 'Even if I haven't said it often enough in the past, I want to say it now. I'm so proud of you both.'

'Gosh, Mum,' replied Hannah. 'What brought that on?'

But Sophie was already turning away to put her jacket on. Martin looked at the girls, raised his finger to his lips and shook his head slightly.

* * *

It was wonderful to be away from the case, if only for a few hours. Sophie could afford to indulge in the intense pleasure of being in the company of the three people who meant more to her than she could ever put into words. Even so, she was quiet and thoughtful while they ate. Her two daughters gossiped amiably, with an occasional interjection from their father. Sophie merely watched, basking in the warmth of their cheerful happiness. Up and down the country there were families indulging in all kinds of activities together. Eating, like her and her family, going for walks together, watching TV. People should be able to do all these things without fear and violence getting in the way. And that was the essence of her job — to give them that chance. She looked again at her daughters. Hannah was talking about her first few months at drama college, and the kind of acting roles she aspired to. Jade had her own very different ambition to become a doctor. These were worthy aspirations, and she felt immense pride at having two such intelligent and warm-hearted daughters. She reached across and squeezed Martin's hand. Then her mobile phone rang. She gave a wry smile.

'Hello, Jack.'

She listened intently. 'Interesting. Okay, thanks.' She looked up to see her family watching her.

'Sorry, I can't tell you what that was about. But I do think that you should finish that wine off.'

'Mum, you've hardly had any,' said Jade. 'These two have guzzled the lot.'

'Got to keep a clear head, young lady. I'm driving, remember.'

* * *

Sophie was back in the incident room by late afternoon. Melsom and Marsh were looking at the board. She went over to join them.

'Jack Dunning phoned from Hampshire about the third possible victim of abuse,' she told them. 'Debbie Martinez. They think the boyfriend's name was Andrew Renshaw, but can't be certain. The details are not on record, since the case was dropped soon after the charges were brought. Jack's managed to trace one of the officers involved. Apparently she remembers interviewing him, and describes him as a fairly tall man with a strong build. He wasn't overtly aggressive or confrontational. She saw the girl a couple of times after the case was dropped. She'd left the boyfriend, and seemed happier. She told the officer that she was thinking of moving away, so her disappearance probably isn't suspicious. Maybe she's gone back to her parents. Maybe she's got married and changed her name. But we need to trace her, if only to check that she is still alive and well. Barry, can you try get across to Southampton tomorrow to see the officer involved?'

'Of course.'

'Anything turned up here?' she asked.

Marsh said, 'I've got a possible address for Tracy Beck in Poole. She's in a flat on the Bourne Valley estate. Nothing so far on Sasha Purfleet.'

'How did Tracy show up?'

'Traffic violation last year. Driving without insurance.'

He handed her a slip of paper.

Sophie glanced at it then looked at her watch. 'I'll go and see her now. Do you want to come, Jimmy?'

'Oh yes, ma'am.'

'Barry, take a break. You've done a lot this weekend.'

'Thanks, ma'am. By the way, we haven't managed to think of a way of pumping Rogers, that reporter.'

'No, me neither. I've been puzzling over it, but I end up rejecting every idea I come up with. They're all too chancy. We can't afford to breach investigation guidelines and risk the chance of making any evidence inadmissible. And I can't interview him and ask him to keep it quiet because of the friction between us. He might promise one thing, but do another, just to get even with me.'

'What about interviewing him with his editor? That way he couldn't break a promise not to publish.'

'Useful idea, but still not secure enough, Barry. He could still spread the story about it deliberately but quietly and then deny that it was him. Too chancy. But keep thinking. One of us may have a brainwave. Let's get off to Poole, Jimmy.'

She let Melsom drive. 'Did you get anywhere with the university report about Donna's disappearance?'

'A couple of Bournemouth PCs visited all her known addresses when the university reported her missing, ma'am. Drew blanks. But at least it was followed up.'

'It might be worth revisiting those places. Now she's a murder victim people may be willing to talk a little more. Murder can have that effect. I'll mention it to Bob Thompson tomorrow.'

* * *

The Bourne Valley estate housed its share of troublesome families. But it was always a minority who gained press attention and gave the area a reputation that it didn't really deserve. As they drove through the estate they could see that most of the houses were well-maintained. There was an occasional weed-infested property, often with a broken-down car in the garden. Tracy's flat was in the middle floor of a three-storey block. Melsom parked and they took the stairs to the second floor. A young man answered the door, and eyed them suspiciously. He was of average height with short blonde hair, dressed in a faded T-shirt and clean chinos.

'Does Tracy Beck live here?' Melsom asked.

'Yes. Who wants to know?'

Jimmy showed his warrant card. 'We'd like a word with her, please. Nothing to worry about.'

The man pulled the door to and disappeared inside. They heard the sound of voices, and a young woman appeared. She had curly brown shoulder-length hair.

'What do you want?' she asked, her freckled face looking suspicious.

'I'm DCI Sophie Allen. We're investigating a series of assault-based crimes from several years ago, one of which involved you. There are a few questions we need to ask but they are rather sensitive. Can we come in please?'

Tracy led them through a tiny lobby to a small neat lounge, where a young child was playing on the floor with her dolls. The man who had answered the door was sitting on the floor with her.

'Tracy, we need to speak to you alone and in confidence, if that's possible.'

'Well, we were about to take Rachel out to the park. Jerry, could you take her? Maybe I'll join you later.'

'Tell me what you want,' Tracy said, once the door was shut behind them. 'I thought that was all in the past. Why are you so interested now?'

'A current enquiry that we are investigating has shown up some similarities to what you went through. There have been several other young women assaulted besides you and we wonder if it's the same man. Since you dropped the charges, we don't have any details on record. It's very important to us to see if there are any connections. We'll be grateful for anything that you can tell us.'

'Have you got someone under arrest?'

'No. We're just trying to build up a picture of the person at the moment.'

'I've never seen a chief inspector before. It was just a couple of ordinary coppers when I reported the assault. Does this mean it's really serious?'

Sophie nodded. 'Tell us the details, as you remember them.'

Tracy took a deep breath. 'I was only nineteen, and it was my first serious relationship. At first I was in heaven because Andy was so wonderful and caring towards me. He seemed so sensitive to my needs, and so protective. After a few months it dawned on me that he was starting to run my life. He made all the decisions. He didn't want me to see my friends. He got angry if I went out without him. Then he started to hit me, usually when he'd had a bit to drink. But he always made up to me afterwards, and bought me expensive presents. I was really confused.' She paused. 'This is so hard. I still think about it, but I've never talked about it to anyone. I made statements when I started the charges against him, but they were more about the assault itself, not what had happened before.'

'Do you feel that your case wasn't dealt with correctly?' asked Sophie.

'No, it's not that. I know they were busy. It was the same time as the London bombings. I wasn't made to feel unimportant, but I felt I was taking up police time. Anyway, Andy bought me a pearl necklace and promised me a holiday somewhere exotic. So I decided to give him another chance. That's why I dropped the charges.'

'What happened after that?'

'The holiday didn't happen. He started hitting me again a while later, so I did a runner. I never saw him again. I've kept quiet since then. I got together with Jerry about three years ago, and we've been together since. He's completely different, a really decent bloke who's very gentle and thoughtful. Just the opposite of Andy. He looked decent most of the time, someone you thought you could trust, but he changed completely when he lost his rag. He was evil. He could really scare people just by giving them one of his looks. I wish I'd never met him. All of my friends are happy-go-lucky. They like to enjoy life. Nowadays I feel anxious and nervous, and I wasn't like that before I met him. It frightened me, and I'm still scared now. I don't know if it will ever go.'

She began to cry.

'Tracy, that's very helpful, what you've told us so far. But I now need some details. Are you okay to continue with that, if I ask you some questions?' Sophie said.

'Yes. Maybe it will help me get over it all finally.'

'What was his full name?'

'Andrew Ridgway, but he was always called Andy. I don't know if he had a middle name.'

'Do you know his date of birth?'

'His birthday was on August the twenty-fifth. I think he was born in eighty-one.'

'That makes him thirty now?'

Tracy nodded. 'But I can't be absolutely sure of his age. I may be wrong.'

'Do you know where he lives?'

'No. And I don't want to. I never want to see him again.'

'What about when you were together? Where did you live then?'

'I rented a small flat in Poole. He came to live with me, so I don't know where he lived before. He was always a bit vague. He must have had a place of his own somewhere, because he used to disappear for a few days sometimes. But I only asked him about it once. He told me I was a nosey bitch and to keep my mouth shut.'

'Did you ever meet anyone else in his family? Parents for example?'

'No. He said that he had an elderly mother in a nursing home. I didn't think about it much at the time but if it's true, she must have had him very late in life. He was only about twenty-five when I was with him.'

Sophie drew the photofit images out of her bag and placed them on the table.

'Is this him, Tracy?'

Tracy started crying again. 'Yes, the one without the beard. That's him.'

'I think we need to give you a few minutes' break, Tracy. Could we make a pot of tea or coffee?'

'I'll do it. It'll help if I do something.'

When she brought the tea, Tracy looked more composed. Sophie decided to press on with her questions.

'Tracy, how did you meet him?'

'It was at a club. I was single at the time, and went with a group of friends. He was by himself, and we just got dancing together.'

'Do you remember what kind of a job he did?'

'He was a maintenance engineer of some type, but he was very vague about it. I do remember that he worked in lots of different places. Factories, shops, even ships sometimes.'

'According to our records he attempted to strangle you. Is that correct?'

Tracy nodded.

'Could you take me through the events that led up to that attack? I know it's not easy, but please bear with me. I'll explain later. When did you first experience the violence?'

'About three months after he moved in with me. He used to shout at me when I did things that didn't please him. He'd come right up to me and put his face up against mine and shout. His face would be red with rage and his spit would fly all over my face. But I never knew what I'd done to set him off. Not exactly. I knew I was doing something wrong, though. And the other thing was that he'd tie me up in bed and gag me. I know lots of people do it, but it was different with him, not like in magazines and books where people use soft cord or fluffy handcuffs. He was getting vicious and he used ropes that he'd tie so tight that they bit into my skin. And he'd put his hand on my throat and squeeze. He'd say really vile things when I was like that. I knew he got a huge thrill from it. The more pain I was in, the more of a turn-on it was for him.'

She paused and took a gulp of tea. 'Then I went out to a friend's hen party. We were all a bit pissed and started talking about sex. Some of the others had tried a bit of tying-up, and said they enjoyed it. When I told them what Andy did with the ropes, and showed them the marks on my wrists they were gobsmacked. The next day one of them met him in the street and had a go at him about it. I could tell something was wrong when he came in, but it was far worse than his usual temper. He was white-faced. He told me I was a gossiping slut and worthless. He grabbed me round the throat with both hands. I nearly fainted.'

Tears were streaming down her face now, but she seemed oblivious to them.

'Tracy, it's important that you try to remember if he hurt you somewhere else while he was strangling you.'

Tracy looked puzzled for a moment. 'Yes, he kicked me on the legs really hard,' she whispered. 'I'd almost forgotten about that.'

'You've been brilliant, Tracy. Really helpful. I know how hard it's been for you.'

'It's a relief in an odd way. I've never talked it through like this. Not with anyone. So is that it?'

'Not entirely, no. How long have you been in this flat?' said Sophie.

'I got it when Rachel was a year old. I've been here for four years.'

'It might be safer for you to move out for a short while in case he knows where you live. Is there anyone you can stay with for a week or so? Anyone this man Andy wouldn't know about? What about someone in Jerry's family?'

'What? What are you saying?'

'He's more dangerous than you realise, Tracy. Trust me. Your lives might be at risk.'

Tracy Beck's face went pale. 'God. Is it that bad? What's he done?'

'I'm sorry but I can't go into the details. Now, can you think of anywhere else you can stay for a while? You'll need to keep quiet about it. The fewer people that know the better.'

'Jerry's sister manages a hotel near the quayside. They'll have empty rooms this time of year. Would that do? But how am I going to explain this to him?'

'No need, Tracy. Leave it to me. We'll walk to the park, and I'll do the explaining. By the way, did Andy ever find out about Rachel?'

'Do you think I was going to tell him after what he did to me? No, he never knew. I left him before I was big enough to start showing. And I never want him to know. She's such a sweet-tempered little thing. My little darling. He mustn't ever find out.'

Jimmy Melsom looked stunned.

CHAPTER 15: No Excuse for Violence

Monday Morning, Week 2

The Monday morning briefing took place in the incident room as normal. Matt Silver was present as an observer. After it was over, the five detectives remained behind.

'What's going on?' whispered Melsom to Pillay.

She shrugged her shoulders. Marsh moved a few desks, and a technical support worker set up a laptop with microphone, video camera, data-projector and loudspeakers.

'The boss wants us to take part in a video-conference with Wendy Blacklock.'

'Why can't we just use Skype?' Jimmy said.

'Not secure enough. We have to go through the central police system so that we can't be hacked. That's why we've got all this paraphernalia. Bigger stations have a permanent room set up for this kind of thing. We could have all gone across to county HQ, but that would have knocked the morning out for us, and she didn't want to lose that much time. This is a mobile set that they keep at Winfrith for times like this.'

The technician switched on and nodded to Sophie.

'Okay, Wendy. We're connected.'

Suddenly Wendy Blacklock's head appeared on the screen.

'Hi, Wendy. Good to see you,' said Sophie.

Wendy smiled. 'Morning. I hear that you've got some interesting information for me.'

'Yes. But can you do us a favour first, Wendy. Can you give us a simple summary of the latest ideas on domestic violence?'

'Okay, a potted account. Please interrupt as things occur to you. It's helpful to subdivide the problem of abusive and controlling behaviour into categories. Since you're not experts, I'll use a system devised by some American counsellors who've spent many years working with violent and controlling men. They've come up with about eight or nine categories of control and abuse. By the way, most experienced workers in the field insist that there are no real excuses for what these men do. The perpetrators come up with all kinds of reasons for their actions, and analysts love it. But it's all hogwash, according to this guy. It just makes the victim feel partly responsible for the abuse, the "It's my fault. What did I do to set him off?" syndrome. In fact, they bear no responsibility whatever. The experts reckon these men do it because they like doing it and can get away with it.'

'What about the idea that men abuse because they were victims of abuse themselves as children?' asked Pillay.

'There's little statistical evidence to support that idea, apart from in the most brutal types. Even then, although there is some evidence for a link, it's not a clear-cut one. The manipulative and controlling behaviour is learned from a range of sources. Role models, peers, exposure to pervasive cultural messages. The list goes on.'

'What about low self-esteem? Isn't there a link?' Barry said.

'Again the jury's still out because there are plenty of men who have low self-esteem who don't try to dominate their partners. These are all just excuses used to justify a behaviour trait that has no justification. We, as police officers, have to uphold the law, and the law on it is absolutely clear. Domestic violence in all of its forms is entirely wrong.'

Wendy took a sip of water.

'I'll give you an example. I was involved with a recent case where the man threw stuff around when he wanted to control his partner. Things went flying, got smashed and broken up. She was expected to clear up, despite being terrified by the ordeal. She genuinely thought that he had lost control when he got into one of these tantrums. When he calmed down, he'd tell her that it was just his temper. That he was "out of it" and it was things she did that set him off. When I got her to list what had actually been broken, we discovered that it was almost always her possessions. He was in control enough to avoid breaking his own things. Now doesn't that tell you something? Some researchers are coming to the view that feelings, and even emotional problems, do not cause the abusive behaviour. It is more likely that beliefs and values are the driving force, even if these are largely subconscious. But the decision to act abusively on any given occasion has a rational component to it. Anyway, I won't go through all of the types in detail, especially since these men may move from one category to another, as they see fit. And they don't even always involve violence or intimidation. One type of abuser is nicknamed 'the water-torturer'. He never raises his voice, but uses intense sarcasm and derision to gain control. This type is also often found when a woman is the abuser, and the victim is a male.'

'I was going to ask you about that,' said Marsh. 'Isn't it often forgotten that the abuse can be that way round?'

'Yes, and we need to be aware of it. It is more common than people think, but it rarely reaches the extremes of violence that characterise the worst cases. In these severe cases there's an element of sadism present that is terrifying. The perpetrator reminds the victim that extreme violence and murder is a possibility, sometimes overtly. One guy even cut out newspaper articles of cases where husbands murdered their wives, and pinned them up for his wife to see. Can you imagine the effect that had on her? She lived in total and absolute terror. And your current case is a typical example of this extreme, terror-based domination. What Tracy Beck described yesterday to you, Sophie, clearly puts your man into this category. We don't need to try and understand the reasons for him doing it. It's not our problem, and frankly, as I've said, the research is all over the place. He likes hurting people, it's as simple as that. He gets a kick out of beating-up on his women.'

'Can you offer any thoughts on the murders?' said Sophie.

'He killed Donna because she left him and ended up with another man. He can't accept rejection. He couldn't go on living knowing that a woman who had rejected him completely was still alive and enjoying life. It's inconceivable to him. So she had to go. Her mother was killed for a couple of reasons. She probably knew too much about him, for one. But mothers are also identified closely with their daughters in the minds of men like this. Donna had turned against him, and he might have seen Brenda as a partial cause.'

'But he didn't murder his previous victims,' Pillay said.

'No, you're right to mention that. It could mean that Donna was more special to him than any of the previous women. It's also possible that he managed to trace her whereabouts, but couldn't do so with the others. We can only speculate.'

'And Susie?' prompted Melsom.

'She may have died simply to shift the line of enquiry over onto your Latvian guy. But I don't think that was the only reason, convenient though it is. Isn't there some evidence now that he might have known her?'

'Yes. We also now know that Donna and Susie knew each other. They took a holiday together. In fact we are trying to discover if Donna moved in with Susie when she left him.'

'I was just about to say that it's likely that she upset him in some way, and that the relationship was deeper than the normal one between prostitute and punter. I'm guessing here, of course. But if she sheltered a girlfriend who was on the run from him, then that would provide him with a good enough reason.'

'Wendy, it's possible that he has used different surnames with his early victims. We can't be sure about it yet. Tracy knew him as Andy Rule, but one of the other possible assaults that we haven't checked out yet had an Andy Ridgeway down as the perpetrator. There's also an Andrew Renshaw showing up in our database searches. Yet they all share the same birthday, so it could be the same man. Have you come across anything like this before?'

'No. It's disturbing. If what you're saying is the case, then there's an astonishing level of calculation. It means he introduces himself to these women with a false surname. Why would he do that under any normal circumstances? He knows in advance that the relationship is just going to be a temporary thing. And presumably they've lasted six months, a year or even longer? The level of subterfuge is quite astounding. I wonder how he gets away with it. Are these women stupid? Hardly, from what you've told me of Donna's background. What about Tracy?'

'She's a bright young woman. She worked at managerial level in a local retailer.'

'It's almost as if each relationship is a game of some sort. No, I haven't seen it before. Sorry, can't help you on that one.'

'Might she be in danger if he thinks that we're on to him?'

'Most definitely, in my opinion. He's killed three. Why stop now? He doesn't know that you've already identified some past victims, so as far as he's concerned he's still ahead of you. He'll go after them, if he hasn't already done so. But this is not part of the pattern of abuse. It's now down to a question of survival for him. In a way, Sophie, you don't need my expertise on this. The abuse took him close to the line of causing violent death. Once he went over that line, with Donna last week, he's into your realm rather than mine. I can't guess what's driving him anymore, but I think he'll look at the women in his back-catalogue, and he'll wipe them out, one by one.'

'Wendy, I do have one further item that you might be able to help us with. I've kept quiet about it because I don't want our man to find out at any time, even when we catch him. Tracy has a daughter by him, but he doesn't know. She left him before he knew she was pregnant. The little girl, Rachel, is nearly six. From your knowledge of violent men, how might he react if he did find out? Would it alter the way he views Tracy?'

'Well, you've saved the juiciest bit till last. Domestic violence rarely changes when children arrive. Children put more stress on a relationship, and there are fewer opportunities for the couple to seek help or talk through any problems. It often gets worse, with the victim feeling even more downtrodden than before, with the possibility of just upping and walking out removed. But in this case? I'd guess that he'd feel enraged by Tracy's decision not to tell him. He's had the wool pulled over his eyes for nearly six years. He won't see it from her point of view. These people can't see it from the perspective of their victims. No, by what she's done she's managed to turn the tables on him and gained the upper hand. He'll be really vindictive if he finds her. You need to keep her safe.'

'Are you sure, Wendy?' Matt Silver said. 'We're taking resources away from the search for this man and putting them into the task of identifying previous victims and keeping them secure. I know there's a big overlap, but we do need to know that the temporary switch in emphasis is worthwhile.'

'Absolutely. By definition, we are dealing with the unpredictable whenever we make decisions about violence of this nature. I think it probable that he will do two things. Firstly, start to seek out these women that he's harmed before and left alone for these six years or more, particularly if they could identify him. And secondly, he'll go ballistic when he finds that Tracy has concealed his daughter from him. The three women he's killed so far have died quickly from stabbing or strangulation. There's a good chance that he'll be not just brutal but sadistic if he catches up with Tracy. She needs protection. Trust me.'

'Okay. That's good enough for me.'

Sophie said, 'Wendy, this has been invaluable. I think we are all more aware of what we are up against. Thanks.'

The line was cut. Sophie spoke to the detectives before they went to their different tasks.

'The existence of the little girl is strictly confidential and on a need-to-know basis. The rest of the team don't know about her, and won't know unless it becomes absolutely necessary. We keep it between ourselves. Clear?'

They all nodded.

'When we spoke to Tracy yesterday she gave us some information about our man's line of work. She mentioned that he worked in some form of engineering in shops, factories and sometimes on boats or ships. What line of work would give that kind of spread? Give it some thought and put a list together. We don't seem to be getting very far with the name Andrew Rule at the moment, so it's probably false. For all we know every surname we'll find for him could be false. The common factor is his first name, Andy, so we'll assume for now that it's genuine.'

She glanced at her watch.

'Time for me to be off to Bournemouth. We're looking at student photos, then following up that mobile phone number this afternoon. We'll be back later. We'll see you when you get back from Southampton, Barry.'

Sophie and Melsom drove via Corfe Castle. Sophie wanted to call in to the hotel that had employed Brenda Goodenough. She wanted to speak briefly to the manager who'd been on holiday the previous week. He took them into his office and closed the door carefully behind him. He was hesitant, often pausing as he spoke. Sophie interrupted him.

'Mr Blake, we don't have time to pussy-foot around here. I sense some reservation on your part, but please be honest with us. Clearly there was a problem. What was it?'

He told them that Brenda was often suffering from the effects of a hangover. Moreover she could be moody and irritable to the other staff and guests.

'Thank you for your honesty. Please contact us if you think of anything else that might be relevant.'

* * *

The session at Bournemouth University proved to be very helpful. David Bell and the two women students interviewed on Friday must have worked for much of the weekend contacting others and collecting the photographs. They had set out the ones with Donna in them. Each table had the photos for a different event or function. 'They're all in date order,' said Bell. 'The first table clockwise from the door holds photos from freshers' week, then we work around the room and finish eighteen months later when she dropped out. You can see there are far fewer for her second year. She was withdrawing from the student scene.'

At the top of each table was a large group picture, sometimes official, sometimes a shot taken at a party or club by one of the students. Pictures of individuals or smaller groups were then spread out beneath. The two women had labelled many of the people in the photos.

'This is all so helpful,' said Sophie. 'Have you found any that show Donna with an unidentified male?'

'Yes, several.' She took them to the first table. 'Over here in the early shots there's a guy we couldn't identify at first. But we think he was her first boyfriend here. We've got a name now: George Warrander.'

Donna had her arm around his waist. He was slightly shorter than her, with fair, spiky hair.

'Then there's one here for the Christmas ball in our first year.'

In the official photograph there were several unidentified men, none of whom were standing beside Donna. But in two of the shots by students, Donna was with a taller man. One was slightly out of focus, but the other was clear and showed a man with facial features similar to their photofit.

'Where is he in the group shot?' asked Sophie.

'It's not clear,' she replied. 'But there's someone behind the woman on the far right, mostly obscured by her head. There's a later group shot, taken after the meal. There's someone behind Donna, again almost hidden. We wonder if that's someone's hand on her left shoulder.'

'It would be great if we could take these, and the digital image files. We can get them back to their owners if necessary.'

'We're pretty sure they're all copies, so there isn't any need. I think we're all glad to be of some help.'

The two detectives had a coffee with David Bell and then left.

'What do you think, Jimmy?' Sophie asked as they walked to the car park.

'It looks like him, ma'am. He doesn't appear in anything before that Christmas ball, so I wonder if he met her there. But he doesn't seem to be a student.'

'The early shots of that evening show her with groups of friends, and not with any particular man, so I'd guess the same as you. Either that or he was her boyfriend already and arrived later than her.'

'But if he didn't know her, and he wasn't a student, how did he get a ticket?'

'It's not that difficult, Jimmy. There are all kinds of ways of blagging entry to a student function. I used to do it regularly in my younger days. I once talked my way into a formal student ball at the university in Bristol when I was only sixteen and still at school.'

Melsom was quiet. He glanced sideways at his superior.

'We need to get some of the team to go through these photos carefully. There might be a chance that one of the shots shows him earlier on. If he's on his own then that should settle it. I think we'll work on the assumption that he met her there. I think we should try to trace her first boyfriend, George Warrander. He might be able to confirm some of our suspicions. Can you do that, Jimmy?' She paused as they reached her car. 'Are you okay, Jimmy?'

'Oh, yes, ma'am . . .' But he looked uneasy.

'Are you sure?'

'I've been thinking about the knife, ma'am. The one used to kill Donna.'

'Yes. And?'

Well, he wouldn't want to get rid of it close to the scene, would he? It would be found by our search teams too easily. And it might have something on it that might link it to him.' He paused again.

'Jimmy, are you doing these pauses for dramatic effect?'

'No, ma'am. I'm just getting my thoughts in order. We wouldn't expect a killer to hang on to the knife, would we? If we did trace him in the end, we'd find it and that would be really strong evidence against whoever it was, wouldn't it, especially if it could be shown to be the one used? So he'd want to get rid of it pretty quick, but not somewhere it might be easily spotted. So he'd choose somewhere miles away, like a rubbish skip, and wrap it up well. But the thing is, if he was trying to frame Berzins, wouldn't he want the knife to be found, so isn't it likely that he left it somewhere we'd find it? He went from here to Corfe, to Donna's mum's cottage. What if he cleaned it up a bit, and put it into her kitchen? It wouldn't look out of place there, would it? But he might expect us to check for it. And if it's not there, it could be in Susie's flat.' He thought for a few moments. 'It would be better at Susie's, from his angle. It would make the link between the other two murders and Susie's stronger.'

'Jimmy, you're a star. You're thinking like a detective. We'll do the Bournemouth end now, since we're here, then check on the cottage on our way back. I can remember seeing some knives in the kitchen drawer in Susie's working flat. We're looking for a heavy-duty kitchen knife with a fifteen centimetre blade, if I remember correctly. That's about six inches. I'll phone Kevin McGreedie.'

They were told that a knife of the correct dimensions had been found in the kitchen of Susie's working flat. It was waiting its turn for forensic examination, so Sophie asked for it to be examined next as a priority. She also discussed the plans for calling the mobile number associated with the Andy listed in Susie's contacts. She decided to make another attempt that afternoon.

'If you're right, Jimmy, then the knife will have traces of Donna's blood on it. Deliberately left to implicate Berzins. But is our killer aware of just how small the samples need to be in modern forensics? There might also be something that can be used to identify him. We can but hope. I'm going to call into Poole on the way back to check that Tracy is okay. She phoned me yesterday evening to say she was settled in, but I still want to make sure. But first to the Bournemouth nick. We have a phone call to make.'

CHAPTER 16: Shock

Monday Afternoon, Week 2

A call-tracing system had been set up in the Bournemouth incident room to track the signal if the phone was answered. Sophie was to make the call, since a woman's voice might not arouse as much suspicion as a man's.

She waited as it rang. It was finally answered by a gruff voice saying, 'Yeah?'

'Andy?'

'Who is it?'

The police team had discussed what persona Sophie should adopt. After much debate, they had decided that to use a real name from Susie's contact list might be too risky. The same applied to the women identified on the assault list, such as Tracy Beck or Sasha Purfleet.

'It's Ella.'

There was moment or two of silence.

'Who?'

'Ella. I'm a friend of Susie's,' Sophie added.

There was another pause. Then came a verbal torrent that made the listening police team sit up.

‘Oh no, you’re fucking not. I know who you are, you slutty cow. Prancing around in your posh silver car with your posh law degree and your posh education. I bet you’ve got them all twisted around your finger, haven’t you? Dancing around when you click your fingers. Yes ma’am, no ma’am, three fucking bags full, ma’am. Well, you can just fuck off and screw yourself. I bet you’ve got call-tracing on, haven’t you? Well you’re gonna be shitting yourself in a couple of minutes. I mean, really shitting yourself. I’m laughing. I’m nearly pissing myself imagining the look on your face, you skinny bitch. You can just fuck off and die, and when you do I’ll come and piss on your grave.’

He hung up.

The detectives stood in silence for a few seconds before turning to the technicians operating the tracing equipment. They looked grim.

‘Our kit here showed somewhere near the riverside in Wareham, but nothing more precise. The call was just a bit too short. But we’ve got a link with the service provider. Tom here was on the phone to them as you spoke to him.’

The second technician finished his conversation. Sophie held her breath.

‘We’ve got him located in a residential area north east of Wareham quay, but it’s not exact. The signal was centred on a road called Spider Lane.’

Sophie’s face went white. ‘That’s where I live! He’s at my house, and Hannah’s there alone. Get a squad car there now!’

As she ran down the corridor towards the car park, Sophie phoned home on her mobile, praying that her daughter would answer.

‘Hi, Mum,’ came Hannah’s calm voice.

* * *

When Sophie, Melsom and Kevin McGreedie screeched to a halt outside the Allens’ cottage in Wareham, a squad car was outside with its blue light flashing. Sophie ran to the door and found her daughter in the hallway, in conversation with two uniformed policemen. She threw her arms around Hannah and hugged her so tight that she struggled for breath.

'What's this all about, Mum?'

'Was there someone here, sweetheart?' gasped Sophie. 'Are you sure there were no callers?'

'No, though I was out for a while to take some stuff to the post office. I got back, let myself in and then you phoned. About ten minutes later the police car arrived, with its siren going. If you hadn't been on the phone to me at the time I wouldn't have known what was going on. These two charming officers aren't totally clear either. I've just made a pot of tea for us. Want some?'

McGreedie had just entered the house. 'Sounds like a good idea. I think we all need a cup,' he said.

He took charge. He spoke to the officers from the squad car and asked whether they'd seen anything suspicious as they approached the house. They had noticed nothing unusual.

Jimmy Melsom seemed to have disappeared. Sophie was just about to send one of the PCs out to find him, when he walked into the lounge. He whispered into McGreedie's ear, but shook his head when Sophie looked at him.

'Later,' he mouthed.

'When's your train, Hannah?' Sophie asked.

'About half an hour. I was just getting my bag together when the police car arrived.' She looked at the clock. 'I'm going to have to go.'

'I'll take you. I need to take Kevin back to Bournemouth, so I'll drop you at the station on the way.'

'No need to take me all the way back, Sophie,' said McGreedie. 'I'll get the train with Hannah. That way we can be sure she's on her way safely, and you don't need to waste any time. I'll get a car across to pick me up from Bournemouth station and she can travel on to London.'

'Kevin, I'm so grateful.'

Sophie's face was tense, exhausted.

* * *

They dropped Hannah and McGreedie at the railway station. Then Melsom told Sophie what he'd been doing when she rushed into her house.

'I had a look around but couldn't see anything odd, just like the two car-cops. But then I saw a curtain twitching in a house two along from yours, so I called in.'

'Mrs Bentley? An elderly lady with a walking stick?'

'That's the one. Anyway, she'd spotted a white van sitting opposite her own neighbour's a bit earlier. That'll be three away from you. It was on the other side of the road. She reckons the driver was watching the road. He wasn't doing anything, just looking. But then she saw him take something out of his pocket and hold it up. She thinks it was a camera. And when she looked along the street, Hannah was just arriving at your front gate. Then he took out what looked like a phone and held it up to his ear. I asked if he seemed to dial any numbers, but she didn't think so, although she can't be sure. He stayed another few minutes, just watching again. What made her remember it all was that he left just before the police car arrived. She reckoned he started the engine just after she heard the siren. It was that made her suspicious. It's a shame she didn't get the registration.'

'Do the times match? The phone calls, I mean? Ours and this man in the van?'

Melsom nodded. 'I think so, ma'am, as far as I can tell. That's what I told the DI when I first came in. He's going to put out an alert for the van, even though we don't know the registration.'

'Christ. How did he find out where I live? And why was he watching the house? Did you show her the photo?'

‘Yes. She couldn’t be sure, but she said it looked like him.’

‘God, Jimmy. I just don’t know what to make of this. It looks like it was almost certainly the man I called. But why was he there? What could he have been up to?’

‘It’s a game, ma’am.’

‘What?’

‘He’s treating it as a game. He’s found out you’re in charge, so you’re now his opponent.’

‘So while clever little me has been thinking that I’m one step ahead of him because everyone thinks we’ve got Berzins as the killer, the reality is that he’s done a neat side-step and is probably one step ahead of me. But how did he find out my address?’

‘Probably from the web. If he knew your name it wouldn’t be hard. You’ll be on the voters’ roll. But he isn’t really one step ahead of us, ma’am. It doesn’t alter the investigation, does it? And surely he’d have been better off just putting the phone down rather than giving you all that spite. It shows us what he’s like, doesn’t it?’

‘And we now know a bit more about how he operates, which we wouldn’t have done if we hadn’t made the phone call. He’d have started collecting information on me and my family, and we wouldn’t have known.’ Sophie paused. ‘He may already have stuff. My God. Maybe he already knows about Jade.’

‘Who’s Jade, ma’am?’

‘My younger daughter. She’s only fifteen.’

She glanced at her watch. Three twenty. Sophie stopped the car and began making calls. The first was to the head of Jade’s school, asking her to keep the girl on site and under supervision until collected. The second was to the Dorchester school where Martin was head of the maths department, asking for an urgent message to be sent to him. She then swapped places with Melsom, asking him to drive the rest of the way to Poole so that she was free to handle phone calls. Her husband called back quickly. She explained that Jade might be in danger. She would remain at school until collected by Martin.

'I can't collect her myself, Martin. I'm up to my eyeballs in this thing. Can you do it? Okay, love you.'

Sophie looked at the silent phone for several minutes before putting it back in her bag.

* * *

The hotel in which Tracy Beck, her daughter and partner were staying was several streets away from the quayside in a tourist area of the town. They found Tracy and Rachel in the small secluded garden.

'I want you to stay in the hotel, Tracy. This garden is fine, it can't be seen from the street. But please don't go out.'

'But what about Rachel? I don't want her to miss more than a day or two off school. And if she is here all day she'll get bored. I took her to the quayside for a walk this morning, and she loved it.'

'Not a good idea. Find someone else to take her if she needs to go out, but I don't want you outside these walls. It's just too dangerous for you. Look, let me be more explicit. If he finds you, there's a chance that he might try to kill you. We think he's already murdered a young woman, which is why we're looking for him. I've decided to allocate an officer to stay with you for the present. She'll be down later today.'

'What good will that do if he's turned as violent as you say? He's really strong, believe me.'

'We know that. Don't worry, she'll be able to handle it. But try to keep Rachel inside as much as possible. Hopefully this will all be over in a couple of days. And trust me, Tracy. It'll be fine as long as you do what I say.'

* * *

When they got back to Swanage they found that Marsh had managed to interview the owners of the flat above

Donna's. The couple had heard several bumps as they'd passed by Donna's door on the previous Monday evening. They confirmed the time at mid-evening, when Donna and Berzins were both at work.

'That's good. Now we need a statement from the residents who saw someone leaving Donna's building mid-evening. Is that coming, Barry?'

Marsh hadn't been able to contact them at the weekend. They'd been away at a family wedding, but were due to return the following day. He and Pillay had made some progress in tracing one of the other assaults, on Sasha Purfleet from Bournemouth. The name hadn't shown up on any of the police databases, but the hospital had treated her for a leg injury in 2006. The record gave an address but no telephone number, so Lydia had gone to check on the lead.

'What did you discover in Southampton, Barry?'

'Debbie Martinez started assault proceedings in January 2005, but dropped charges within a week. I spoke to the officer in charge, Gwen Davis. She was a DC then, but she's a sergeant now. I like her. She seems a thorough and genuine sort, so I trusted what she said. Apparently Debbie dropped the charges because she just couldn't face the thought of a court appearance, and because she didn't believe that her injuries were serious enough. Gwen tried to talk her into continuing, but it was no use.'

'And she remembers the man? Andrew Renshaw?'

'Yes, although her memory's a bit vague. It was six years ago. She just confirmed that he was tall and heavily built, though not fat. He looked as if he kept himself fit.'

'Did she remember anything about his character?'

'She found him fairly quiet. He didn't say much, as far as she remembers. But she does remember that he made her feel uneasy. She couldn't explain why. He was apologetic, and assured her that it wouldn't happen again. But she wasn't entirely convinced.'

'When did the girl disappear?'

‘A couple of months later. Debbie left Renshaw. She paid off her rent, and moved away. Gwen wasn’t too concerned, because the girl had talked about doing exactly that when they’d last met. She talked about going to find a job in London, where she had family.’

‘Does she know what happened to Renshaw?’

‘No. The flat they shared was rented in Debbie’s name. She’d been there alone before Renshaw moved in with her.’

‘That matches the story that Tracy Beck told me yesterday. Him moving into her flat. We need to trace this woman, if only to check that she’s still alive and well. A statement from her would be a real bonus.’

‘Gwen Davis has offered to do it. She said she feels a sense of responsibility. I said I’d be back in touch with your decision.’

‘If you’re happy with her, Barry, then it’s okay with me. I think we’ll also be getting names from Susie Pater’s address book today. The Bournemouth lot are going to send across details of anyone that might be in the age-range we’re looking for. It’s interesting that he moved into Debbie’s flat. I wonder if it means that he did the same with Donna? Maybe we need to find out more about where she lived after she pulled out of her course.’

Sophie sat down on the nearest chair. She looked tired and drawn.

‘Ma’am, I’m worried about the incident at your house and the fact that our suspect may be targeting you and your family. Who’s dealing with it?’

‘Matt Silver, so I’m sure we’ll be okay. I just don’t know what this man’s game is. It’s frightening, but at least it’s brought him out of the woodwork. That might make him more vulnerable. But it does mean that the kind of protection that I’ve been pushing for Tracy Beck has now got to apply to my family. It’s a weird feeling. It also means, I’d guess, that he’s given up on Vilis Berzins being prosecuted for the murders. Maybe he only set that in motion to gain time.' She paused. 'Sod it, let's get that journalist Rogers in and get him to tell us what they spoke about on Friday. I'm fed up with pussy-footing around the issue. See if you can find him, Barry. Get him in now if you can. And can someone get me a coffee? Please? With two sugars? And a couple of biscuits?' She smiled at Marsh. 'Don't worry, I'll be fine.'

Just then a courier arrived with a package from police HQ. It was the previous week's CCTV footage from the Poole to Studland ferry.

'Well, that's Jimmy's job for the next couple of days sorted,' said Marsh.

* * *

They sat in the interview room. Bill Rogers looked nervously across the table at Sophie.

'So you say he'd been there earlier in the week?'

'I think it was on Wednesday. I thought I recognised him when he appeared on Friday. When he spoke to me it gave me a chance to look at him closer up. I thought he was a new hack from one of the local rags, but he said he was just passing by.'

'Anything unusual about him or what he said?'

'No, not really. Nothing that stuck out. He was quite tall, medium build. No, maybe a bit heavier than average. Looked fit.'

'Could you tell anything about his attitude?'

'Difficult to say.' Rogers swallowed. 'He did look kind of determined. Focussed . . . Look, I'm sorry about what I told him.'

'What was that, Mr Rogers?'

'That you were leading the investigation.'

Barry Marsh asked, 'Was he trying to find out?'

'No. I just happened to see the Chief Inspector's car come in at the back.'

'Why did you ask that question about the car we were looking for? How did you find out about it?' asked Sophie.

‘One of the other guys had just got news of it on his mobile. He told us but didn’t seem keen to ask the question himself, so I thought, nothing to lose. I’ll ask.’

Barry looked at Sophie. ‘Ties in with what we know.’

She nodded and turned to Rogers. ‘What about your new friend?’

‘What do you mean?’

‘How did he react, if at all?’

‘I felt him kind of tense up slightly, but I thought it was just my imagination. You know, it was just a feeling I had. And you were looking directly at us at the time.’

‘What difference does that make?’ asked Sophie.

‘It sure makes me nervous. Like now.’

‘What did he do when I’d finished answering your question?’

‘He just turned and walked away. He crossed Kings Road and stood at the brook for a couple of minutes. Then he walked down towards town, I think.’

Marsh looked at him. ‘Have you told us everything, Mr Rogers? It’s just that I get a sense that you’re holding back on something.’

Rogers seemed happier talking to another man. ‘I told him about the DCI’s reputation. I said that she was one tough cookie, or something like that. I told him about our run-in a couple of years ago and that she’s got a law degree.’ He looked at Sophie. ‘Look, it wasn’t illegal. It was all stuff that was common knowledge.’

‘Absolutely, Mr Rogers,’ said Marsh. ‘It’s just that there was a possible attempt to kidnap one of the DCI’s daughters earlier today, almost definitely by the same man. And knowledge of this is not in the public domain, and never will be, we hope. Do you understand our concern?’

Rogers gulped.

‘And do you understand why I’ll be *personally* very displeased if you spread or report any of this until I give you the nod to do so? In exchange, Mr Rogers, you have my word that you can have first claim on any story once it's all safely tucked up and put to bed. Okay?'

Rogers nodded.

'For example,' Marsh went on, 'it might be in your interest to call me tomorrow morning. Say about nine-ish? Information you get then would make it into tomorrow evening's edition, I expect?'

'Sure.'

Sophie stood up. 'Thank you, Mr Rogers. You've been very helpful.' She left the interview room. Marsh accompanied the reporter out of the building, then returned to the incident room.

'Ma'am, you need to go home. There's nothing immediate going on just now. It's just a question of Jimmy getting on with the CCTV footage and me following up a bit more about this man, Rule. I just wonder whether his possible birthday on August twenty-fifth might give us a lead, so I want to do a bit of digging. But nothing requires you to be here. I think you should head off, and try to be home when your daughter and husband get back. They'll need you there, really they will.'

'Okay, Barry. Thanks for your concern, and I'll do what you say. I'll be on the end of the phone if you need me, and we'll see what Rogers makes of the news about Berzins tomorrow morning. Should be interesting.'

* * *

Sophie was home ten minutes before Martin and Jade arrived. She watched from the lounge window as the car backed into the drive, then opened the front door.

'Hi, Mum. What's this all about?' asked Jade.

Sophie gave her daughter a hug, 'A bit later, Jade. I need to talk to your dad first.'

Jade shrugged and disappeared up to her room.

Martin put his arms around his wife and squeezed hard. 'A bit of a fraught day, I take it?'

'Just a bit.' She felt tears welling up in her eyes. 'More than a bit. It was terrifying when I realised that he was somewhere here, near the house. I thought he might be inside. I was so scared.'

'How did Hannah take it?'

'She didn't seem worried in the slightest. When I phoned I asked her to lock all the doors and windows until the local police arrived. I stayed on the phone to her all the way here from Swanage until I could see she was safe. Rather than being worried, she was calming me down.'

'Just like Jade just now. She kept saying, "Don't worry, Dad. It's all fine." I wish that was true. They're real treasures, aren't they?'

Sophie could only nod. 'Kevin travelled on the train with Hannah as far as Bournemouth. She phoned me when she got to Waterloo.'

'Shall I phone for a take-away this evening?'

'No. We're moving out to a hotel for a couple of days. It's just not safe to stay here for the next day or two.'

'I noticed some men just along the road. Are they the forensics officers?'

Sophie nodded. 'The mud on the side of the road means that they've got a good tyre print. They don't think he got out of the van, and Mrs Bentley didn't see him outside of it. We think he was just watching. The local police are doing a house-to-house to check if any of the other neighbours noticed anything. Nothing so far.' She hesitated. 'He took a photo of Hannah.'

'Christ, this is appalling. What if he finds out where she stays in London?'

'The college will look after her. I spent a while on the phone to the principal late this afternoon. She'll be staying with one of the tutors, and getting a cab into college with her. I'm hoping it will take just a couple more days, Martin. We're getting closer. I can sense it.'

CHAPTER 17: Friction

Tuesday Morning

Despite the comfortable rooms, the night spent in a nearby hotel hadn't been restful. The Allen family had made good use of the pool, eaten well and enjoyed a late evening drink in the lounge bar. But Sophie had not slept well. Neither had Martin. Only Jade reported sleeping through the entire night. But the breakfast was worth savouring. Instead of the usual rush of cereal and toast, the two adults had enjoyed fresh fruit and smoked salmon with scrambled eggs. Jade was now worried that she'd put her morning training session for the school hockey team at risk because of all the food she'd consumed.

'I'm stuffed,' she announced solemnly, as she made her way to Sophie's car. 'I'm going to turn into a porky if we stay here too long.'

'No one's forcing you to try everything on the menu, Jade. There is such a thing as self-control, you know.'

'Mum, if you only knew how much I love bacon and eggs and all the other stuff, you'd understand that I just can't refuse it when it's all there, inviting me to gorge on it.

It's like I'm in heaven. I really didn't think I'd manage anything after that meal last night, but then I saw all the breakfast stuff laid out, there was my appetite, back in a few seconds.'

'Maybe I'd better explain all this to Mrs Wentworth when I see her. I'll tell her that, because of all the anxiety and tension that you suffered yesterday afternoon, you were forced to eat a plateful of bacon, eggs, black pudding, mushrooms and tomatoes. After a dinner of venison casserole last night. Not forgetting your pudding of banoffee pie. Two helpings, wasn't it?'

Sophie unlocked the car doors and watched her tall, slim daughter climb in.

'I just don't know where you put it all. Well I do, actually. I was the same at your age.'

'And you've kept your figure brilliantly, Mum. Everyone says that you're the best-looking mother among all my friends.'

'Well, they won't be saying that if we stay at this place for much longer.'

It was eight o'clock. A low sun was peeping through the clouds to the east. Once she'd dropped Jade at school, and had a word with her head teacher, she'd be back on this road heading into the sun as it climbed into the sky above Swanage.

* * *

'Did you find Sasha Purfleet, Lydia?' asked Sophie.

'Yes, ma'am, but she wasn't at all helpful. She's a druggie and where she's staying, well it's just a hovel really. It's not as though the area is too run down, but her house was one of the filthiest I've ever been in. It stank. And she seemed as if she was in a world of her own. You know, completely out of it.'

'So nothing really helpful from her?'

'Not really. She was just so vague. She couldn't even remember what year she'd been with this Andrew

Ridgway. She did confirm his name, and said the photofit could have been him, but she wasn't totally sure.'

'Could she remember anything about how her injuries happened?'

'He'd hit her, that's all she'd say. But it was all too vague to be useful. She wouldn't be a reliable witness unless she got herself off whatever she's taking. Otherwise it's pointless. She'd be torn to shreds in court by any half-competent barrister.'

'I still think we need to get her somewhere safe. Did you suggest it to her?'

'Yes. She mumbled something about her parents. I called her mother after I left. She hasn't seen her daughter in over a year.'

'Are you surprised?'

'Well, I expect things haven't been easy between them. Anyway, her mother said that she'd do what she could, if only for a few days.'

'Could you follow it up later this morning? If nothing has happened, we may need to do something ourselves. I don't want her to be at risk, particularly if she's not aware of what's going on around her. She'd be easy prey for our man if he did decide to wipe his history. By the way, have there been any updates from Walsall?'

'Yes. Liz Angel had time to do a bit of digging. She phoned me yesterday, and is sending down some documents later.'

Marsh walked over to them. 'Jimmy's just about to start working his way through the CCTV footage for the Sandbanks ferry. It could take days, ma'am, and might not produce anything useful.'

'Get him to start with the second half of Friday morning, when we know he was out front here. He would have heard about us looking for the car, so my guess is that he'd have avoided using the main road out of Swanage. Opting for the ferry would have been safer. Say from about ten thirty. We think he was also here on

Wednesday morning, but we weren't looking for the car then. He'd probably have come by road. Make that his second priority, okay? Apart from that, you're right. We don't want anyone's time wasted, so he can start looking for the student who was Donna's first boyfriend at university. George Warrander was his name. He may know something. Meanwhile, we've been emailed the list of contacts from Susie Pater's address book. That's for you and Lydia to start on. I want the locals who might have been friends. Check each one, then we'll shortlist those that might be worth a visit. I don't understand the relationship between Susie and our man Andy. What was it? Were they just friends? Was he just a punter? Were they lovers? It niggles me. I've got to visit HQ for a meeting but I should be back before the end of the morning.'

Sophie visited the station's senior officer, Tom Rose, before she left.

'Tom, I'm in a rush and all my team are up to their eyes in chasing stuff up. But I want to find out the details on the transfer of ownership of Donna's flat when it was left to her in her grandmother's will. Can you put someone local onto tracing the solicitor who handled it? I want them to get as much detail as they can about the will and the transfer. That would be great.'

'Of course. Anything else I can do?'

'Donna went on a holiday sometime in the past year with Susie Pater. I think it was Corfu. I wonder if she booked it locally. Could someone pop into the local travel agents and see? I'd like to know when she went and if anyone else went with them. That's if we can trace the company. And thanks.'

* * *

The meeting in the assistant chief constable's office was an informal one, chaired by him. They were seated in comfortable chairs around a low coffee table. Silver and Dunnett sat either side of Sophie.

The ACC, Jim Metcalfe, began, 'Can I say, Sophie, how shocked we all were to hear of yesterday's events? It's rare to hear of a criminal targeting an officer's home or family, outside of the gangland world. This man is obviously very disturbed. There has been a suggestion that we take you off the case and you go away on holiday with your family for a couple of weeks. You'd all be out of harm's way.'

'No.'

Dunnett shifted in his chair beside her.

'Sir, you know me better than that. Things are coming to a head. We're homing in on him, and he's starting to panic. That's why he was watching my house. He knows that the pressure is on. He'll also know that time spent watching me and my family is time wasted, time that he could be spending removing some of the traces that he's left behind. And he was nearly caught. So he won't do it again. He's not some berserk individual who's lashing out uncontrollably. That's just not his style. Everything he does is careful and controlled.'

'So why was he watching your house and family?' Dunnett asked.

'It was just a game to him. Curiosity. And the speed of our reaction would have scared him. He shot off like a bullet when he heard the sirens, according to my neighbour. It was a serious error of judgement on his part, and he'll have realised it. I don't think he'll try it again. I think Matt's precautions are perfectly adequate. Our man now knows that the case against Berzins has been dropped. He'll go back into his hole. He'll only venture out to remove another link that he realises could be used to trace him. The people at risk are his ex-partners, Tracy Beck and Sasha Purfleet, not me, and not my family.'

'I'm not convinced,' Dunnett said.

'We couldn't take a holiday anyway. Jade is in the middle of a heavy year at school, and Martin's a senior teacher. Do you think he could just walk away like that?'

‘He would if the lives of his wife and daughters were at risk, surely?’

‘But they’re not. Look, the house is empty. None of the neighbours know where we’re staying. They’ve all been asked to look out for anything suspicious and report it. The same applies to Martin’s colleagues and Jade’s school, including her friends. You’d be putting the investigation at risk if you did this.’

‘Are you saying that Matt and Kevin McGreedie couldn’t cope?’ asked Dunnett.

Sophie looked at the ACC. ‘Jim, I’m not responding to that comment. It’s completely below the belt. You know how I feel about Matt and Kevin. They’re friends as well as colleagues. Kevin even accompanied Hannah, my elder daughter, on the train as far as Bournemouth to make sure she was safe when she went back to London. I will not accept this suggestion. If you want me off this case, you’ll have to order me off. And accept whatever decisions I make as a consequence.’

The ensuing silence seemed to stretch for minutes.

‘We’ll review at the end of the week,’ Metcalfe finally said. He stood up. ‘We’ll leave things as they are until then. I suggest Friday morning at ten. Sophie, can you stay, please?’

Dunnett and Silver left. Dunnett’s face was red and angry.

Metcalfe waited until the door closed behind them. ‘Don’t pull that stunt again, Sophie. You’re only a DCI, remember. It might just backfire on you.’

‘What makes you think it was a stunt? I always mean what I say, Jim. You should know that. That son of a bitch has been needling me from the start. Maybe you didn’t know that, but you do now. If I thought that he was genuine in his wish for my family’s safety, I wouldn’t have responded in that way. But he’s as shallow as a rain puddle. I just wish I knew what I’ve done to upset him.’

'I don't want to hear this, Sophie. Just make it work, that's all I'm asking. I can't have two of my middle-ranking colleagues at logger-heads like this. So get over it. And I won't be so understanding on Friday if we're no further forward. Okay?'

'Thanks, Jim.'

'And if you're right, then we need to look after your man's exes. Do whatever you think necessary. You've got one out of her home and into a hotel. Now do the same for the others. We can't afford to lose any previous victims.'

He put a hand on her arm. 'Just take care, Sophie. I don't want to lose you, and I don't want this case to go down the pan. The wolves are beginning to circle, even though you can't see them.'

Sophie called in to see Berzins at the safe house on her way back to Swanage. She told him of her decision to release the news that charges against him had been dropped. She advised him that it would be safer for him to remain where he was for a few more days.

* * *

Sophie was back in the incident room, talking to Marsh. 'How's the check on Susie's contacts going?'

'Reasonable. We've managed to talk to about half of the ones we've phoned. I expect a lot of them will be at work. It would have been a lot worse if they'd all been landlines. At least with mobiles we can get through to people even if they aren't at home. I reckon we'll be through the list by mid-afternoon. That's the first trawl. We'll then start trying again for the half that didn't answer first time round. It could take until mid-evening, and I can guarantee that there'll still be a couple left.'

He took a sip from his coffee mug.

'Another thing, ma'am. Gwen Davies from Hampshire was on the phone just now. She hasn't been able to trace Debbie Martinez anywhere. She managed to get a number for a cousin in London but she hasn't seen Debbie for a couple of years. None of the other London family members have either. Her cousin assumed that she was still in Southampton, but there's no trace of her there. She seems to have vanished.'

'I just hope we're not too late. I'll phone Jack Dunning and let him know. We need to start a major search for her.'

'How did Donna's brother take the news about the decision to drop charges against Berzins?'

'He was angry at first. But he finally accepted it. And he was mollified by the fact that he can move into Donna's flat now we've finished with it. Berzins, of course, was pleased for it to be out in the open.'

'So David Goodenough is staying?' Sophie said.

'Yes. He said he's taken some overdue leave from his job, and will stay until after the funeral. It makes sense. There's so much for him to organise, with both mother and sister's affairs to settle. It must be a shattering time for him.'

Tom Rose came into the room. 'We have the details on the flat transfer. But I think it just confirms what you already knew. Her grandmother was Deirdre Goodenough and she'd lived in the flat for a good ten years. I have the details here. There was no luck with the local travel agents, so I sent someone up to the hotel to speak to Maria, Donna's workmate. She said that Donna had mentioned booking it on the internet, and had gone with a friend, singular. But it was before Donna started working at the hotel, so Maria doesn't know any other details.'

'That's great, Tom. Thanks for your help.' Sophie looked puzzled. Just then, Melsom burst into the room, a broad grin on his face.

'Gottit!' he shouted. 'Got the car!'

They went through to a small room that had been darkened for the video search. A frame was frozen on screen. It showed a grubby Ford Fiesta disembarking from the Sandbanks ferry. The frame was timed at twelve thirty on the previous Friday. The driver looked like their suspect, his face almost identical to the photofit image. The car registration plate was obscured by mud.

'Jimmy, see what you can do about getting that number plate identified. Can we clean up the image somehow?'

Marsh said, 'Ma'am, there's someone at county forensics who's an expert at this kind of thing. I'll phone through, get their email address and give it to Jimmy. He can do a screen grab and email it across. It'll be a lot quicker than wasting time on it ourselves.'

'Good idea, Barry. Now where does this get us?'

'He left here and went east. That means he probably lives in east Poole, Bournemouth or somewhere further along the coast. And because of Debbie Martinez, we have to go as far as Southampton. In fact, I'd suggest Southampton as a strong possibility. Gwen Davies always assumed he was local. As far as we know, Debbie was the first person to report him.'

'Where's Lydia, by the way?'

'She got Donna's student address. She's across in Bournemouth trying the neighbours. Kevin McGreedie has arranged for some uniformed bods to help her. She's also using his influence to get Sasha Purfleet moved to somewhere safe.'

'That's not going to be easy if she's an addict. She's not going to manage a fix if she's in a safe house, is she?'

Marsh shrugged. 'What else can we do?'

'Nothing, of course. By the way, did anything come from the photos from the university?'

'I've got a couple of the local guys checking them in the back room downstairs. Maybe we should go and check.'

Several of the photos taken by students showed their elusive quarry by himself early in the evening. He was beside Donna only in the photos from mid-evening onwards.

'So it looks like he met her at that Christmas ball. He came by himself, met Donna and stayed with her. They started a relationship and things were fine for a few months. But then the violence started. It's so similar to the story that Tracy Beck told us. I think we have a pretty clear idea of how he works. We'll get Lydia back in once she's made the arrangements for Sasha Purfleet. I need her in Poole, looking after Tracy. That's now one of the main priorities.' She thought for a moment. 'Barry, can you get onto Bob Thompson? I want to know if he's found any evidence that confirms it was Susie Pater who went to Corfu with Donna. Ask him to find out if Susie's friend Bernice knows.'

She left to make the phone calls from the main incident room. Marsh followed her.

'He's only just out of reach now, Barry. We're getting close.'

'I wish I could share your optimism, ma'am.'

'I want to know more about Donna's grandmother. Can you organise some visits to all of the neighbours in Gilbert Road? Find out about her. How long she'd had the flat, whether she lived locally before then, whether people remember her. The usual stuff. There's something here that doesn't sit easy in my mind.'

Melsom waved from his desk. 'I've traced Warrander, ma'am. He's with one of the big finance companies in Bournemouth.'

'Get onto them, Jimmy. Confirm it, then we'll go across and see him right now before he finishes work. And well done.'

* * *

George Warrander still sported the spiky hairstyle from the student photos, although his eyes were serious. His voice was surprisingly deep. He was waiting for them in the lobby of the building. He stood up as they entered, walking forward in order to shake their hands, Sophie first. He was wearing a deep blue suit, a red tie and smartly polished black shoes. The only similarities to the university photographs were his hairstyle and his fresh complexion.

He ushered them across to a collection of seats set out around a small, low table with publicity brochures spread across the surface.

'Have you worked here long, Mr Warrander?' Sophie asked.

He ran his fingers through his hair. 'Just over a year,' he replied. 'I started the autumn after I graduated. I landed a summer job here while I was still a student and worked most holidays after that when they needed extra staff. I even did a few weekends. I got on well with everyone, so they offered me a permanent job once I finished my degree. I was really lucky.'

He seemed an open and amiable young man and Sophie guessed that it wasn't mere luck that had secured him the job. 'What do you do exactly?'

'I'm a trainee business manager specialising in links with France. I kept up a French language option while I was a student, and it's paid off well. I don't think I'd have landed the job without it.'

'Why didn't you contact us when you saw the press reports about Donna's murder?' Sophie asked. 'The story's been in the press for over a week now, with her name very prominent. Surely you must have known it was her? Goodenough isn't a very common name.'

'I've been on holiday,' he replied. 'I only got back two days ago, so I've been out of the loop. When you contacted me it came as a real shock, I can tell you. I've read every paper I've been able to lay my hands on since then. I can't believe it. I still feel sick when I think about it. She was such a lovely person.'

Sophie glanced across at Melsom and nodded slightly. He walked across to the reception desk, then moved towards the lift.

'Confirming that I was away?' Warrander asked.

Sophie nodded. 'In a case like this we double-check everything. I'd like you to take me back to when you first met Donna. Tell me everything you remember about her. We're still trying to build up a picture of her life here, why she left and what happened to her subsequently.'

'I met her at freshers' week, the September she started. I was on the student committee for the business course. I was just about to start my final year, so I was a couple of years ahead of her. She visited my stall and we got chatting. She was very easy to talk to, and we got on really well. She was very mature for her age. I thought at first that she was maybe an older student, but she was just eighteen. We hit it off right away. I think she wanted more but I was on the rebound from a relationship that had gone disastrously wrong and wasn't ready to get too involved. Anyway, that came out a bit later. I went to the freshers' ball with her and to several other functions during her first term, and we'd meet up for chats.' He paused. 'I really missed her, you know, when we stopped meeting up. Some months afterwards, when she was seeing someone else, I began to think that I'd totally messed up in not taking it further. We got on so well. In some ways better than any other girl I've known. It's just that I wasn't ready for any serious entanglement at the time.'

'So you saw her fairly regularly during that first term, but then it stopped? Is that right? What was the reason?'

'I suppose she got fed up with me dithering about. She started seeing someone else and I'd lost my chance. I regretted it within a few months and missed seeing her for our chats over coffee or in the bar.'

'When did she meet her next boyfriend?'

He thought for a few moments before replying. 'I think it was at the Christmas ball. I took her along, then we separated as usual. I think she got off with someone midway through the evening.'

'Did you meet again very much after that?'

'No. The Christmas break came within a few days, and we both went home for that. When we returned she was clearly involved with someone, and I didn't want to spoil things for her so I kept my distance. I began to realise what a mistake I'd made. But it was my last year and my finals were looming. I really had to get my head down and get stuck into the work. And once the exams were out of the way, that was it. I wasn't on the campus any more, other than when I graduated.'

'I want you to take me back to that ball. Did you know the man she met there?'

'No. I didn't recognise him at all. But then there's a huge student population on the campus. We only ever know a small proportion of the students, mainly just those doing the same subject.'

'Can you remember much about him? What he looked like? Did you talk to him at all?'

'He was tall and quite heavily built. Kind of athletic looking. But I don't remember much else, except that he didn't seem to smile much. I did speak to them very briefly, just to ask Donna if she needed me to see her home. But she said that she was okay. There was something about him that I couldn't put my finger on. The way he looked at me. It was kind of distant and watchful. But maybe I was imagining it. As I turned away I heard her say to him that I was a bit like a brother to her. Then it hit home that maybe I'd misjudged things with her. But it was too late.'

'Did Donna use his name at all?'

'I think she called him Andy, but I can't be sure.'

'One other question, Mr Warrander. Did Donna ever talk about her family background?'

'Once or twice. Sometimes she'd seem a bit quiet and withdrawn. Not quite depressed, but getting there. I used to ask her if she wanted to talk about what was bothering her, but she'd usually shake her head. She did tell me once that family life back home was a bit fraught and she was worried about her dad. The only other time she told me anything, it really threw me. She'd been adopted as a baby.'

Sophie sat silently for a few moments.

'Did she ever mention this again?'

'No, never. It was only the once.'

Melsom returned and nodded to Sophie as he sat down.

'Is it true how she died?' Warrander asked. 'Was she stabbed?'

'Yes. Late at night just after she finished work. She was on her way home.'

'I haven't been able to sleep since I found out. It makes me feel so sick. I mean physically nauseous. She was a really nice person and it all makes me realise how much I miss her. It's just unbelievable.'

'Do you have a girlfriend now, Mr Warrander?'

'Yes. That's who I was on holiday with. But I still keep feeling that I let Donna down somehow. It plays over and over in my mind.'

'None of it is your fault, trust me. All any of us can do is to make the best judgements we can in whatever circumstances we find ourselves in. And from what you've said, I think that you were absolutely right at the time to wait and not rush into a relationship with her. It's pretty clear to us that she came from a broken family background, so she needed a friend as she started something new like university. And you were that friend. There's no need for you to feel any guilt. Not that my words will give you much comfort in the short term, I know.'

'Did you see her?' he asked.

Sophie nodded. 'Yes. I saw her within an hour of her body being found, and several times later. I saw how beautiful she was.'

Warrander looked at her. 'It must be terrible for you. How do you cope?'

'Because it's my job to cope. It's my job to find out who did it and bring them to justice. And I will, Mr Warrander, I will do that.'

'I'd like to be at her funeral.'

'We'll let you know the details when we know ourselves.'

She stood up and shook his hand again before they turned towards the door.

'If I wanted to join the police, it wouldn't be too late for me, would it?'

She passed him her card. 'No, it wouldn't be too late. Contact me, if you decide you're interested.'

CHAPTER 18: A Soured Romance

Tuesday Evening

'Do you like curry?' Lauren pushed her empty plate away, and settled back into her chair with a groan. 'I think I'm going to burst. And you haven't answered. Don't think I haven't noticed.'

'It's okay. There are just too many of them over here.'

'Too many what?'

'Indians. Pakis. Immigrants of all types. Bleeding us dry.'

Lauren looked horrified. 'Did you know that in the First World War India lost seventy-five thousand dead in France fighting for Britain? And the same number wounded? And in World War Two they had about the same number of soldiers killed, but also lost about two million civilians?'

'So?'

'I always quote those figures when people make a racist comment about them. They fought and died for us, particularly in the first war. The least we can do is to show them some respect, surely?'

'Are you saying I'm a racist?'

'No, I didn't say that. I said it was a racist comment.'

'Same thing, isn't it?'

'Not necessarily. A person can be a racist, but not make any comments about it, so no one would know. Or someone needn't be a racist, but could make racist comments without meaning it just by choosing the wrong words, particularly if they've had a few drinks. Like you've had.'

'So you're giving me the benefit of the doubt?'

'This time.'

'Are you patronising me?'

'No, I'm telling you what my dad would say. He was born in India. My grandmother was Indian although my grandfather was a Yorkshireman. He was in the army.'

'But you're blonde and have blue eyes.'

'My brother's eyes are darker. But you still wouldn't know by looking at them. But you'd find out pretty quick if you made that kind of comment in their presence. They wouldn't react calmly like me. They'd have just gone for you.'

'I can look after myself.'

Lauren laughed. 'One is in the local sea-rowing club and is a lifeboat volunteer. The other is an amateur middleweight boxing champion for the region. You wouldn't stand a chance. Don't kid yourself.'

If anything, the comments made him even surlier than he'd been previously. He remained silent.

Lauren frowned and bit her lip before continuing. 'If what you said is really what you think, then there's no future for us. I'll make that clear now. I have Indian relatives, and I love them. I've visited India, and I think it's fantastic. I won't put up with racism. I'm going to leave my share of the bill and go. Think it over, and phone me if you want to continue seeing me. I'd like you to, but I won't compromise on what I know is right.'

She put some money on the table and left.

She cried as she walked away from the Indian restaurant. He had seemed so nice over the weekend. So perfect. Too good to be true — that's what her dad would say. She'd picked up on his new mood immediately. He was withdrawn and irritable. Even his hello kiss seemed half-hearted. What had happened? She was mystified, but just because he was in some kind of a strop didn't mean that she had to tolerate the nasty comments he'd just made. She hadn't done anything to cause his bad mood and he'd refused to say what was wrong.

She stopped to hunt for a tissue in her bag, and loudly blew her nose. She heard footsteps behind her. He was there, reaching out for her elbow. She pulled back, away from his outstretched arm.

'Lauren, I'm sorry. I've upset you, I know, and it's not your fault. I've had a bad day, and I just feel really tense. I don't know what made me say those things. Forgive me?'

He tried again to hold her arm, but she shrugged off his hand.

'I'll forgive you when I know that your apology is genuine. Let's have another couple of evenings out later in the week and see how things go. I'm not saying no, but I'm not saying yes either.'

'Can I at least walk you home? I don't like you being out alone this late at night. I'll be worried about you.'

'Okay, but promise you won't try and come in with me. You leave me at the front door, and just say goodbye. I don't even want a kiss from you until I've thought this through and decided what I want. And I'm only saying yes because I promised my dad I wouldn't be out late on my own.'

As they walked along the quiet pavement together, Lauren was surprised at how much his mood seemed to have changed again. He was almost back to his relaxed and cheerful self. How could his temper have changed so rapidly? And who was he, really? The man who was such good company over the weekend, or the moody one of this evening? She hadn't heard his question.

'What was that?' she said.

'I asked why your father is worried. Why today? Has something happened?'

'Apparently the police are dropping charges against that Latvian guy for the murders over in Swanage. It was in the evening paper. They're looking for someone else now. I told Dad that Southampton's far enough away. But he worries about me.'

'Stupid morons. Releasing him like that,' he muttered. 'Look, let's get a move on. I've got things to do.'

* * *

Shaz was late coming home. She was also unsteady on her feet, having knocked back several glasses of wine too many after finishing her shift at the café. It had been just what she'd needed, bumping into one of her closest friends on her way out of the door. And she was on the late shift again the next day, so why not relax and enjoy herself? Tuesday evenings were always quiet at the nearby wine bar, so they'd settled in for a real gossip-session, running down anyone they could think of, and howling with laughter. Therapeutic, that was the word for it.

She put the key unsteadily in the outer door and turned it, almost falling over as it swung open under her weight. She staggered in, hiccupping, and started to giggle.

'Shushh,' she said to herself. 'Fucking keep quiet, you drunk cow.'

That caused her to giggle some more as she staggered down the hallway to her own door. The landlord still hadn't changed the locks. Was it worth hassling him anymore? That Andy wanker-bastard had vanished completely. He wasn't going to appear now. She leaned against the door breathing heavily, trying to line up the key in her hand with the lock in front of her. Fuck. Why wouldn't it stay still? Finally the key slid in.

'Reminds me of sex,' she slurred to the empty hallway. 'Everything reminds me of sex. Want some.'

The door opened and she stepped forward into the void.

* * *

'Good evening, sir. Sorry to delay you, but this shouldn't take long.'

It was three in the morning and the A31 — the dual carriageway stretching east-west between the Bournemouth conurbation and the end of the motorway network at Southampton — was almost deserted. An occasional car, van or lorry passed. Most of them were waved into the long lay-by by the police traffic team, eerily visible in their luminous yellow jackets. PC Kenny Morton disliked the overnight shift, particularly on chilly, damp, misty nights in the middle of winter. He sniffed again. Must be coming down with the winter cold that so many of his colleagues were suffering from. He walked towards the white van that he'd just called into the lay-by and asked the driver to switch off his engine.

'I haven't done anything wrong, have I?'

'Not that I'm aware of, sir. This is the first night of our anti drink-driving campaign. It'll go on until the New Year. Were you aware of the campaign from our adverts?'

'No.'

Did the driver's voice sound a little strained? It was maybe worth prolonging the conversation and taking a sniff of his breath.

'Do you live in Dorset, sir?'

'No. Southampton.'

'Is the van yours?'

The driver nodded.

'And your name, sir, if you don't mind me asking?'

Again Morton noticed the slight pause before the man replied.

'Why are you out so late at night, sir? I'm just curious. It isn't the most pleasant of times.'

'I've been delivering some emergency engineering parts to a client in Poole. They're needed tomorrow.'

There it was again, a hint of tension in the voice.

'Can you open the rear doors, sir, please?'

'Oh, for God's sake, is that really necessary?'

Morton looked at the driver coolly and nodded without speaking. The driver got out, walked round to the back of the van and unlocked the rear doors. The policeman shone his torch into the interior.

'Seems fine, sir. What are in those boxes?'

'Refurbished heat exchangers for a refrigeration unit. They've just been serviced.'

'Open them, please. I just need to do a quick check.'

The two boxes that lay along one side of the van's interior contained exactly what the driver had described.

'So why are you really stopping people?'

'Illicit booze and fags. We think there's a consignment coming in tonight at Poole, and being driven along to London. Nothing yet.'

'Can I go now?'

Morton nodded, running the beam from his torch over the mud-spattered wheels and sills. He'd already noticed the mud on the driver's boots and trousers. 'Drive safely. The road's a bit slippery with the rain, and you were speeding a little as you approached us.'

'Sure.'

The driver locked the van and returned to his seat. He started the engine and drove back onto the main carriageway heading east, passing the police team who waved him on.

'Fucking wanker,' he mouthed through his smile as he waved back in return. He obviously wasn't aware that a high proportion of the Dorset Force were trained to lip-read. It had formed part of their inclusivity workshop, designed to help them understand the problems faced by deaf people. Morton watched the van disappear out of sight. I'll have you one day, he thought.

CHAPTER 19: The Dark Pool

Wednesday Morning

Lydia Pillay was tired. She'd spent the night in the hotel room next to the one used by Tracy Beck and her family. She'd woken regularly through the night, looked at the clock and then lain awake for what seemed like hours before drifting off once more. She'd seated herself at a table near the family while they ate breakfast, until she was finally relieved by another officer. Now here she was in Bournemouth, knocking on the door of a ground-floor flat that seemed to be unoccupied, judging from the lack of response. The building was dingy, with a badly soiled carpet running the length of the ground floor corridor. The walls looked as though they hadn't been painted in a decade. The interior light didn't work so the sole illumination for the landing came from a dirt-encrusted window that looked out onto a small paved yard. A slightly raised bed of earth ran down the side of the yard, looking as though someone had once made an effort to grow a few flowers or shrubs. There was nothing there now but weeds.

A middle-aged Asian couple came out of the front flat.

'We heard you knocking,' said the man. 'She may be at work.'

They looked frightened. Lydia took out her warrant card and held it out for them to see.

'Dorset police,' she said. 'I'm DC Pillay. The lady who lives here may be able to help us with an investigation. Her name is Shaz Fellows. Is that right?'

The woman nodded. 'Sharon is such a pretty name. Why do girls have to alter their names like that? She was here last night because we heard her before we went to bed. There was some bumping.'

'Where does she work?' asked Pillay.

'A café ten minutes' walk away towards the gardens. It is called Waterside café, though it is away from the stream. But you can see the flower beds in the park gardens from the front tables. It is nice for tourists. Good food. What is the word when nothing has been put on the food?'

'Organic?' suggested Pillay.

'That is it. It is an organic café. Expensive.'

'Do you know Shaz well?'

'No,' came the hesitant reply. 'Some local girls are good, and courteous . . .'

'But Shaz isn't?' prompted Pillay.

'You know what some young girls are like in these days,' explained the man. 'They have no moral centre to their lives. It is the drink. She can be nice but we would be ashamed if our daughter were to behave like her at night. It is good to see a young Asian woman like you in the police. Why do these English girls have no dignity?'

Pillay didn't answer. She still enjoyed her wilder moments at parties, but was careful to keep the gory details well away from her immediate family. She smiled at the couple.

'Well, thank you for your help. We may want to speak to you again.'

She took a note of their names and telephone number. Then she walked outside to call back to the incident room. As well as the name Shaz Fellows on the list of Susie Pater's contacts, Pillay remembered also seeing the word Waterside. Sophie's instructions were for her to visit the café.

The café owner was harassed and short-tempered.

'She's let me down again,' he hissed at Pillay, as he passed with a tray of coffee and buns. 'I'm sick and tired of it. And she knew I was depending on her today. I told her when she left yesterday evening. I really don't want her back, but I just can't find anyone else to fill the mid-week slots. It's a nightmare. I've got someone coming this afternoon for an interview and if she seems any good I'll take her on right away, and Shaz can just fade into oblivion as far as I'm concerned.'

'Does she often take days off without warning?'

He stopped to think, wiping his hands on his pristine white apron. 'Now you come to mention it, this is the first time. She's always let me know by phone before.'

'So why do you feel so negative about her?'

'She's slow, lazy and rude. Thank God she's never sworn in front of any customers, but once she's out of their earshot she's as crude as they come. But she can be really surly to them if she's in a bad mood. The last few days have been awful. Her boyfriend has walked out on her apparently, and she's been absolutely foul. And her cold sore didn't help. Who wants to be served by a surly, moody waitress with a weeping lip for goodness' sake?'

'She had a cold sore?' Pillay asked.

'Well, that's what she told me. I think they'd come to blows, and that's why he left. There were some marks around her cheeks. She'd done her best to cover them with make-up, but I could still see something. I didn't mention it though. She could fly off the handle at the slightest provocation. And she only got the tattoo done a couple of weeks ago.'

'Can you explain, please?'

'She had a big heart tattooed on her right arm with his name inside. I'm not a great fan of tattoos, but some can look alright. You know, a flower or butterfly. But this was a real monstrosity.'

'What was the name?'

'Andy. The message inside read 'Shaz for Andy' but with the word 'for' written as a number. You know, like text-speak. Really tacky, and that sums up Shaz.'

A sudden thought struck Pillay. 'Was Donna Goodenough ever an employee or customer here?'

'Yes,' he said. 'I had her as a waitress about three years ago. She was a student, and worked weekends. For about six months, I think. She was about the best waitress I've ever had.'

'And Susie Pater?'

'No. But there was a customer called Susie who became friendly with Donna.'

'Don't you read the papers or watch the news?' Pillay looked across at a couple of tabloids lying on a side table, provided for customers to read.

'Not really, apart from the sports section. Don't have much time.'

Pillay was already moving to the door. 'Thanks. We'll be back in touch.'

She could hardly get her phone out quickly enough.

* * *

Marsh replaced the phone carefully into its cradle. He tapped his finger on the desktop for a few moments, then stood up and went in search of Sophie.

'I've just had an interesting conversation with someone from Wareham nick, ma'am.'

'Go on, Barry. I can see by the look on your face that you might be on to something. Don't leave me in suspense.'

'Well, I've been keeping my eye on the log of calls coming in to various stations around the county, just like you suggested. Apparently there's a squad car out at a pool in Wareham Forest just now. A nature reserve ranger called in to report that she suspected something was dumped in the water last night.'

'Any other details?'

'Not a lot. But a squad car doesn't usually get despatched just because a bit of rubbish has been chucked in the water somewhere. There must have been something suspicious about it. I was thinking of Lydia's news. There's probably no connection, but even so . . .'

'Is it possible for us to be put through to the squad car?' Sophie said.

'I don't see why not. I'll get the control room, shall I?'

After a minute or two, Marsh handed over the phone, mouthing, 'One of the guys out there.'

'Who am I speaking to?' she asked.

She listened to the slightly crackly reply, and jotted down a map reference.

'You know why we might be interested. What can you see?' She listened intently to the reply. 'Listen, don't disturb anything any further. We're on our way, and I want forensics there just in case. We'll arrange that. Just stay where you are and keep the ranger with you. We should be with you in about half an hour.'

She replaced the phone and unhooked her jacket from the back of the chair.

'What was that you said yesterday about not sharing my optimism, Barry? Good job I didn't take you seriously. And well done for spotting that report. It just might be the breakthrough we've been looking for. We're on the move.'

'Could they see anything?'

'No, it's too murky. They spent some time poking around with a pole. There was something there, but they couldn't tell what it was.'

* * *

The pool was set back about three hundred yards from the road, approached by a muddy track that seemed to lose itself in the shadowy gloom created by the overhanging trees. The trees thinned out close to the edge of the pool and the surface of the water showed few reflections. The part of the pool they could see was about half a mile in length, but less than half that in width. A group of people was standing midway along the northern side, where the track ended at a small grassy clearing alongside the water's edge. Sophie peered into the dark, peaty water as the ranger recounted her tale. Alice Llewellyn was a tall, fair-haired young woman dressed in olive-coloured outdoor gear and boots. She told them how she carried out a reconnoitre of the area regularly each morning, and had spotted fresh tyre tracks leading close to the water's edge. The edge of the bank had drag marks on it, as if something heavy had been pulled across it and into the water. She had spotted something just below the water line, looking as though it was a bundle in plastic, but it had slid further under when she'd tried to hook it with a pole. She'd felt uneasy about it and so had reported it to the police.

'What made you feel uneasy?' asked Sophie.

'Maybe I watch too many crime dramas on TV, or maybe I'm over-imaginative, but it gave me the creeps. It was lodged on the edge of those reeds, but below the water line. And it had the shape of . . . well, you know. As I tried to hook it, it got dislodged, and it was gone in an instant. It must have been heavy. These guys arrived and we poked around. We hit something solid but the pole just slid off it.'

She looked rather frightened.

'Look, you don't have to stay. It'll be a little while before our forensic and underwater squads arrive. Would you prefer to wait back in your office or at home?' Sophie said.

The ranger shook her head. 'Are you kidding? This is my patch. I'm responsible for it. Anyway, you might find something, and I don't want to miss that. Things can be a bit dulls out here. Don't think that I'm complaining. I chose this job. But some excitement is no bad thing. What I can do is to go and get some coffee for everyone. Would that be okay? We've got a stack of flasks in the centre — we use them when we have school groups here.'

'That would be just perfect, Alice,' Sophie said.

'Any chance of choccy biscuits?' asked the younger of the two uniformed men, with a wink. Alice smiled and nodded before heading off down the track.

Sophie moved to one side and rang Pillay for an update. McGreedie's team had been due to arrive at Shaz Fellows's flat in Bournemouth in order to carry out a search.

* * *

Alice had only just returned with the coffee when the first of the vans arrived, disgorging a mass of equipment, followed by a Land Rover with the underwater squad. It was an hour before the divers were kitted out and ready to start the search. Sophie didn't envy them as they slid into the dark cold water. The pool was about seven feet deep at that point and the divers' underwater lights could only just be seen by the group standing on the bank. Within a few minutes one of them surfaced and called for a sling to be taken down. Two of the divers then resurfaced at the waterside with a bundle wrapped in black plastic sheeting. It was carefully hauled onto the bank, a few bedraggled strands of weed still lying draped across the surface. Sophie turned to the white-faced ranger who nodded.

'That's it.' She held her hand to her mouth.

Sophie turned to the senior forensics officer. 'Let's get it open for a quick look. If it is what we think, we'll need a tent up, so be ready. It may have only gone in last night.'

She took hold of the ranger's arm and steered her away. 'Alice, thanks for all your help. This is where things might get nasty. You can remain if you wish. But you could be in for a shock if you wait around here. Believe me, if it is a body, then this won't be a very pleasant place to be in the next few minutes. You'd be better off away from here. I can keep you informed by phone if you wish. Alternatively, you could sit in your jeep.'

'Yes, I'll do that. I want to know what's happened and I'd just fret if I was back at home or in the office.'

'Can we see all of the pool from here? It's just that I can't make out the western edge. It disappears behind the trees. Is there any more?' Sophie asked.

'Yes. It widens again round the corner, but that part doesn't belong to the nature reserve. It's fenced off, and the land is owned by a gravel extraction company. You can see the start of the fencing if you look carefully. Here, use my binoculars.'

Sophie could just make out the posts of a chain-link fence between gaps in the trees that ran down to the water's edge.

'It's deeper than this end, but it isn't accessible. The whole of that area was owned by a mineral company, but they went bust before they could start extracting. Some kind of conglomerate has it now, but they haven't done anything about using it. I'm quite glad, because I don't want a lot of noisy trucks here.'

'So how do you get into it?'

'There's a rough track that comes off the road a mile or so further along. It loops around the higher ground and doubles back. But there's a locked gate at the lower end as the track leaves our land and access to the pool area is barred at the top end by a high security gate set into the fencing. It's kept padlocked.'

'Do you check it each morning as well?'

'No. It's off my normal route, and the approach is very rough. But it is kept secured. I check the top gate once a week or so but, as I said, the area inside the fence doesn't come under our responsibility. Its upkeep is still down to the mineral company.'

'When did you check the gate last?'

'Middle of last week, I think. Why are you interested?' She paused. 'Sorry, that's a stupid question.'

'So there shouldn't be any possibility of illegal dumping of any kind there?'

'No. It's so out of the way that very few people go anywhere near it. The approach track has deteriorated badly and is full of potholes. There's never been a problem, as far as I know, probably because free access is impossible.'

'Can we have a look later? It seems foolish to be here and not to check.'

'Only from the outside. I don't have a key to the top gate, that's easily accessible. We do have one for emergencies and for my annual check, but it's kept in the safe at the office. It's not our land, you see.'

Sophie nodded. The ranger went to sit in her jeep. Sophie and Marsh returned to the poolside and watched the forensic team start their work. They slit carefully down the side of the plastic, and peeled it back. The body was wrapped in an old rug, weighted down with a length of chain. It was a young woman with streaky, blonde hair. Her eyes gazed upwards. Water had not yet penetrated through the outer plastic layer which had been sealed with waterproof tape, so the corpse still looked as though it could be brought back to life, if only someone could wave a magic wand and chant the right spell.

'We need to see the right upper arm and shoulder,' Sophie said.

One of the team carefully loosened the thin, white, waitress's blouse to show the tattoo on her upper right arm.

'That's her. Don't do anything else other than check her body temperature. I want Benny Goodall brought in to do the rest.' She turned to Marsh. 'Phone Lydia and let her know.'

She went outside to speak to the diving team, who had finished their search of the immediate area with no further discoveries. They were asked to wait on site a little longer. The two detectives joined the ranger in her jeep and asked her to take them to the fenced-off section. She drove the jeep back to the road and further north for a mile. She stopped at a pull-in beside a metal five-barred gate and unlocked it. It moved easily on its hinges as she pulled it open.

'It looks new,' said Marsh.

'It is. We only replaced the old timber gate two days ago. It had been here for decades and some of the wood was rotting badly. We had this one spare back at the centre, and it was an easy job to swap them over.'

'Was the old one kept locked, Alice?' Sophie asked.

'Yes. We had a padlock on it, probably as old as the gate itself. This one has an intrinsic lock fitted, so it should be more secure.'

The ranger had been right about the track. The jeep bounced and swayed up the rutted path. Pebbles shot away from under the moving tyres and struck the rocky ground at the side of the path.

'You said that the mineral company owns this track,' Sophie said.

'That's right, but we have access as far as the security gate. That's why I had the key for the bottom gate on me. It's convenient for getting to the north end of our land, although it's pretty rough, as you can see.'

It took ten minutes to drive to the start of the fenced area. The high, steel-mesh gate across the rough track was still in good condition, and the fitted lock holding the two gates together was still rust-free and securely locked.

Barry Marsh inspected it closely. 'Have you opened it recently?' he asked.

'No, no one's been inside for months. Someone from the mineral company checks inside once a year. If I'm free I come with them. The last time was in the spring.'

Marsh sniffed the lock. 'Someone's used a lubricating spray on it, and not very long ago.'

He looked at the ground immediately below the lock. There were a couple of tell-tale drips of the lubricant on the gravel. He rubbed the end of his finger in one of them, then sniffed it cautiously.

'Yes, fairly fresh.'

'Could someone from the mineral company have come up here without your knowledge?' asked Sophie.

'I suppose it was possible until two days ago when we replaced the lower gate. We haven't sent them their copy of the key yet. It's still lying in my in-tray at the office. So no one could have come up here since then. To be honest, I don't see how anyone could have been up here before then. The company always phones to let us know when they want to carry out a visit, and that hasn't been since last year.'

'And you don't hold a key for this gate?'

'Not on me. It's not our property, you see. The key's kept in a safe at the office and I take it once a year for my site check.'

'We'll need to get inside, Alice. I'm afraid you'll have to get it. I'll come with you, while Barry waits here.'

'Okay. It'll take us about half an hour.'

Marsh didn't look particularly pleased about having to wait by himself in this desolate spot.

'Could I borrow your binoculars?' he asked. 'I may as well have a good look round while I wait.'

The jeep was back within twenty minutes. Sophie was nursing a slight bruise on the side of her head caused by bouncing into the door after one particularly vicious lurch.

'There's a faint mark of tyre tracks just inside the gate,' Marsh reported on their return. 'But no other signs of recent access, as far as I can see. The tracks might be old indentations from years ago.'

The lock opened fairly easily, but the gates were stiff on their hinges.

Grass and weeds grew in the stony surface, but there were two or three muddier patches in the track. It was here that Marsh thought he could make out the faint imprint of vehicle tracks. The only wildlife in sight were some ragged-looking crows that flapped lazily away as their vehicle approached. A final turn brought them to a hard surface overlooking a still area of water, shadowed all around by the dark trees and a grey rock face. It looked like strong, black tea.

'How many times have you been up here?' asked Sophie.

'Only a couple of times. As I said, someone from the parent mineral company does an inspection once a year, and if I'm free I come with them. It always gives me the creeps.' Alice wrapped her arms around her midriff.

'How do they carry out the inspection?'

'Mainly visually. They check the vertical rock face for signs of slippage. They also poke down into the water surface with a pole.'

'Well, let's have a look. Try using the extending pole just here.'

Alice nodded and pulled the pole out to its full length. She walked over to the water's edge and started to poke below the surface.

'It's rather deeper at the edge compared to my end of the pool, and a lot deeper in the middle. There's no way of checking the middle without a boat or raft of some type, so they just poke around down here close to the edge. There's never anything here, though.'

'Let's hope that's still the case,' Sophie answered.

'What am I looking for?' Alice asked.

'I don't know. Anything out of the ordinary, I suppose. Anything that shouldn't be there.'

Alice's arm stopped moving. 'That's odd, there's something hard down there.' She pulled the pole partly back, and prodded a few times. 'It feels solid, maybe metallic. The pole skates across the surface.'

Barry Marsh took over and felt around the area that Alice had been probing.

'It feels like a car.' He looked at Sophie. 'What are the chances of it being a red Ford Fiesta, do you think?'

He pulled out his phone and called through to the diving team at the other end of the pool.

* * *

Within an hour, the two divers drove up with their support squad and disappeared below the surface. The water was deeper here, so little could be seen. It was several minutes before one of them rose to the surface.

'There's a car there, but we've spotted something else. Can you get the sling over again?'

Sophie looked at the ranger who held her hands to her mouth.

'There aren't going to be any more bodies, are there?' asked Alice. 'I couldn't cope with any more of those horrible bundles coming out. How can anyone do that? Really?' She was almost weeping. 'I don't know if I can ever walk by that side of the pool again. How will I be able to do my job? I'll be forever looking into it and wondering. God, this is all too awful.'

'Go back to your jeep, Alice, please,' Sophie said.

Minutes later, one of the divers surfaced again and signalled for the ropes to be pulled in. The grey-wrapped bundle dragged onto the bank was the right shape and weight for a body, but it had clearly been in the water for some time. The plastic was discoloured and had deteriorated badly. The taped-up edges were peeling back in places, and a brown ooze was seeping out of the gaps.

'Get that forensics tent up quickly,' said Sophie. 'I don't want this left outside any longer than necessary.'

They masked-up for the opening of this second bundle. Even so, the smell was sickening and the sight of the corpse horrific. It was little more than a putrefying mass adhering to the skeleton.

‘Another young woman, I’d say, judging from the hair remains,’ the forensic officer said to Sophie. ‘It must have been in there for years. Is Dr Goodall on his way?’

Sophie nodded. ‘He’s just arrived at the other end. He’ll do a quick examination there, then come up for this one.’

‘Were you expecting this?’

‘The thought had occurred to me, but I was just hoping for the car.’

She looked across the surface of the dark, brooding water. This was as bad as her job got.

CHAPTER 20: The Girl on the Swing

Wednesday Afternoon

The police divers surfaced and signalled that the winch lines were secured. The crane began to winch and the cables tightened, groaned and began to move. It was several moments before the car appeared, gushing filthy water as it rose above the surface of the pool. A red Ford Fiesta. The vehicle was swung onto a low-loader truck, parked close by. Marsh looked at Sophie and nodded. They were inching closer to their elusive prey. The ranger had returned to see the raising of the car so Sophie spoke to her.

'It links in with a crime we've been investigating. Barry's been looking for that car for days now. I'm afraid you're going to have to keep all of this to yourself, Alice. This morning's events will all form evidence in a court case, so please don't mention it to anyone.'

She walked across to the officer in charge of the divers. 'Can you keep looking? There's a possibility that our man might have dumped other stuff here, and back in the other location too. We're not expecting any more bodies, but we have to make sure.'

She turned back to the ranger. 'We need to find out how he managed to get keys for the gates. Can we go back to your office to talk?'

Alice nodded her agreement but didn't speak.

'Barry, would you keep your eye on things up here? I'm going back with Alice, but I'll call in to see the forensics at the other end of the pool on the way. Maybe we can meet back here in a couple of hours?'

The ranger drove the jeep back to the temporary tent at the first site. She remained in the vehicle while Sophie talked to Benny Goodall who was about to leave.

'You keep creating work for me, Sophie. Don't you think I'm busy enough?' he said.

'A bottle of red for you, Benny. Anyway, I'm keeping you in business. What can you tell me?' Sophie replied.

'This one has only been in there since last night. Absolutely no doubt, since she's been dead for less than twenty-four hours. Strangulation. But a different method to the two from last week. This was brute strength, with hands only. I'll have a look at the other one now. I need to get back to base for mid-afternoon, though.'

'I'm off to the rangers' office for a short while, but I hope to be back before you finish. It's not nice up there, Benny.'

'Is it ever?'

* * *

The rangers' office was attached to an outdoor centre displaying exhibits of local wildlife, along with charts and maps of the most popular forest walks and viewpoints. Alice's boss was waiting for them. He was a tubby middle-aged man with friendly eyes and a cheery smile. They shook hands.

'George Panakis,' he said. 'From what I hear, you and Alice have had a grim morning. I'll do anything I can to help.'

'We need to know who has had access to the keys for the two gates, Mr Panakis. Someone has managed to dump a car and a body in the private end of the water. He could only have done that with easy access over a number of years. Are all the keys accounted for?'

'We've never had a problem with lost keys. None have gone missing in the ten years that I've been here. We keep the key to that top gate in the safe, as Alice will already have told you. I'm mystified.'

'Let's do it logically. Can you make me a list of all employees over the past six years? Names and known addresses, plus dates of birth if you can. Do you have voluntary helpers, student placements, temporary workers?'

Panakis nodded.

'They all need to be added, but keep each group separate. When was this place built?'

'Over twenty years ago, long before my time.'

'Any recent developments or additions to the building?' Sophie asked.

'The public toilets were built about eight years ago, at the same time as the staff kitchen. That was in my time.'

'Who did the building work? Can you add their names, please? If no keys have gone missing, then they must have been copied. The only alternative is that the key has come from the office of the mineral company, but I understand that they don't hold a key for the bottom gate. Is that correct?'

Panakis nodded. 'I'll get our admin person involved. She'll know where to find the records, and she's been here longer than me. She's only part-time, and isn't in on a Wednesday, but I'll give her a call and ask her to pop in. Is that okay?'

'Of course. That list needs to be as comprehensive as possible.'

* * *

Edith George, the administrative assistant, bustled in within fifteen minutes. By then the list contained more than twenty names, but she was able to add another five almost immediately.

After another fifteen minutes, the rangers and their assistant decided that the list was as complete as it was going to be.

'I don't know the names of the individual builders,' Edith said. 'You'll have to contact them for that.' She looked triumphantly at the list in front of her. 'The only people not there, as far as I know, are the young offenders.'

Alice and her boss looked perplexed.

'Young offenders?' queried Sophie.

'Yes. A group of them put the fence and top gate up in the first place for the mining company when they thought they might develop the site. A group came over from Hampshire each day to put it all up and build the track.' She looked at Panakis. 'Oh, this was a good twelve years ago, a couple of years before you came, George. Apparently there was a government project that tried to get young offenders trained in the work environment ready for when they were released. They were working on that track for about a month. But they weren't really a problem, as far as I remember.'

'But they were the ones who put the fence up, and fitted the gate?' asked Sophie.

'Yes.'

'And they must have had the key for the bottom gate in order to get up to where they were working?'

Edith nodded. 'The two staff did. They borrowed it each day.'

'They were from a Hampshire centre?'

'Yes. Most of the lads were from the Southampton and Portsmouth area.'

* * *

Alice drove Sophie back to the second site, but returned to the rangers' office immediately. Sophie guessed that the young woman had experienced enough shocks in one day to last a lifetime. She didn't want her exposed to the horrors of the second corpse.

She walked into the tent as Goodall was packing up.

'This one? Difficult to be exact, but my guess is anywhere between three and six years, judging by the state of decomposition. But I did use the word guess, as I'm sure you noted. We'll need some experts to look at the gunk that's living on the body residues to be any more exact, and I don't know how possible that is. What I can say is that she was a young woman of under thirty, five feet four inches tall and probably of medium build. And she had a dislocated jaw,' he said.

'What?'

'A dislocated jaw — out of alignment on the right side. I spotted it as soon as I looked at her skull.'

'But that's easily treated, isn't it? People don't normally ignore jaw dislocations.'

'The joint area didn't show signs of any long-term damage, so I'd guess that it hadn't happened long before she ended up being dumped here.'

'For pity's sake.'

Goodall put an arm round Sophie's shoulder. 'He's not a nice individual, your killer. He's been nastier than we thought for longer than we thought. You need to catch him, Sophie.'

'Well, thanks, Benny. As if I'm not trying hard enough.'

'I'll start on the full PMs once I'm back at the lab. And I promise to get the results to you as soon as I can. I'll call you if I spot anything else unusual. Okay?'

Sophie gave him a brief, weak smile. She went over to Marsh, who was standing looking into the pool.

'Anything else?' she asked.

'No, just a few things from inside the car. It's a bit disappointing to be honest. I was hoping for some stuff from the houses. Odd.'

'It makes me wonder a bit too, Barry. Let's leave them to it. We've got a lot to think about on our way back to the office. And we haven't had lunch yet — if you can stomach anything after all this.'

* * *

The two detectives decided that their first priority was to chase up the names of the young offenders who had erected the security fence and gate ten years previously.

Marsh drove, and Sophie phoned through to the governor's office to warn them that she was coming. She asked for the relevant records to be made ready.

'It would fit, Barry. The team leader would have had both sets of keys each day in order to get onto the site. One of the lads in the squad could have got hold of a copy somehow, and kept it all these years. That end of the pool is so cut off that it's an ideal site for dumping things. Then just a couple of days ago, the rangers finally got round to changing the lower gate. Our man pays a visit late last night but can't get through the new lower gate because his key no longer works. So what does he do? He's got Shaz's body wrapped up, all ready for disposal, but he can't get to his planned disposal site. He decides to dump it in the nature reserve's end of the pool.'

'We're in the run-up to Christmas, ma'am.'

'That comment is too cryptic, even for me, Barry. What do you mean?'

'We'll have had several teams from traffic out on the roads last night, looking out for drunk drivers. Shall I contact them when we get back? See if they spotted anything unusual?'

'Absolutely. Brilliant idea, Barry.'

* * *

The governor's secretary was a stout, middle-aged woman who appeared to see her main task as protecting her boss from excessive demands on his time. Sophie was annoyed that nothing was ready for them when they arrived.

'I'm running an investigation into multiple murders. I just don't have time to go through the usual channels. Either get me the information I need or get me someone who can find it. Is that understood?'

Her voice had evidently penetrated the governor's inner sanctum, because the door opened and a head peered out.

'Chief Inspector?' The man looked at his secretary. 'I'll take over from here, Babs. If you can just find the details that the chief inspector has asked for? And quickly, please?'

The governor ushered the two detectives into his office and introduced himself.

'I'm Des Bartlett, the acting governor. I must apologise for the attitude of my secretary. I've only been in this role for a week and a half, and I'm trying to get things shaken up a bit. Babs was trained by my predecessor into thinking that her main role was a cross between a door-guard and a human filter, keeping out anyone and anything that might prove to be too demanding. I am trying to convince her otherwise. Was she trying to delay things?'

'I could maybe understand it in normal circumstances, but I'd explained to both of you on the phone why this is so urgent. I need that list, and I need it now. I don't want this delay causing another death.'

'I'm sure it will appear, Chief Inspector. Would you like some tea while you wait?'

A man out of his depth, thought Sophie. He can't see that murder doesn't wait for the bureaucratic niceties. Assisted by a woman who thinks she's a Rottweiler.

'I really thought you would have the information ready for me by now, Mr Bartlett. I phoned well almost an hour ago.'

He failed to meet her stare. Sophie guessed what had happened. He'd merely asked his secretary to find the information, maybe once she'd completed the task she was working on.

'We have two vulnerable young women out there. They know something, and our killer knows that they know it. We have to find him before he finds them. Do you understand? Normal rules and procedures don't apply. I explained all this to you. So why leave it to your secretary? How would you feel if one of those young women was your daughter?'

Looking sheepish, Bartlett left the room.

'Christ, people like this drive me mad,' Sophie said to Marsh. 'So many people bury their heads in the sand when there's a crisis, hoping someone else will deal with it. Bartlett's one of them. I bet he doesn't get the permanent job.' She sighed. 'Although maybe he will. I don't know what kind of person they want for this type of role.'

Marsh said nothing.

* * *

Finally they were on their way back to Swanage, with Marsh driving. Sophie looked at the list.

'There's an Andrew Renshaw on it, Barry. That's the name supplied by Southampton CID in the Debbie Martinez case. It's got to be him. So why can't we trace him? I'll phone Lydia.'

Pillay was waiting for them when they got back to Swanage.

'Ma'am, I think I've just found something in the old records. There was a teenage lad who was in a lot of trouble in Southampton some fifteen years ago. He was called Andrew Renshaw. Arson, animal cruelty, petty theft, violent and abusive behaviour. He ended up in a young offenders' institute. His date of birth tallies exactly.'

'Those offences are the key signs of a psychopath in the making. But we haven't been able to find anything else on that name, have we? Every single man with that name in Dorset and Hampshire has been checked and cleared. Yet clearly he's the man we're looking for.'

'Either he's moved outside the area, or he must have changed his name. Officially, I mean. I can't think of any other reason, ma'am.'

'I'd go with the second. We already know he's been using different names. And I think he's still in the area. If his parents didn't marry, or they split up, he may have got used to using two surnames, and that's what gave him the idea. If so, he uses Ridgway and Renshaw. But neither has come up with anything. Nor has Rule, the alias we think he's been using.'

'So his current name isn't any of those, and that's why we haven't made much progress in finding him?' added Marsh. 'It could be anything.'

'Well, if that's the case we may be in for a hard slog. At least we have his car now. Fingers crossed, we might get somewhere with that once forensics have finished.'

* * *

Tracy Beck was restless and bored. Living in a hotel with views across Poole's picturesque quayside was okay for a day or two, but now she just wanted to get back to her normal life. She liked the reassurance of everyday life with her daughter and boyfriend in their small flat. She was beginning to appreciate what a home really was. It wasn't just a set of rooms behind a door, but somewhere she could let down her defences and be herself. Here in this hotel room she was restless and on edge. She looked out of the window and saw Rachel on the swing in the garden below. It was beginning to get dark so she opened the window to call Rachel in. She heard her daughter singing to herself as she swung to and fro, and decided against it. She leaned on the sill and watched her. Then, Tracy became aware of the smell of cigarette smoke and she wondered where it was coming from. She leaned further out and could just see a man's legs stretched out below. Someone was sitting in a chair directly under her window, smoking. And watching Rachel? She closed the window, hurriedly slipped a cardigan over her shoulders and left the room. Uneasy now, she hurried down the stairs, past the reception area and nearly cannoned into a tall, heavily built man coming in from the patio area. She gasped, but he was past her and gone.

Her sister-in-law called from the corridor behind her. 'When do you want your tea, Trace?'

Now Tracy was in a blind panic. She ran outside and stood on the patio. There was Rachel, still on the swing, still singing to herself. The little girl smiled and waved when she saw her mother. Tracy was shaking, her hands at her mouth, her eyes wide with fear. That man. It was him. Rachel's father, Andy. Why was he there? What had he been doing, watching Rachel like that? She ran over, sobbing, and hugged her daughter.

'What is it, Mummy?' asked the little girl.

Tracy couldn't answer. It was all she could do to prevent the vomit from rising in her throat.

* * *

Back in the incident room Sophie's mobile phone rang. 'Hi, Tracy . . . What? Are you sure? Did he recognise you?' Sophie scrabbled for a sheet of paper on her desk. 'It should be Kim Lockwood with you at the moment, Tracy. Is that right? Is she there? Listen carefully. Stay in your room with Rachel and Kim, and lock the door. Get Kim to tell the manager what you're doing. I'll come across right now. Expect me in about half an hour. Can you put Kim on please?'

Sophie listened to the policewoman and told her what to do. 'Don't let anyone in, even Jerry, until we arrive. We'll phone when we get to the hotel. Is that clear? Phone back to your station and get a squad car to sit outside. Put them onto me if there's a problem. Okay?'

Sophie grabbed her jacket and ran to the door. 'You got the gist of that I expect, Lydia. Tracy says that our man Andy was in the hotel garden just now, watching the little girl.' As they rushed across the incident room she called out to Melsom. 'Jimmy, our man seems to have turned up at Tracy's hotel. Hold the fort while we're gone.'

* * *

Tracy had calmed down somewhat by the time they arrived. After a few words with her, Sophie left Pillay there while she and Marsh went downstairs to speak to Tracy's sister-in-law.

'I served him a pint in the bar. He wanted to smoke and asked me where the garden was,' she said.

'Did he give any clue about why he was here?'

'I think it was sheer chance. While I was pouring his beer, he went to the loo to wash his hands. They were oily, as if he'd been working on machinery. I asked if he'd been working nearby, and he nodded. He didn't say anything else. I got the impression that he was a bit surly. I can't remember ever seeing him in here before. He drove off in a small, white van. Plain. No name on it.'

She could add nothing else. Sophie glanced at her watch and spoke to Marsh.

'If we're quick we might be able to check some of the local businesses before they shut for the day. Let's think. Oily hands and machinery? Some of the premises across on the quay might be the best bet. I'll get Lydia. With three of us and a couple of the local plods we might strike it lucky if we get a move on.'

They gave up after an hour. Most of the businesses were already closed when they started the search, and the rest shut as the enquiry progressed. The only positive news was a probable sighting of the van earlier in the afternoon. It had nearly collided with a local worker's car at a mini-roundabout. The car driver had noted that the van drove off along the quayside and indicated left. From there he could have driven straight to the hotel.

'So it does look as though he was working locally,' Marsh said. 'Should we come back tomorrow?'

'Yes. We can kill the proverbial two birds. I'll get the local squads to check the warehouses, while we keep an eye on the hotel in case he decides to return. He doesn't seem to have recognised Tracy when he passed her. But he would have heard the sister-in-law calling her name out. So he may well be back, if only to satisfy his curiosity. We'll move Tracy and little Rachel to somewhere safe, and leave a watch on the place overnight. Then we'll all come back tomorrow morning, first thing.'

CHAPTER 21: Coffee and Bruises

Thursday Morning

Sophie wanted every member of the team to be aware of what they were confronting. 'Psychopaths often look absolutely normal. The wild-eyed and manic stereotype is a complete myth. It's just not possible to identify a psychopath from his or her appearance. They can be short, tall, slim, tubby, young, old, male or female. The only thing that sets them apart is their inability to feel empathy. They are incapable of feeling real emotional attachment to other people. Any emotions they do feel are shallow, so they tend to drift in and out of relationships. But most are not criminals. As far as I know, it's not clear what drives some of them to step over that line. Our man Andy is an example of the most extreme type. He's moved in and out of relationships, quite possibly carrying on several at the same time. He's lied to his partners. We know that because of the different surnames that he's used. In each relationship he's moved from casual bullying to extreme violence in a matter of months, and he won't see anything wrong with this, if he's true to type. To him, other people are present only to please him. He'll use them and then abandon them when it suits him. He won't feel remorse or a sense of shame. Any situation will be manipulated to give maximum benefit to himself. The extent of the lying is quite extraordinary. You and I feel a sense of guilt when we lie, so we give off tiny signals in our body language. It really doesn't work with an extreme psychopath. How can it? These tiny clues are the result of tension and guilt at telling a lie. But a psychopath feels no such guilt, so will give no clues. They'll just lie and lie until presented with hard evidence that they are lying. Then they'll switch their story immediately. But there is still no sense of anxiety created by the new lie, so it will be as smooth as the previous one.

'Andy won't be feeling bad about any of these murders. At best he will feel irritation at the trouble they caused him. In each case it was the fault of the victim for boxing him into a corner where the only way out for him was to kill her. He will view each of these killings as a necessary act.

'You all need to understand why I'm telling you this. I believe that we are getting close to him, and he knows it. That's why he killed Shaz Fellows on Tuesday night. She must have known something that could have identified him. It's just so tragic that we got to her a day too late. From what we can tell, he split with her last week but left her alone for the intervening time. He came back for her on Tuesday evening.

'If we find him, I don't want him approached by any one of us alone, or even in pairs, not without major backup. He's a well-built man, and he's extremely violent. Whereas he murdered Brenda Goodenough and Susie Pater with a ligature, Shaz was strangled with his bare hands using brute force. Her face had been severely knocked about. It's possible he's started to lose control. But you also need to remember that psychopaths are very charming on the surface. They are experts at making people feel they are easy to talk to. He might attempt to schmooze you into a false sense of security if he suspects that you're unsure of him. We don't know whether he carries any weapons, so don't gamble. We aren't aware that he has firearms, but we must consider the possibility. I don't want us to put our lives at risk, nor any member of the public. So once we find him, we tread carefully. Is that clearly understood by everyone?'

She looked at each member of the team in turn. 'We work in pairs. No one is to go out on any part of the investigation on their own. We don't know when we might bump into him, who he might be considering targeting next. Our priorities must be the two exes we know about — Tracy Beck and Sasha Purfleet. Both are now in safe houses.'

'Ma'am, has there been any further confirmation of who yesterday's second body was?' asked Lydia.

'No. We're assuming it's Debbie Martinez. Our Southampton colleagues still can't trace her, and the hair colour matches. But we won't know for sure until the DNA tests are done. We'll be looking at a week before confirmation, I expect.'

Sophie paused. 'Finding the car was an extraordinary piece of luck. Okay, so the car number plates were missing, and he's removed all of the VIN plates. But there are still some readable digits on the engine.'

Marsh broke in. 'Ma'am, I didn't even realise that there was more to that pool than we could see from the first body-site, and I'm fairly observant. It was due more to your single-mindedness than to luck.'

'Unfortunately, Barry, my single-mindedness, as you call it, wasn't enough to save Shaz Fellows. I regret that. At least we know that Sasha Purfleet's been moved somewhere safe, though Bob Thompson didn't find it easy to convince her. Kevin is organising a team to keep an eye on Sasha's old place to see if our man turns up there.' She glanced at the clock. 'We're all going to Poole to watch the hotel where he called yesterday. I'll have some backup available there in case we need it. I'm hoping that he'll have recognised Tracy and has decided to pay her another visit.'

* * *

They arrived in Poole early in the morning. Marsh drove Pillay in his car — which had not been used so far — and parked in the hotel car park. They waited inside the building. Sophie and Melsom found a parking slot on the quayside. They could see the hotel. The weather was dry, although a cold wind was blowing in from the sea.

'Let's just stretch our legs before settling back in the car. I want to get a feel for the layout,' said Sophie.

She buttoned up her long coat, pulled on a hat and wrapped a scarf around her neck. They walked along the quay for several hundred yards until they were well beyond the hotel. Then they crossed the road and turned into a side street. Alongside the hotel were small shops selling tourist gifts, as well as an estate agents and a newsagents shop. The side street took them inland away from the quay for almost a hundred yards before they could turn west again. This road was composed of old, terraced houses, in keeping with the ancient port district. As they turned left once again, they could see the harbour in front of them. Sophie could see the top of the children's swing over the high wall of the hotel. Across the road was a triangular grass area, dotted with trees and bushes. Beside the small park were several cafés, each with a few tables set out on the pavement. In the cold early morning no one was sitting at the tables.

They returned to the car. Sophie took a small pair of binoculars from her bag.

'How have you found the past two weeks, Jimmy?'

'What do you mean, ma'am?'

'Well, it's not every newly appointed DC who gets a chance to take a prominent role on a murder case, even a simple one, in their first few months. Yet here you are on a multiple murder investigation. They don't happen very often.'

'It's been just the best thing, ma'am. I know that probably sounds a bit off, and I wish that murders didn't happen, but it's been great working with you and the others. I've learned so much. It's almost as if I've had more excitement in the past two weeks than all of the previous six months put together. And it's been so good that you've put me in charge of a couple of things, like the university stuff, and allowed me to get on with it.'

He looked out of the window, across to the hotel building.

'Do you think he will really turn up here, ma'am?'

'It's all speculation and probabilities, Jimmy. Why was he here yesterday? Was it him or was it just someone who looked like him? If it was him, why didn't he react when he saw Tracy? Assuming it was him, then it's likely that he'll go for Tracy rather than Sasha over in Bournemouth. And why was he so open about it? But then, maybe that's all part of his bravado. So yes, there's a chance he'll be back. I still think he wasn't looking for Tracy yesterday. Remember that Tracy told us that he was an engineer, and he worked in lots of different places. That sounds to me as if his work involves repairing or fitting machinery of some type. When he was living with her he spent a fair amount of time in Poole, working somewhere on the quayside. It sounds very much as if he did a job of some type here yesterday, and called into the hotel for a drink after work. Tracy's sister-in-law thought Andy behaved just like any other workman out for a quick drink before heading home. He didn't try to hide himself away in a corner. He went outside and had a smoke in full view of anyone from the hotel, and was there for a good ten minutes. And he didn't seem to recognise Tracy. But then that kind of bravado is typical of a psychopath. So it doesn't prove anything.'

'But how could he have found where she was staying? The only people who knew were us and her partner.'

'She's been there a couple of days, Jimmy. Word might have got out. But I'd rather go for the coincidence theory. And whether he'll turn up again depends on whether he realised who she was.'

* * *

Marsh and Pillay sat on a sofa and chair in the front bay window of the hotel. From there they could see the area outside, and the hotel entrance, as well as the interior reception area.

'You've worked with the boss before, haven't you?' asked Marsh, sprawled in his soft chair.

Pillay nodded. 'About a year now. I don't work with her all the time, but this is the third case I've been on with her.'

'How do you find her?'

'It's always hard work, but she's absolutely straight. There are no hidden agendas with her, unlike some of the others I've worked with. But she does expect total dedication when a case is on. The first case I was involved with, there was a DS who wasn't pulling his weight. She dumped him within a few days. I haven't seen him since, but he's probably doing something mind-blowingly boring. The thing is, she's totally tenacious. She never gives up and she's got this incredibly logical brain. I think she's a bit of a one-off.'

'I was amazed last week when she told us about her background. Did you know already?'

'Some of it. She doesn't hide her background, but she wouldn't want it spread about unnecessarily. Apparently she told Jimmy a couple of days ago that she used to sneak into university dances when she was way under-age and still at school. He was gobsmacked. But it'll be true. I met her elder daughter, Hannah, once when I was waiting at her home, and she's pretty lively. But then, the boss is phenomenally clever. She did some kind of research paper as part of her master's degree, and it's still one that people refer to even now, some ten years later.'

'It makes me feel a bit inadequate.'

'Well, join the club, Sarge. Her family are lovely. Her husband runs the maths department at one of the big county secondary schools, and he's really nice. He came to the Christmas party with her last year. That was some event.'

'Why?'

'I put it down to a mix of personality and looks. She really likes nice clothes and you see a different side of her at a social function. She loves dancing, and she gets a lot of attention. She wore this incredible, long, jewel-encrusted dress that fitted her like a glove. We all noticed that the chief constable danced with her more than his wife, including a couple of slow numbers. Apparently his wife went into a sulk and wouldn't speak to him for a week — but I bet that's just gossip.'

Marsh was silent.

'. . . And the other one was a big charity do at Easter with a roaring-twenties theme.'

'I remember seeing the publicity for that. I decided not to go in the end.'

'Well, that really was something. She turned up with her elder daughter, Hannah, in matching, fringed flapper-dresses, both in deep red. They were just astonishing. They were on the dance floor most of the night. Hannah's at drama college, so you can understand it. But if the boss hadn't joined the police, she could have had a career as a professional dancer, believe me.'

'I heard that one of her daughters was training to be an actress.'

'That's the one. They looked so alike, it was uncanny. She really likes her clothes.'

'She told me last week that was the way to a woman's heart, buying her some nice clothes.'

‘Probably just teasing you. Life’s a bit more complicated than that, isn’t it?’

They lapsed into silence, looking out over the quayside in front of the hotel.

* * *

Lauren Duke had woken early feeling conciliatory. She decided to give her new man another chance. Maybe his mood earlier in the week had a rational explanation. Maybe something had happened that he couldn’t share with her.

She sat on the arm of the chair in her small student study and called him. The number rang three times before it was answered.

‘Hi—’ was all she managed. Then he began.

‘If that’s you, Tracy, I’ll fucking find you wherever you are. Don’t think I didn’t recognise you. Think you can get one over on me? You stinking cow. Just you fucking wait. You always were full of pathetic shit.’

The line went dead. Lauren stared at her phone with horror and placed it slowly on the table. She backed away, tears beginning to trickle down her cheeks. She had phoned him in order to suggest they meet for coffee. That seething, spitting voice — what on earth was going on in his head? One thing was clear. If he could speak like this then she was better off without him. She felt swamped by a feeling of total betrayal. The pleasant, protecting, safe and gentle giant of the weekend had somehow morphed into a raging monster. Which one was the real person? Or were they both real? Monday evening had been bad enough, with him switching moods so quickly. The changes had been astonishing, almost as if he had no real depth to his feelings at all. As if each of his moods was a skin he could step into, and which he could shed when it suited him. And finally, the vicious attack on the phone just now.

She decided to visit her father in Poole. She needed comforting, and her dad was the perfect person for this.

He lived in a flat near the quayside. It would be peaceful there at this time of year.

* * *

Lauren took a fast train from Southampton to Poole and walked to her father's flat near the quay. He hadn't answered the doorbell, so she'd let herself in with her key. She'd just poured herself a glass of water when he arrived back from an early morning walk with his dog. His face lit up when he saw his daughter.

'Lauren, sweetheart! You're a sight to gladden an old man's heart.'

She ran over and flung her arms around him.

'Oh, I'm glad to see you, Dad!'

'Something wrong?'

'Well, sort of. But I think I'm okay.'

'Let's sit down and you can tell me about it if you feel like it. But I don't want to pry. Is it trouble with that new man of yours?'

She burst into tears. 'I thought he was so lovely when we met at the weekend. But he was really foul just now. I feel like I've met some kind of monster. Something happened to him early this week, and it's almost as if it's turned his mind.'

'Best to leave it, Lauren. I've met men like that on the docks. Cheerful and chatty one day, vile and moody the next. They never change.'

'Oh, don't worry, Dad.' She wiped some tears from her cheeks. 'I've already decided. He was so abusive on the phone this morning, and I don't even think he knew it was me that had called him. I've been so upset. I needed someone to talk to.'

'Have you had anything to eat?'

She shook her head.

'I haven't had much either. Why don't we walk to the café on the corner and get some comfort food? A big breakfast is just what we both need. I'll treat you.'

She gave her father another hug. They left the flat and walked towards the quayside. They were halfway across the local green when Lauren saw him. He was sitting on a bench, reading a newspaper. She stopped dead, about five yards away from him. She stared at him, still holding tightly onto her father's arm. The man looked up and the spell was broken.

'Are you following me?' she shouted. 'You evil bastard. What are you doing here? Why are you doing this?'

She held her father's arm more firmly, and almost pulled him along as she walked away, fast, turning once to scream back at him.

'Andy Riley, leave me alone! Don't you ever come near me again. I don't want to see you and I don't want to hear from you. I wish I'd never set eyes on you. You're sick!'

* * *

It was mid-morning and Sophie was beginning to feel stiff from sitting in the car.

'I'll go for a wander and get some coffee for us from one of those cafés,' she said. 'Keep your eyes open while I'm out. Here's the binoculars.'

She walked along the quayside. The local detectives were being discreet in their enquiries, and none could be seen. She opened the door to the warm, steamy interior of one of the cafés. It was a homely place, where several groups of locals were enjoying coffee, or a plateful of bacon and eggs. She bought two coffees to take out, and backed out of the door. Her mobile phone rang just as the door closed behind her. She stood the coffees on a nearby wall and took the call. It came from the local DS, in charge of the team working their way through the warehouses along the quayside. They had just been to a cold-storage unit, where a repair engineer had been booked in the afternoon before to fix a faulty cooling unit. The repairman had apparently been irritable, moody and full of complaints. His last comment before leaving had been that he needed a drink.

'Have you got a name?' Sophie asked.

'The foreman is chasing up the paperwork now, but he thinks his surname might have been Riley. But there's more. He thinks that he passed the bloke's van just twenty minutes ago on the quayside. He was out collecting some goods and reckons he saw it parked about a quarter of a mile along from where you are.'

Sophie picked up the coffees and set off back to the car. She took a shorter route, across a small grassy area, dotted with bushes and shrubs, opposite the hotel.

She was halfway across when a young woman walking towards her, with her hand through the arm of an older man, suddenly froze with a look of horror on her face. She seemed to be staring at a figure sitting on a seat beside the path, his face half-hidden by the newspaper he'd been reading. Sophie kept walking. The woman suddenly began to haul her companion past the seated figure, almost at a run.

Sophie heard her scream out, 'Andy Riley, leave me alone! Don't you ever come near me again. I don't want to see you and I don't want to hear from you. I wish I'd never set eyes on you. You're sick!'

By now the young woman was sobbing and shaking. The man on the seat had been looking east towards the hotel. Now he rose and stared at the couple, with a look of astonishment. It slowly changed into one of venom. He started to move towards them, then he saw Sophie. Their eyes locked. Sophie's mind whirled, adrenaline began to flow, and she broke into a run.

She passed the two walkers, shouting, 'Police! Stop. Now.'

The tall man began to slide his left hand inside his coat. By now Sophie was only three yards away from him, running at full speed. She hurled the hot coffees towards his face, then launched herself at him. The first carton hit him on the shoulder, the second full in the face, followed by Sophie crashing shoulder-first into his chest. He fell back, groaning from the pain of the scalding liquid. Sophie landed on top of him. She hit him as hard as she could in the middle of his face, using both gloved fists together as a club. She then rolled over onto her knees away from him and pulled out her Taser from its holster beneath her coat. She pointed the weapon directly at his torso.

'Police. Taser. Don't move!' she shouted.

Andy Riley opened his eyes and pulled a knife from inside his coat. Then he caught the look on Sophie's face and slowly dropped it. Sophie's shoulder felt as if it had been in a collision with a tree trunk. Her knuckles were grazed and bleeding, and her left knee was starting to ache. But she was filled with total and overwhelming exultation.

'Got you, you fucker,' she said.

CHAPTER 22: Snapshots

Friday Afternoon

They were in the corridor outside the interview room. 'He's still not talking, ma'am,' said Marsh.

Sophie sipped her tea. 'So I heard. He's playing a waiting game. Seeing what we have on him. At the moment he knows we can charge him for possession of the knife, but that's all. He's obviously aware that we know about the three murders, but he may still think he's in the clear for them. What he doesn't know is that we have the two bodies from the water, and that we also have his car. He thinks he's been playing with us, but we know different. I think it's time to rattle him a little, don't you? I've got everything ready. Let's go.'

Sophie and Pillay had spent the morning in Walsall. They were back by early afternoon, and Sophie had asked Marsh for a summary of the morning's events. It had been a hectic time.

She put her cup down on a shelf, collected a large brown envelope from her desk and followed Marsh back into the interview room. This was the first time she'd been in Riley's presence since he'd been arrested at Poole Quay the previous day. The rest of Thursday had been spent reassuring Lauren and her father, tracing the warehouse where he'd worked on Wednesday and getting statements from the foreman and manager. Information had also started to come in from the forensics department, as they began to inspect the material from a bag dumped in the pool beside the car. Riley's van had been taken apart and meticulously inspected, as had the car. Lauren had spent an hour with Sophie and Pillay, gradually calming down in the warmth of the hotel lounge as she'd made her statement. Marsh had returned to the station with the squad car taking Riley to the cells.

* * *

Sophie saw a slight flicker in Riley's eyes as she entered the room behind Marsh. It was impossible to guess what it meant.

Marsh spoke into the microphone. 'This is Detective Sergeant Marsh resuming the interview with Mr Andrew Riley after the allocated twenty minute break. Also still present is the duty solicitor, Mr Charles Murray. We have been joined by Detective Chief Inspector Allen.'

Sophie spread a set of documents on the table. 'These are all yours, Mr Riley. Some are in the name of Renshaw, but they still clearly relate to you. We also have witnesses to the fact that you have sometimes used the names Rule and Ridgway. I wonder why someone would see the need to for multiple identities? Anyway, let's move on.'

She opened the envelope and pulled out a pile of photos, all face down.

Marsh spoke. 'For the benefit of the tape, DCI Allen is about to show Mr Riley a sequence of photographs relating to a series of violent crimes that have occurred recently. We believe that Mr Riley knows a great deal about these crimes.'

Sophie turned over the first photo. It showed the body of Donna Goodenough, lying face up on the damp surface of Spring Hill. It had been taken by the forensic photographer on arrival at the scene.

'Is there anything you want to tell us about this murder, Mr Riley, that of Donna Goodenough?' Sophie asked.

Riley glanced at the photo, then looked at Sophie. He shook his head.

She turned over the second print. This one showed Brenda Goodenough, lying dead in her bed. The livid marks around her throat were clearly visible.

'And this one?' Again, a slight shake of the head.

The third photo showed the slender body of the almost childlike Susie Pater, pale-faced against the dark, satin sheets and pillows of her bed. Sophie raised her eyebrows questioningly. Riley's response was the same. It was impossible to read anything from his expression.

She turned over the next picture. It showed a kitchen knife.

'This knife was found in the flat used by Susie Pater, the third victim. Traces of Donna's blood were found on the blade. We believe it to be the weapon used to kill her.'

No reaction from Riley. Sophie sat silently, watching his face. She sat without moving, one hand resting on the pile of inverted photos, the other resting on the edge of the table. The only sound in the room was the ticking of the clock and the regular breathing of the people inside. She continued to sit without speaking and without moving for almost a minute. All the time she was looking directly into Riley's eyes. Slowly her right hand slid the next photo from the pile, and turned it over in front of him. Riley glanced down at the image. It showed the corpse of Shaz Fellows, still lying on the black, plastic sheeting that had just been cut open at the waterside. Marsh looked quickly at the image, and then watched for a reaction from Riley. Sophie never took her eyes from Riley's face.

The next set of photos followed more swiftly. The first showed a view of Riley's van, the rear doors open wide. The second was a still from a low-quality video camera, but it clearly showed a traffic policeman talking to Riley by the roadside in the dark, at the rear of the mud-splattered van. The image was imprinted with the time, date and location — Tuesday night, three days previously. The following photos each showed a set of tyre prints, the first in the soil that had spilled across the paving outside Shaz Fellows's flat. The second marks were in the mud near the bank of the pool in Wareham Forest, and the third in the damp soil of Spider Lane, near Sophie's house. They were followed by a shot of the tyres on the van.

'The tyre prints match exactly, Mr Riley. There is little doubt that they are from that van.'

Riley looked down at the set of pictures, this time taking a little longer.

'How long is this game going on for?' he finally said.

'We're not there yet, Mr Riley.'

She turned over the next image. It was a still from the CCTV camera at the Sandbanks ferry crossing. It showed the red Ford Fiesta with a bearded Riley in the driving seat, the time stamped at midday on the previous Friday. The vehicle's registration was just discernible through the dirt that was smeared across it.

Sophie paused again. When it appeared, the photo showed a similarly coloured Fiesta with its number plates missing, gushing water as it dangled from a crane above the dark water of the pool in Wareham Forest. It was swiftly followed by an image of a number on the underside of the engine. The subsequent image showed an extract from a database, linking that engine number to the vehicle registration.

Riley's eyes shifted from the most recent image to the remaining photos, as yet unrevealed. He looked back at Sophie, who returned his gaze without moving. The room almost hummed with tension. Sophie waited again, her hand resting on the diminished pile of images.

Slowly Sophie turned the next image over. It showed the decayed corpse found in the pool beside the car. It still hadn't been incontrovertibly identified, but evidence was pointing more and more towards it being the body of Debbie Martinez. Riley stared at the image for longer than the previous photos. His eyes returned to Sophie's.

'We believe that the body is that of Debbie Martinez. Only another two to go, Mr Riley.'

The next photo was identical to the first. It showed Donna's body sprawled across the sodden surface of Spring Hill. Riley looked puzzled. Sophie turned the final image. It was of the same scene, but with the body removed. The photo was focussed on the wall, which was illuminated with ultraviolet light to show up the bloodstains. Blotchy marks and streaks showed up brightly on the treated surface, and low down, just above ground level, faint lettering could be made out, traced as if by a young child. The characters spelling 'andy' could just be discerned in the mess of blood splashes and stains.

'She didn't die straight away, Mr Riley. She died slowly over fifteen minutes or so, from severe blood loss, and was probably drifting in and out of consciousness. But she still had time to nail you.'

Sophie nodded slightly, a signal to Marsh. He cleared his throat before speaking.

'Andrew Riley, we are charging you with the murders of Donna Goodenough, Brenda Goodenough, Susan Pater, Sharon Fellows and Deborah Martinez. You do not have to say anything, but anything you do say will be taken down and may be used in evidence against you.'

Sophie hadn't taken her eyes from Riley's face. Now she spoke to him for the last time. 'Remember what I said to you yesterday, Mr Riley. Did you think I was bluffing?'

She got up and walked out.

Marsh joined Sophie later in her office. She was standing near the printer, leafing through a batch of documents that had been emailed to her.

'How's his latest girlfriend taking it all, ma'am?'

'Lauren? She'll be fine, I think, but it will take a while. She's coming back in later with her father to make a written statement. She doesn't know what we've hauled Riley in for, so it will come as a shock. It's always going to be a problem for her, that she had a short, intense relationship with a mass-murderer, but no doubt she'll survive. That's one of the problems with this totally casual approach to sex. Who exactly are you sleeping with? The charming guy who picks you up at the nightclub could be evil incarnate, as he was on this occasion. Another few months and things could have been so much worse for her.'

She looked at Marsh. 'It's not all over yet, Barry. We turned up some interesting stuff in Walsall this morning that probably explains why Riley isn't talking. He hasn't thought everything through yet. It's proving to be a real can of worms. I've left Jimmy and Lydia ploughing through piles of documents and cross-checking the details.'

She looked at the paper she'd just picked up and glanced at her watch.

'It's just after two. Can you and Jimmy shoot across to Southampton as fast as you can? I want you to visit his old school and check something out for me. Take this with you. I need to know if it's true, and if so whether they knew each other. I'll phone ahead and ask them to find some staff who were there at the time.'

She handed over a second sheet.

'Then call in at the city's adoption agency and the fostering agency. They're both together in the City Chambers in the Guildhall. Check to see if both these reports are true. Again, I'll phone through first to tell them that you are on your way. Then visit this street here.' She pointed to an address on the top of the page. 'Speak to neighbours and see if anyone remembers them, particularly the youngsters. All of them. You can imagine what we need to know. Get Jimmy to drive and you stay handy with your mobile. I'll probably need to contact you to update you during the drive. And phone me with any information. Okay?'

Marsh stood with his mouth open, skimming through the content of the papers in his hand.

'Get a move on, Barry. Don't stand there like a goldfish. It's Friday afternoon. If we don't get it all checked now we may have to wait until Monday and our friend may well have left the area by then.'

Marsh suddenly came to and hurried away to collect Melsom. As he reached the door of Sophie's office, she called after him. 'If you want to swear then feel free, but please wait till I can't hear you.'

Sophie finished her tea and walked through to Pillay in the main incident room. 'Any luck with forensics?'

'Yes. There are some scrapes on the nearside front wing that are consistent with a body collision. Liz Angel has just emailed a forensics report on the paint fragments found on his clothes. Should be here in a minute or two. But the description of the colour seems to match.'

'Can we just double-check everything, Lydia? I want to be sure that we have all the statements and details, and that it is all consistent. Okay?'

The young detective spread the pile of documents out in front of her, picking up each paper as Sophie listed it.

'GP statements about parents. GP statement about Donna. GP statement about David Goodenough. School admission dates from Walsall. Three statements from neighbours. Statement from Mr Goodenough senior's employer. Statement from Relate counsellor.'

Lydia's computer pinged, indicating an incoming email message. She read it carefully.

'Yes. Confirmation. The paint matches the colour code on the van. Shall I print it?'

Sophie nodded. Pillay added the new page to the sheaf.

'Copy of section from Donna's grandmother's will. Copy of ownership transfer documents for the flat.

Statement from solicitor.' She paused. 'That should be it. Have I forgotten anything?'

'No, ma'am. We just need whatever Barry and Jimmy find this afternoon.'

'And the West Midlands team are on their way?'

'Yes, ma'am. Liz Angel said they were just leaving.'

'Good. In that case I'll phone him now.'

Sophie sat down and dialled. 'Hello, Mr Goodenough. Is the flat okay?' She listened. 'We finished with it as a crime scene a couple of days ago, so it's no problem. It's probably a lot more convenient for you than staying in the guest house. And more comfortable?' Pause. 'That's good. I've phoned because some more information has come to light that I need to check with you. Could you call in to the station this evening? Maybe about seven if it's convenient? That's great. Bye.'

She replaced the handset.

'That was very smooth, ma'am. I can see where your daughter gets her acting talents from,' said Pillay.

Sophie laughed. 'Time for me to stir up some people in Southampton, I think. I want Barry to have as smooth a ride as possible. I think I might ask Tom Rose to allocate someone to keep an eye on Gilbert Road. Just in case our friend smells a rat.'

* * *

David Goodenough arrived promptly at seven and was shown through to the largest of the interview rooms, where Sophie and the detective from Walsall were waiting. A large jug of water sat on the table in front of them, with several glasses. Goodenough was offered a glass of water, and took a sip. Marsh, Pillay, Melsom and Liz Angel were watching on a TV monitor that had been set up in the incident room. Tom Rose joined them.

Sophie opened the plain folder in front of her. 'Mr Goodenough, last week when we first spoke, you agreed with me when I suggested that your mother had moved to

Purbeck to be near her own mother, who owned that flat in Gilbert Road at the time. Yet your Swanage grandmother's name was Deirdre Goodenough, which means she was your paternal grandmother and not directly related to your mother. Why did you let me believe otherwise?'

Goodenough took a sip of water. 'I must have been confused. I wasn't thinking straight. You'd just given me the worst news I could ever receive, and my brain was fuzzed up.'

'Your grandmother had always lived in this area, hadn't she? Apparently she was a pillar of the local community. Your father was born here, wasn't he?'

'Yes, I think so.'

'And he was well-thought of, too. Several locals remember him as a young man. They say that he didn't have an ounce of badness in him.'

'Well, they weren't on the inside, were they? The kind of bullying we suffered from is easy to hide from outsiders, you should know that. Look, what's going on? You said that you had information for me.'

'I'm just trying to get a couple of things straight in my mind.' She picked up the first sheet of paper. 'Your GP in Walsall has made a statement that there was never any hint of physical abuse to your mother, nor any history of heart trouble. If anything, it was your mother who had the temper, not your father. He visited the doctor several times for cuts and bruises to the face that were consistent with being struck with household objects. On two occasions the police were called by neighbours and found your father nursing mild injuries, and your mother under the influence of alcohol. But he never pressed charges. Isn't it the case, Mr Goodenough, that the break-up of your parents' marriage was down to your mother's unstable behaviour rather than your father's? That's what the evidence would seem to suggest.'

Goodenough didn't speak.

'Donna was in fact closer to your father than your mother, wasn't she? You said yourself that she was "the apple of his eye" but went on to add that didn't apply when he was drunk. But no one in the neighbourhood of your family home in Walsall ever remembers him drunk. People recall him as a sober, thoughtful man. But they do remember that your mother was fond of the drink.'

'Like I said, they weren't on the inside.'

'You told me that your father was apparently killed in a car accident in August.'

'As far as I know, that's true. We only heard later. We were out of contact with him by then.'

Sophie picked up the next sheet.

'This is a summary of the police inquiry into your father's death. He was apparently the victim of a hit and run incident.'

'I didn't know that.'

'DS Black here is from the West Midlands police, and was involved in the subsequent investigation. No one has yet been apprehended for the crime.' She paused. 'Would you like a solicitor, Mr Goodenough?'

'I don't see why I need one. I haven't done anything wrong.'

Sophie took a photo out of the folder. It was an image of the van that Goodenough used for his job, owned by his cousin's delivery company.

'Were you using this van during August, Mr Goodenough?'

'It looks the same colour as mine. The company owns three.'

'This is the registration.'

He glanced down at the slip of paper that she slid across in front of him.

'My van does have that registration.'

'Its paint matches the fragments found on your father's clothing exactly. It has slight marks on the front offside wing consistent with the injuries that your father suffered, although they have been sprayed over. I say again, would you like a solicitor, Mr Goodenough?'

'I don't have one.'

'That's not a problem. I have our duty solicitor outside. Shall I call her in?'

Goodenough shrugged. Sophie glanced across to the constable standing by the door. The solicitor was with them within five minutes, and Sophie summarised what had been said. She continued. 'When we spoke last week, I gave you the opportunity to tell me anything important about the family that would help me in my investigation into the deaths of your sister and your mother. Do you remember?'

'I've already told you, I was confused by everything that had happened. My brain wasn't thinking straight.'

'Why didn't you ever mention that you were adopted? And that Donna was adopted as well? Didn't you think it important that I should know your mother and father were not the birth parents of your sister? She'd just been murdered, for goodness' sake, as had your mother. What on earth caused you to believe that wouldn't be information of vital importance?'

'Adopted children should be treated the same as the birth-children. I did nothing wrong in not telling you.'

'You are right, of course, from a legal perspective. But in my role of trying to find your sister's killer, knowing she had been adopted could have saved a lot of time. So, Donna was not your natural sister?'

'No.'

'You also led me to believe that you grew up in Walsall, but that isn't true is it? You moved there in your mid-teens. Donna would have been about eleven. Where did you live before then?'

'Southampton.'

Sophie turned another page of notes. 'Your father worked in the docks? As an electrician?'

Goodenough nodded.

‘Soon after the Goodenoughs adopted you, they fostered another boy for a few months. Can you remember that?’

‘No. I was too young.’

‘You were seven. He was eight. Granted it was for a short time, but I would have thought he would have left an impression. His name was Andrew. He never settled, and proved to be a real problem for your parents. He was almost uncontrollable. Do you remember him now?’

‘No.’

‘But you did meet him again some years later, didn’t you? He went to the same school as you. He was a year ahead of you, wasn’t he?’

‘We didn’t speak to people who were a year above us. You must know what kids are like. I didn’t know him.’

‘That’s not what some of the staff say.’ She glanced down at the next document in the pile. ‘A couple of older staff members state that the two of you were as thick as thieves. According to them, the reason your family moved to the Midlands was to get you away from him. Your parents saw him as a trouble-maker and a bad influence on you. They told the head so. Your uncle in Walsall had spotted an ideal job vacancy in his area, told your father about it, and it seemed a good solution to a difficult problem. The family moved and the link was broken.’

‘I have nothing further to say.’

‘The boy’s name was Andrew Renshaw. Renshaw was his mother’s name. His father’s name was Riley. He discovered that quite recently, and uses either name as he sees fit.’

Silence. Sophie watched the man seated opposite her. He dropped his eyes.

Back in the incident room the group of officers were huddled in front of the monitor.

‘Christ, she’s doing it again,’ Marsh said.

‘Why? What else has she got?’ asked Melsom.

'I don't know. Something got emailed to her late this afternoon, and she kept it closely guarded. She's too bloody dramatic for words. It's unbelievable.'

In the interview room, Sophie finally spoke:

'Mr Goodenough, your own birth-mother's name was Renshaw. He's your brother or half-brother, isn't he? You stayed in touch, despite the wishes of your parents, and he moved in on Donna when she came back to this area as a student. Did you tell him that she was coming? I bet she wasn't even aware of the history, was she? I bet she thought this charming man, Andy, was just another guy. But you knew, didn't you? You knew full well what was going on. And the two of you planned and schemed and plotted. And you stood to gain from the acquisition of three properties with a total value, I'd guess, of about three-quarters of a million pounds. But do you know what really makes me feel sick in my stomach, Mr Goodenough? It's that you knew what kind of man he was. You knew what he did to his girlfriends. And yet you still let him loose on your step-sister. He might be a psychopath, Mr Goodenough, but what are you?'

She waited for a while before continuing:

'You need to know that earlier this afternoon we charged Andrew Riley with five counts of murder. More interestingly from your point of view, DS Black and his colleagues in Walsall have found the ashes and residues from some recent attempts at incineration at your home. Burned photos, they think. We found keys to Donna's flat and your mother's cottage hidden at Andrew Riley's home in Southampton. How could he have obtained possession of those keys, Mr Goodenough? All this leads us to believe that you were heavily involved in the planning and execution of three of those murders, so you will be charged accordingly once we have assembled all our evidence. Meanwhile I will leave DS Black to charge you with the murder of your father in August in Walsall.'

CHAPTER 23: Sequins and Shimmy

Saturday Morning

Sophie drove directly to the county police headquarters the next morning. Matt Silver was waiting for her in the car park. He walked across to her as she got out of her car and gave her a hug.

'You do realise that this is going to turn you into a bit of a celebrity, don't you? And not only within this force?'

'Shield me from it, Matt. I'm sure that's part of your job.'

'I'll do what I can. The big chief wants to see you.'

'Do you mean he's missed his Saturday morning golf just to see me? Maybe the world will end this year, after all.'

They walked down the corridor to the chief constable's suite, and were shown straight in to the inner sanctum. The ACC in charge of criminal investigation, Jim Metcalfe, was already there, as was Neil Dunnett. They rose to greet her.

'I want to say, Sophie, what a brilliant job you've done.' The chief's voice always sounded slightly strained, no matter how hard he tried to sound sincere. She knew he meant what he said. 'Clearing up five murders in twelve days is exceptional. We're all so proud of you.'

'It was six, sir. Don't forget the father in Walsall. We solved that for West Midlands. It was a payback if you like. I was aware that they didn't want to lose me when I came here. And thank you, sir. You and the ACC have always made me feel wanted, as has Matt here. I know you gambled a bit when you appointed me, and I'm grateful.'

'The next superintendent's job that comes up, Sophie, you can just walk right into it.'

'Thank you sir, but no. I'm a hands-on person. I think you all know that. I'm already in the right job for me. I really don't want anything else, and you certainly wouldn't want me anywhere in the vicinity of your office doing a desk job. It would be sheer hell for me and for all of you. You'd probably have to fire me within a year. I just want you all to tolerate my quirks and know that I'll always do the best job I can for you.'

Metcalfe broke in at this point. 'But none of us are getting any younger, Sophie. I know that's a cliché, but it's a true one. What you do places enormous stresses on you. You have to think of your future.'

'I might try to return to academic life when I can't do this anymore, Jim. I loved the year out doing my master's degree when I was in London. They told me at the time that it wouldn't be difficult to extend the area I worked on into a doctorate. My dream would be to get a lectureship somewhere. I was so apprehensive when I started university as an eighteen-year-old. I was from a single parent background, and came from a council flat in Bristol. I was terrified. Yet my years at Oxford were among the best of my life.'

'And your husband? Martin?'

'We met while we were students there. He feels the same. It has good memories for both of us. But don't worry, that's years away yet. You've got me for a good while longer, so keep indulging me. And thank you again for your support.'

'I sometimes think you're the toughest person I have in my team,' Metcalfe added.

'Well, I am a woman, Jim.' She laughed. 'But seriously, if you think I'm tough, you should see what my mother had to go through. Pregnant with me and turned out onto the streets at sixteen. She's always been my inspiration.'

'Are you returning to Swanage today?' asked the chief.

'Yes, directly from here. Just to clear up, and say goodbye.'

He passed her a sealed envelope. 'Don't refuse it, Sophie. It's to take them all out for lunch or whatever you think is most appropriate.'

'Thank you, sir. I'll do that and let them know of your thanks.'

They left the office and she turned to Silver. 'I hope you're coming down to join us for this shindig, Matt. We got used to having you hanging around.' She looked at him and laughed at his solemn face. 'Please?'

* * *

'Have you had any congratulations from HQ?' asked Marsh. They were sharing a coffee in the incident room.

'Yes, and I'll be passing that on to everybody later. But we were very lucky, Barry. Not that I told the chief constable that. Riley and Goodenough were such total dumb-asses, despite thinking themselves so clever. They just couldn't control it all, there was just too much for them. And one of our lucky breaks came from Riley's poor driving — the near-miss in the lane outside Corfe that you found out about. That gave us the lead about his car. The other was the sheer chance of the nature reserve changing that gate when they did. I wonder what went through his mind when he drove up on Tuesday night with Shaz's body in the back of his van and found he couldn't get through? It resulted in him dumping it in the nature reserve part of the pool with the consequences that followed. If it hadn't have been for that, where would we be? I've no doubt we'd have found him in the end, but it could have taken weeks. And that's more normal in a case like this. Let's face it, that set-up framing Berzins was a totally crackpot idea. It was paper-thin. Surely the two of them didn't seriously think that it ever stood a chance of surviving any close scrutiny? Did they seriously think we were all such fools?'

Marsh said, 'I don't think I've been on a case like this before, you know, with a psychopath. That stuff you told us the other morning was really useful. It explains a lot.'

'It's useful as far as it goes. But it doesn't explain why. It's all based upon observation of criminally inclined psychopaths, and the way they behave. It's a kind of syndrome, a set of behaviour patterns. You can read about the clues in text books. You know the kind of thing: look for this kind of behaviour; he might do that; he feels no normal emotions such as these. What's really interesting, though, is the way that the latest research shows some lack of connectivity inside a psychopath's brain. Which leads to the real problem for society. Is he ultimately responsible for the crimes he commits in the same way that an individual with a normal brain would be? After all, he's not responsible for the wiring of his own brain. None of us are. Those pathways are most likely developed during infancy. Dangerous stuff, Barry.'

'What did you say to him on Thursday, ma'am? That you referred to as you left the incident room yesterday?'

'You'll never know. That's between him and me. Although it's just possible that the pretty Miss Duke overheard.' She paused. 'We'll need to get a press statement together, Barry, then let family and friends know. It's all over to the CPS and the Coroner's Office now. Donna's aunt can maybe start planning for the funeral.'

'There have been a lot of people enquiring, ma'am. Berzins and his brother, university people and all the hotel staff. She was very popular.'

'A young life snuffed out. It's the worst tragedy that can be thrown at us. And let's not forget the others: Susie, Shaz, Debbie Martinez. And Donna's mother. Is it down to pure evil? God knows.' She shook her head. 'By the way, confirmation came in this morning about Donna and Susie. They met at the café where Shaz worked, but a couple of years ago, while Donna was still a student. Donna was a part-time waitress there. Kevin confirmed that Donna moved in with Susie for a while when she left Riley.'

* * *

They went out for a celebratory lunch in the Red Lion, one of the local pubs and the closest to the scene of Donna's murder. They returned to the police station in the middle of the afternoon. Sophie asked Melsom to photograph the incident board, and watched as it was carefully cleared of its contents. The items were all filed for future reference. Marsh sidled up to her.

'Ma'am, it's our Christmas bash on Friday evening, next week. I've organised it this year. We're holding it at one of the local posh hotels, and we've got a four-course meal, a live blues-rock band, plus a disco. It's in aid of charity. There are a few tickets left. Would you like a couple for yourself and your husband?'

'Barry, I thought you'd never ask. I've had my eye on a gorgeous, ice-blue, sequinned dress for a few weeks now. It'll be just perfect.' She paused. 'Listen, Barry, could you get two more tickets for me? I'm afraid both Hannah and Jade take after their old mum in the shimmy department. I'm sure they'd love to come as well. Would that be alright?'

Barry Marsh nodded, but looked bemused.

'Shimmy, Barry. Look it up in the dictionary,' Sophie said, winking at him.

THE END

Acknowledgements

This novel would not exist without the help and support of a number of people. Firstly, to my wife, Margaret, for being who she is: the most important person in my life, now as always. Secondly to my daughter-in-law, Kat, who made many suggestions for improvements, particularly in grammar and structure. Lastly to my three sons, their wives and my grandchildren.

If you have never visited the Isle of Purbeck on Dorset's Jurassic Coast, then you really should. The area has beautiful scenery, wonderful beaches and some of the best pubs in the southwest of England. The DCI Sophie Allen novels are partly dedicated to this jewel of an area.

I'd also like to thank Jasper Joffe and the staff at Joffe Books for helping to add the final touches to this novel. Anne Derges, as the crime editor, has done a first-rate job.

Thank you for reading this book. If you enjoyed it please leave feedback on Amazon, and if there is anything we missed or you have a question about then please get in touch. The author and publishing team appreciate your feedback and time reading this book.

Our email is office@joffebooks.com

www.joffebooks.com

33503579R00168

Made in the USA
Middletown, DE
16 July 2016